THE MAN HE NEVER WAS

This Large Print Book carries the
Seal of Approval of N.A.V.H.

THE MAN HE NEVER WAS

JAMES L. RUBART

THORNDIKE PRESS
A part of Gale, a Cengage Company

Farmington Hills, Mich • San Francisco • New York • Waterville, Maine
Meriden, Conn • Mason, Ohio • Chicago

Thorndike Press, a part of Gale, a Cengage Company.

Thorndike Press® Large Print Christian Mystery.
The text of this Large Print edition is unabridged.
Other aspects of the book may vary from the original edition.
Set in 16 pt. Plantin.

LIBRARY OF CONGRESS CIP DATA ON FILE.
CATALOGUING IN PUBLICATION FOR THIS BOOK
IS AVAILABLE FROM THE LIBRARY OF CONGRESS

ISBN-13: 978-1-4328-4939-9 (hardcover)

Published in 2018 by arrangement with Thomas Nelson, Inc., a division of HarperCollins Publishing, Inc.

For Theo

"With every day, and from both sides of my intelligence, the moral and the intellectual, I thus drew steadily nearer to the truth, by whose partial discovery I have been doomed to such a dreadful shipwreck: that man is not truly one, but truly two."

— ROBERT LOUIS STEVENSON

"Everyone is a moon, and has a dark side which he never shows to anybody."

— MARK TWAIN

CHAPTER 1

Toren Daniels rolled over in bed and light pierced his closed eyelids, which meant five a.m. had come and gone. Which meant Quinn was already at the gym, into his third set. Which meant Toren would be buying lunch at the end of the week. And Quinn ate like a whale when he was training heavy. Toren groaned. He'd set two alarms on his phone and still overslept. Not good.

Toren opened his eyes for a second, then immediately closed them against the sunshine, far too bright. His head. Yeah, he'd been pushing his conditioning hard for the past seven weeks, but the haze swirling through his mind along with the dull ache that pressed in from all angles in his skull didn't feel like the usual day after hard sprints and heavy weights. It felt like the day six years back, the only time he'd ever been rip-roaring drunk, after he'd made the team and all the vets forced Toren and the rest of the rookies to drink far past a rational level. At least he hadn't puked. Right now? Same feeling. And his stomach might win this time. What was wrong with him?

He lay still, head on the pillow, eyes closed. Took in a deep breath, a vain attempt to clear his senses. Didn't help. He ignored the pain in his head. He had to ping Quinn, apologize for blowing the workout. Toren covered his eyes with one hand and with his other reached for his cell phone, which he always placed in the same spot on his nightstand, a few inches from the edge, a few inches from the front. His fingers searched the smooth surface of the wood in widening circles. He blew out a sigh of exasperation, turned his head to the side, and opened his eyes again. The phone wasn't anywhere on his nightstand.

Worse, this was not his nightstand. Toren's heart hammered.

"Sloane?"

He twisted and clutched a handful of the white sheets on the king-size mattress, blinking. Except for three pillows lumped up against the headboard, the bed was empty. His wife wasn't there. His heart pumped. This wasn't their bed, their room. The increased pulse brought a new level of throbbing to his brain.

Toren did a slow half-circle spin until he sat upright on the edge of the bed, still squinting against the light. Why was it taking his eyes so long to adjust? He blinked and rubbed his eyes as he took in the room. A hotel room. Why? It made no sense. He'd gone to bed last night at home after a movie night with the kids, Sloane next to him, his alarm set for four forty.

Toren staggered to his feet and wobbled over to the bathroom door. "Sloane?"

No response. Toren pushed open the door. No lights. No Sloane standing under a rainfall of steaming water. He was alone.

His pulse increased as his gaze swept the room and spotted nothing familiar except a pair of Nike sweats and a Seattle Seahawks T-shirt lying over the back of the overstuffed chair next to the window. Toren slipped on the sweats but hesitated with the shirt. His old team. The one he wanted to rage against for releasing him — but the cutting truth was he'd pulled the pin on that grenade all by himself. Still, whoever was behind this had a distorted sense of humor.

A quick inspection of the room revealed no wallet, no cell phone, no keys, nothing. A TV. A coffeemaker. A clock that read eight thirty-nine. That was it. Toren strode over to the beige phone on the faux mahogany

11

desk and stared at the name of the hotel stamped in tiny letters at the bottom of the keypad.

THE WILLOWS LODGE
Woodinville, WA

Toren snatched the phone and pressed zero. The front desk picked up after one ring.

"Yes, Mr. Daniels, how can I help?"

"How did I get here?"

"Um, I'm not sure I understand the question."

"How did I get here?" Toren repeated. "And what am I doing here? I need answers. Now."

"I'm, uh, I don't know." The kid on the other end of the line sounded nervous.

"I go to sleep last night in my home and wake up twelve hours later feeling like I'm drugged, with nothing in the room except a pair of sweats and a T-shirt. That's a problem. Major problem."

"Yes, I can certainly see how that would be."

"And?"

"I don't know why you're here, but —"

"Can you help me find out?"

"Yes. I'll do whatever I can."

"Thanks much, I appreciate that."

As the words slid off his tongue, an emotion hit Toren so hard he slumped into the chair. An overwhelming sense of patience. He should be freaking out, riding a wave of frustration and anger till he got an explanation for what was going on. It was there, but so deep he barely felt it. The overwhelming sensation was tranquility.

"Of course, sir. If I'd been here when you checked in last night, I might have an answer, but I wasn't. And there aren't any notes next to your entry in the computer. Would it be a problem if I put you on hold for a moment while I go find out what I can about your situation?"

"No, that's not a problem at all."

Light instrumental music drifted through the phone.

Toren puffed out a puzzled laugh. What had he just said? Not a problem at all? It was a massive problem. He had no cell phone, no clothes, no wallet, no idea how he'd gotten to this hotel. And yet he felt no compulsion to raise his voice. He wasn't ticked off. Even mildly. The shortest fuse in the universe, his all-too-familiar companion, simply wasn't there. Yes, he'd been getting more control over his anger lately, but this was different. A complete serenity from no

13

place he could fathom surrounded him like cool water on a blistering day.

As he waited for a response from the front desk, Toren wandered over to his window and stared out at two massive maple trees, thick with green. Not much longer. Another four weeks, six at most, and half the leaves would be on the ground. It would be three or four games into the season, and the odds said a few guys would be hurt. If God was still answering prayers, Toren would get a call from at least a few teams asking him to come try out.

He was ready. He'd stayed in shape, been working on his emotions. Mastering methods to keep himself in check. Succeeding. Definitely in public. And even with Sloane and the kids, he'd made some strides. Not nearly enough, usually just inches at a time, but he was trying.

"Sir?"

"Yeah?"

"My apologies for the length of time it took to get you an answer."

"No worries."

There it was again. Patience. Then a peace that flooded his mind in a way he hadn't known in years. Not a quality anyone had accused him of having in abundance since he stopped playing ball.

"I checked with my manager, and there's a package here that we were instructed to deliver to your room as soon as you called us. Would it be okay if someone brought that up to you now?"

"More than okay. I'm grateful for the help."

Through the phone, Toren heard the concierge direct someone to bring the package.

"Sir?"

"Yeah?"

"I followed your career at the University of Washington. You were one of the best defensive ends ever to play for the school. I played the same position in high school. I wasn't good enough to go on and play for a major college, or even a small college, but during high school you really inspired me. And I love that they used to call you Torenado at UW."

"Wow." Toren laughed. "Haven't heard that name in forever."

"It fit you like a custom-made glove. Powerful. Unstoppable."

"That's kind of you to say." Toren smiled. "Thank you."

"You're welcome, sir. And I'm sorry you didn't last longer in the pros. What they did was wrong."

No, it wasn't wrong. The Hawks had done the right thing. They'd given him multiple chances to keep his boat from sinking, but he kept punching holes in the hull till the whole thing went under.

"I appreciate you saying that, um . . ."

"Landry."

"Thanks, Landry."

"That package is on its way, sir."

"Not sir. Toren."

"Yes, sir . . . Toren." A nervous laugh floated through the phone. "If you don't mind, can I ask you a question?"

"Sure. Anything."

"I don't want to pry — it's none of my business or anything."

"No, really, it's fine."

"Okay." Landry hesitated. "Where have you been, Mr. Daniels? I mean, my manager says we're not supposed to tell anyone you're here, like TV people or the radio or . . . but a lot of people are curious, you know? And since we're talking, I just thought I'd ask. I won't tell anyone. I promise. But if I'm stepping over a line, please just tell me to keep my questions to myself."

"What? Who's curious? Tell anyone . . . I have no idea . . ." Toren squeezed his forehead. "What are you talking about?"

"I'm wondering where you've been for the past eight months."

A shiver shot through Toren's body. "I haven't been out much if that's what you mean. But I've been here in town. I've been working out, going to the gym, doing stuff with my wife and kids, that's about it. Staying around the house."

"Oh, I see."

But by the way Landry said it, his vision wasn't even close to clear.

"But when they . . . Why didn't you let folks know after they started searching . . . and . . . I mean, it's just that . . ."

Landry trailed off, and heat shot through Toren's body.

"Searching for what?"

"For you."

"What are you talking about, Landry?" Toren paced on the dark-brown carpet. "What do you mean searching? Why would anyone be searching for me?"

Landry's voice sounded puzzled. "You vanished eight months ago. No one has seen you since."

"What are you talking about? I was at the Seafair Parade three weeks ago and saw a bunch of people. Took a few shots with people who recognized me."

A deep sigh came through the phone.

"What?"

"I'm not sure how to say this, Mr. Daniels."

"Say it."

"Everyone thought you were dead, sir."

"Dead?" The heat pushed through Toren's skin and sweat broke out on his forehead. "Why would anyone —"

"It's been over eight months since Seafair," Landry said, his voice soft.

"What?"

"Eight months. Are you all right, sir?"

"What are you talking — it's only mid-September." Toren stopped pacing and stood at the end of the bed.

"No, sir, it's not." Landry paused. "It's the middle of May."

CHAPTER 2

Toren drew ragged breaths through his nose as he slumped onto the bed and braced himself with his free hand.

"Landry?"

"Yes, sir."

"Quinn put you up to this, didn't he?"

"No, this is —"

"Then who did?"

The question was stupid. No one had put Landry — or anyone else — up to anything. But that logic didn't help. It only made the growing fear in the pit of Toren's stomach more intense.

"Mr. Daniels, three guests just arrived. Can I put you on hold?"

A rap on the door jerked Toren around.

"Take care of your guests. The package just arrived."

Toren hung up and let the phone drop onto the bed. Eight months? Not possible. How could he have been gone for eight months and not known it? And if the impossible had happened, where had he been? Sweat now seeped, it seemed, from every pore in his body.

The sound of rapping on the door to the hallway filled the room a second time and Toren lurched to his feet. He stared at the door as he shuffled toward it, desperate to open the package and get answers, yet terrified at the same time.

Toren placed his hand on the knob, paused for a moment, then pulled the door open.

"Mr. Daniels?"

"Toren, yeah."

The young woman at the door handed him a brown package the length and width of a shoe box, but only a few inches high. "Is there anything else I can get you?"

"No, thanks for bringing this up."

"Yes, of course." She nodded and trekked back down the hallway.

Toren stared at the package as he meandered to the chair by the window and slowly sank into it. The package stayed on his knees for more than three minutes before he finally tore it open.

A folded sheet of paper lay on top. He lifted the paper and opened it as he examined the contents of the package. His driver's license. A credit card. Fifty dollars in cash. A small booklet of sorts with a blank cover. That was it. He pulled the sheet of paper closer. No company name. No address. No phone number. Just a piece of paper with a handwritten note on it. Toren sighed and began to read.

Dear Toren,

Hopefully as you read these words your breathing has returned to normal. Having been involved in numerous cases like yours for quite a few years now, we know this transition back into society isn't necessarily an easy one. But you will be fine. We promise.

You of course want to know where you've been and why you don't have any memories of your time away.

You've just completed eight months unlike anything you've ever experienced. A life-altering eight months. Consequently, you'll notice changes inside. Significant ones. Most notably, specific to your case, your struggle to control your temper will have been eradicated. Embrace that revolution. You have earned it. It did not come without cost, but that cost will give you a freedom you've never known until now.

To continue in that way of freedom, we highly encourage you to study the enclosed booklet. It will provide exercises to reinforce what has occurred, and keep you on the narrow path.

Now to practicalities: You'll find enclosed your driver's license and a credit card for anything you need, such as clothes, a cell phone, etc. Also you'll find a bit of cash. Your hotel room is taken care of for the next three weeks, should you choose to stay that long. A car has been rented for you for one week starting today. After that, you'll need to take care of transportation arrangements on your own. The hotel manager has the details and assured us he would be happy to deliver you to the rental lot.

Finally, you'll undoubtedly be anxious to return home and see your wife and children. We advise against this. Not only have you been through significant change, but they have been as well, due to your long, unexplained absence. We encourage you to get to know yourself, your new self as it were, for a few days, maybe a few weeks, before engaging with them. Give yourself time. Find out who you are now. Who the new man is that you have become. That will be best for all of you.

With deepest belief in the
true you,
Your friends

Toren pawed through the box, then pulled the thing apart, looking for any clues as to who had sent the package, but even as he did, he knew he'd find nothing. Whoever had done this to him hadn't provided any answers, only more questions. He pulled out the booklet, white, three inches by five inches, about sixteen pages, nothing on the front. He leafed through it. Meditation techniques, studies on maintaining calmness, prayers, spiritual disciplines. He tossed the booklet onto the ottoman and fell back in his chair. So he'd been to some kind of spiritual retreat center.

New man? Temper gone? That would be the greatest gift he'd ever received. As the thought rushed through his mind, hope filled his soul, because he knew it was true. But how? And where? Toren clenched his fists with determination. He'd go to the moon and back to get answers.

And he would get to know this new man, yes, but sorry, he wasn't going to put off racing to see his family. Were they kidding? Not even an All-Pro offensive line could stop him from getting to his wife and kids in record time. He had no idea what he would tell them, no idea how they would react, but he was going to see them. Now.

CHAPTER 3

As Toren sped toward home, he marveled at how easily a spring day in mid-May could impersonate a sunny day in mid-September. Yes, now that he knew, he saw the differences, but they were subtle. More a feeling in the air than anything concrete. He had checked the date on a newspaper at the rental car lot three times.

Eight months. Gone. With no memory of those weeks. How was that even possible?

As he pulled onto the street that held his home, his hands grew damp. He remembered everything in detail up till September 14 of the previous year. Too much detail. The months leading up to another NFL season without him in it had been brutal. And he'd taken out his frustration on Sloane. Wave after wave of fights, him losing his temper again and again, screaming at her, her finally screaming back, the kids hearing far more than they should, even when they were upstairs in their rooms. Then the apologies, his hard work to keep his rage in check, all for nothing when a few weeks or days later he'd blow the doors off whatever semblance of an emotionally safe home he'd built.

The counseling sessions? They always started out with hope and always ended with a rising crescendo of shouting. Too many times to count, Sloane had threatened to divorce him and he'd always talk her out of it.

Toren eased his car to a stop five yards from the entrance to his driveway, his fingers gripping and regripping the steering wheel. He'd pictured Sloane overjoyed to see him, but what if she wasn't? Toren pushed the gear shift into park as he stared at the driveway. Sloane loved the entrance to their home, long and accented with gentle curves.

Just as he was about to turn in, a green truck appeared, whipping down his driveway toward the street, faster than made sense. Rakes, shovels, and a lawn mower poked out from the bed of the truck. Ten yards from the street, the truck slowed down, moving at just over a crawl now. The driver wore a red hat. Sunglasses. Goofy grin on his face. He glanced Toren's direction, and in spite of the glasses, Toren sensed the man was staring directly into his eyes. The guy jabbed a finger at Toren, and the smile grew wider. Then he turned the truck onto the street and sped off.

Toren knew the guy, didn't he? He was ninety-eight percent certain. But exactly who it was flitted just out of reach. Something reeled in Toren's gut. Whoever the man was, the feelings his image stirred up weren't pleasant ones.

Toren shook his head, shot up a quick plea for God to make this reunion a joyful celebration instead of a disappointment, and turned into his driveway. He stopped the rental car fifty feet from the house, got out, and sent up another silent plea. Good, bad, or horrendously ugly, this meeting was guaranteed to be a little weird.

Toren shuffled up the rest of the drive and shoved his trembling hands into the front pockets of the jeans he'd bought an hour earlier. He glanced at the massive front lawn, the grass greener and mowed shorter than he'd ever gotten around to cutting it. Looked elegant. Purple flowers cascaded from baskets hanging from both corners of the roof. The sun was out and spring had kissed the Pacific Northwest with full force.

The mid-May sunshine brought a lightness to the air he should have felt as he stared at the front door, now just ten yards away and at the same time a million miles from where he stood. But the lightness didn't reach his heart. Of course it didn't. How could it? The truth settled on him hard: he'd been gone for eight months. He was about to rock the world of his wife and kids in a way they couldn't imagine.

The house had been painted beige. All six thousand square feet of it. Good for her. Sloane had always wanted that color and Toren had always fought her on it. But he knew, deep in his gut, those days were over. If the miracle he'd been feeling for five hours now had truly happened and he was a new man, then fighting about idiotic things like the color of their house would be a thing of the past. All he wanted at this moment was to wrap her in his arms, tell her he loved her, and then do the same with his kids. During the time he'd picked up the car, bought clothes, and snagged a lunch on the run, he hadn't found any memories of his time away, but the sense he'd been gone a long time did engulf him, and his heart ached to be back with Sloane, back with Callie and Colton.

Enough stalling. He had to get up there, pull the brass knocker back and let it fall three times, and let be what would be. It would be good. A whisper of a voice told him he'd changed in ways he couldn't fathom. He had great hope where before there had been only darkness. He truly was a new man, and Sloane and he could get back to the way they'd been before the Seahawks cut him loose.

He took the last step slowly, as if the concrete under his shoe might crumble. Sloane's muted voice floated through the door. She was giving directions to at least one of the kids, maybe both, and Toren drew in a sharp breath. Then a deep breath. Hand up. Grab the knocker. Rap once, twice, three times.

What had he just done? Eight months gone with no word, no clue as to where he'd been. He should have called first. Should have bought a cell phone and called. Did he have time to leave? He glanced behind him. Not a chance. He stumbled down the porch steps till he stood in the driveway, as if a little more distance between them would prevent her from feeling ambushed the second she opened the door.

Toren staggered back another step, his poor balance threatening to send him sprawling onto the asphalt. He tried to take a breath. Seconds till her slender hand would grab the doorknob, open the door, and reveal an image she likely wouldn't be able to comprehend.

An instant later the deadbolt slid, the knob rattled, and Sloane pulled the door wide. She stood in the center of the doorframe. Her hair was shorter. She opened her mouth slightly as her right hand gripped the edge of the door. Her other groped for the doorframe. Her eyes blinked once, twice, and she pulled in air as if she'd just surfaced after being under water far too long. Her hands shook, and a moment later her body joined in.

"No." Her legs started to give out, but somehow she steadied herself.

"I should have called." Toren took a halting step toward her. Sloane shook her head. Tiny little shakes. Though she stared right at Toren, she wasn't seeing him.

"I'm sorry, Sloane. I just thought getting the shock over all at once might be best, rather than seeing me . . . Then I realized I should have done the opposite . . . That would have been better . . ."

He trailed off. Better than what? Showing up in person after nearly a year away without a shred of communication?

"No. No. No. This isn't possible," she whispered as her body trembled.

"Stay with me, Sloane." Another hesitant step toward her. He held out his hands as if he could steady her. "I'm sorry, but I thought if I called, you wouldn't believe me and that might have made it worse."

For the first time since Sloane opened the door, she looked at him, really looked at him, deep into his eyes.

"You are not standing there. You can't be." She closed her eyes tight, her fingers now white where she clutched the blue door.

"It's me. Really."

"No. You're dead. You wrote a note," she whispered, just before the light faded from her eyes and she collapsed backward onto the hardwood floor.

"Sloane!"

Toren bounded up the steps with two strides of his six-foot-three frame and lurched across the threshold into a world foreign and familiar at the same time. But before he could fall to his knees next to his wife, Toren's ten-year-old son, Colton, rounded the corner of the kitchen. He'd grown at least two inches. His eyes went wider than his mom's had and his face turned ashen.

"Dad?" His lips trembled. "What . . . what . . ."

"I know, Colton. I know. It has to be a

shock to see me." He sucked in a quick breath. "I'm so sorry."

His son's eyes narrowed. "You . . . you're not . . . you're not alive anymore." Colton braced himself against the wall and shook his head, a perfect reflection of what Sloane had done seconds earlier.

"Mommy?" The word floated in from the family room.

Toren froze. He had to check Sloane, make sure she hadn't hit her head, but he knew what was bound to come around the corner in seconds, so he stayed standing, his eyes flitting from the edge of the tan wall leading into the kitchen, to Sloane, then back.

Please stay there, Callie.

She padded around the corner, long dark hair pulled back, dark eyes flashing, more beautiful than he'd imagined they could become. Eight years old. Still living in the land of innocence, but she'd be on the brink of womanhood in an instant.

"Daddy?" Callie's lips trembled and she tilted her head to the side.

"Yeah, sweetie, it's me."

The shock of seeing him skittered away almost instantly — at least on the outside. She didn't shake, didn't speak, didn't gape in disbelief. She simply sank to the floor, sat crisscrossed, and stared at Toren with a look of sorrow.

"Mommy said you were never coming back."

"She didn't think I was."

She responded by turning her head and staring at the wall. How could his daughter understand why the man she desperately wanted to love but had every reason to spurn had slipped back, utterly unannounced, into her young life?

After a quick glance at Colton, who scowled, Toren knelt next to Sloane. She stirred, and he fought the urge to gather her into his arms. Not a good plan. But he couldn't do nothing. He reached for her, but before his hand could take her shoulder, his son's voice sliced into his thoughts.

"Stay away from her. You just stay away from her!" Colton knelt down on the other side of Sloane, one hand on her shoulder where Toren's should be, the other rigid, his finger pointing through the open front door. "We don't need you anymore. Get away from us!"

The thought to take control flashed into Toren's mind, to tell his son the way it was going to be, but the thought was only mist with no substance, and the idea evaporated. All Toren felt for his son was love. And remorse for what he'd been, and the desperate hope that the change inside him was real.

"Okay." He nodded and stood but didn't step through the door.

"Please go!" Colton's finger hadn't moved, though his other hand was tenderly massaging his mom's shoulder as she groaned as if waking from a deep sleep. Colton's voice sank to a savage whisper. "Go! We don't want you here. You need to leave. You're not welcome here. Go, just go!"

As Colton fumed, Toren studied his wife. She stirred. He'd seen enough men knocked out on the field to know she would be fine. Toren nodded again and stepped through the front door onto the porch, hesitated, then turned back. Callie now stood between him and Sloane. Callie didn't speak, didn't have to. The blank look on her face couldn't hide the bewilderment and sadness that seeped out of her soul. Then, just as Sloane and Colton had done, Callie slowly shook her head back and forth. The sentiment sank into his mind like a tattoo that would be with him till death. When she finished, she reached out with her tiny fingers and pushed softly on the door. The door took an age to close, and all he could do was stare as the picture of his family grew narrower and then disappeared entirely.

Toren pressed his lips together and tried to send a request to the heavens, but they seemed shut, and even though he couldn't blame his family for reacting like this, the reality of it took more out of him than he'd expected.

He turned and stumbled down the steps, wound his way down the walkway and then down the driveway back to his rental car. His fingers felt like little stumps and he couldn't seem to get hold of the remote that would unlock the car. He noticed how damp his armpits had become. But that was a good thing. So good. It meant he'd been nervous. Unsure of himself. The old him hadn't been nervous in eons. He'd learned years ago to cover up his insecurity with a false confidence that carried him in every situation. But the lie had ebbed away. Maybe the old man truly was dead now. The verse he'd taped to his mirror years back about his old self being crucified, buried, had come true. He got in, started the car, but didn't put it into gear.

Even though the knowledge of his transformation was only five hours old, he knew wherever he'd been, whatever he'd gone through, had changed him irrevocably. He had to tell Sloane, had to explain and beg for a fresh start.

What to do next? No idea. He hadn't expected a hero's welcome, but hadn't expected a total rejection either. Didn't they at least want to ask where he'd been? No, of course they didn't. He shouldn't have come.

Toren headed back to the hotel with a vise grip clamped around his stomach. What had he expected? That Sloane and Colton and Callie would waltz over to him with birds swirling around them singing a syrupy sweet song about reconciliation? That they would all join together in a powerful hug and they'd laugh and Toren would confess to losing his temper far too often? That even though he understood why they didn't want him in their lives any longer, they'd forgive him and they'd all live happily ever after? A bitter laugh sputtered out of his mouth. If he was them, he wouldn't want him back either. Not for a second. Why would they?

Where did he go from here? He hadn't thought of any steps beyond seeing his family.

Quinn. That was his best option. In the morning he'd call his workout partner and give him the shock of his life.

CHAPTER 4

"Mom!"

The voice of Sloane's son floated down on her as if coming from another decade. She was asleep, yes? She tried to open her eyes, but it was too much effort. Middle of the night — had to be.

"Mom, wake up."

Someone was gently rubbing her cheek. Callie's hand? What had happened? Was she still in bed? Dreaming, had to be dreaming. Needed to get up, get the kids ready for school. No, that wasn't it. Hard floor under her back. She'd been standing in the entry-way . . . hadn't she? Yes. She'd fainted, just a moment ago. Someone had been at the door. Someone . . . an image of Toren flashed through her mind. No, not him. Not possible for that image to be real.

"Mommy? Wake up, Mommy. Please?"

The image of her husband flashed into her mind again. Stayed longer this time, and the truth seeped into her brain. Toren — it really had been Toren. Impossible, but it hadn't been a dream.

"Mom, are you there? Are you okay?"

Colton's voice this time. Sloane raised her heavy lids and looked into the eyes of her son, his dark, curly hair framing a face full of fear. On her other side, Callie squeezed Sloane's fingers, strong then soft, strong then soft. Callie's eyes closed, lips silently moving.

"Yeah, I'm okay."

She squeezed Callie's hand in return, then tried to sit up, but the room spun wildly so she settled back down.

"Just stay there a minute." Colton turned to Callie. "Did you call the 911 people?"

"Not yet."

"Callie! All you do is pick up the phone and —"

"Don't worry. I'm going to!" Callie scowled at him. "I'm not a little girl."

"That's exactly what you are!"

"Guys, relax." Sloane gave a weak smile. "Thank you, but really, I'm okay. You don't need to call them. It was just a bit of a shock seeing . . ."

She trailed off as she rose to an elbow. The room still spun, but manageably now.

"Seeing, uh . . . Dad?"

"Yeah."

"He's gone," Colton said.

"Colton made him go away." Callie gave Colton a smile as she rubbed Sloane's forehead.

"It's over, Mom," Colton said.

Sloane nodded at her son and again tried to smile. Over? No. Not even close. They had just been forced onto a roller coaster, and it was a virtual certainty the track would end the moment they reached top speed.

"I'm good, really I am." She sat up and took three slow breaths. "But can you help me up?"

Colton and Callie made an effort to help Sloane to her feet and shuffled alongside her as they padded over the maple hardwood floor into the kitchen. They sat at the table, pushed their afternoon snacks to the side — any shred of hunger had been stolen — and stared at each other, trying to pretend what had just happened wasn't real.

"I don't get it." Callie pressed her knuckles together, voice pinched. "Daddy's dead, right?"

"It didn't look like it to me," Colton said.

Sloane glanced back and forth between her kids. She had to figure out what to do. What to say. How to explain why their dad had reappeared after everyone had accepted the high probability of his death.

"Why did Daddy come here? I mean —"

"Think, Callie," Colton said. "How in the world would Mom know why he showed up?"

"Why can't I ask Mommy that, you doofus?" She stuck out her tongue. "It's called a question."

"A stupid question."

"Not helping." Sloane leaned forward, arms outstretched, palms on the table. "Let's show a little grace. I'm guessing all three of us are dealing with a little shock right now."

"A little?" Colton puffed out a laugh. "A little shock? Yeah, sure, just a tiny, tiny bit."

"Shut up, Colton-bozo." Callie yanked the end of her long dark-brown hair and glared at him.

"Give me your hands." Sloane extended hers to either side and her children took them, both of their hands warm and a perfect fit with hers.

"Listen. We're going to figure this out. We're going to make a choice right now. A choice to believe that in some crazy, insane, unexplainable-at-the-moment way that the One who loves us is in this, yes?"

Colton and Callie nodded.

"No, we don't have any idea why your dad showed up here. Where he was. What he wants. But for the moment we're not going to worry about any of that. For the moment we're going to worry about the moment. And this moment is about trusting, pressing into what we know is true. We are loved beyond measure by a God who is infinite, who numbers the hairs on our heads."

Colton's eyes grew intense and he gave a tiny shake of his head. "Yeah, that sounds great — until Dad wants to be part of us again, and hang out around here and start yelling all the time and calling us names and calling you names and all that kind of stuff. You know?"

Sloane nodded as her eyes narrowed and she squeezed Colton's and Callie's hands, glancing back and forth at their worried eyes. "What has life been like since Dad went away?"

"Way, way gooder than it was," Callie said.

"Better, not gooder," Colton said.

"Shut up, Colton!"

"Hey, guys." Sloane squeezed again. "Not now. Okay?"

They both nodded.

"What about you, Colton?"

"There's a part of me that's missed him big-time, but most of me hasn't."

41

"Me too, Mommy. There's part of me that still likes Daddy."

"I know. I know," Sloane said. "That's okay."

"But it's way better this way, and how it should be now, and you're way better this way too, right, Mom?"

"Yes." Sloane smiled, genuinely now, full of grit and fire. "Which is why there is no way I'm going to let anything or anyone, not even your father, take that away from us. What we have right now is what we are going to keep."

Colton and Callie nodded.

"Do you believe me?" Sloane looked them each in the eye.

Again, two nods in unison.

"Good."

She released their hands and sat back. "You two have grown up so much over the past eight months. I'm so proud of both of you. And you're not the only ones who have grown up. I have too. So yes, I promise. Whatever happens with Dad, you have my word, I will not allow it to affect what goes on in this home. For that matter, I can't see him being in this house ever again."

"Promise?" Colton asked.

"Yes. I promise."

To keep that promise, Sloane knew she'd

have to wrestle with two massive weights she had just slung around her neck. First, battling the inevitable onslaught of Toren's efforts to work his way back into her life, and second, accepting the truth that her children deserved, if they wanted it, to have their father involved in their lives.

CHAPTER 5

It took far longer than Toren expected to get a new cell phone, so by the time he pushed through the double doors of the hotel lobby late that evening, he had three simple goals on his mind: Get upstairs and take a blistering hot shower, process what was happening to his soul, and crash into bed. In the morning he'd brainstorm ideas for how to win Sloane back, and his kids, then devise a plan for finding out where he'd been for the past eight months. After that, he'd call Quinn.

"Mr. Daniels?"

Toren glanced at the front desk. A tall, thick young man who couldn't be much past high school stood behind the counter, a boyish smile on his face.

"Yeah?" Toren slowed his pace slightly but kept moving toward the elevators.

"It's me, Landry."

The last thing Toren wanted to do was

stop, but an instant later it was the thing he wanted to do most in the world. The bewildered look on his face must have been priceless.

"Mr. Daniels, are you okay?"

"I'm fine . . . I . . ."

"You look like you lost something, or just remembered something surprising."

"No, I didn't."

Then again, maybe he had. Toren eased over to Landry and offered his hand and a wide smile.

"It's great to meet you in person, Landry."

"Yeah, well, wow. Yeah, good to meet you too." Landry let go of Toren's hand and shuffled a few papers that didn't need shuffling. "Is there anything I can get you, Mr. Daniels?"

"Not sir, not Mr. Daniels." Toren grinned. "Just Toren."

"You got it, you got it." Landry returned the grin.

"Any crazy guests tonight, Landry? Besides me?"

"No, not too bad tonight." Landry fixed his eyes on the counter between them. "Um, hey, you know, if this is wrong to ask, you totally don't have to, but if you're okay with it, do you think you might be able to sign something for me?"

"Sign something? You mean you want my autograph?"

"Yeah, but really, only if —"

Toren's laughter interrupted Landry. "I appreciate you asking, really, I do. But why would you want the autograph of a ball player who only started one game in his entire five-year NFL career, and only because the guy ahead of him got hurt? I was practice-squad fodder, that's it. I could walk down the streets of Seattle during my playing days and maybe, maybe, one out of fifty thousand people would recognize me. I was never a big deal, Landry."

"Uh, well, like I said on the phone earlier today, you were a big deal to me. I loved you at the UW, and you were a big deal there, enough to make it to the pros, right? And I think it's pretty cool that you have a faith that you talk about and trust in God and all that, and I would love that signature . . . but only if you feel like it."

"I feel like it. Right now." Toren leaned into the counter. "You got a pen?"

Landry handed him a pen and a pad of paper and Toren wrote, *To Landry — You're stronger than you know, and if you follow God's commands, he will make your paths straight,* then signed his name underneath.

"Thank you so much, Mr. . . . Toren."

"You're entirely welcome."

Landry tilted his head to the side. "Do you miss playing?"

The question pierced him.

"Yeah." Toren stared at the thick wood beams over Landry's head. "Every second of every day."

"Is that why you're still in such great shape? I mean, it looks like you're in great shape."

"Thanks, Landry, and yes, I'm still hoping, still praying a team will take a chance on me."

"I hope so too."

Toren smiled, gave Landry a fist bump, and strolled toward the elevators. When he stepped in, turned, and waited for the elevator doors to close, Toren spotted a man at the far end of the bar in the adjacent restaurant staring directly at him.

It was him, wasn't it? The same guy who was in the truck, the landscaping guy. From this distance it was hard to be certain, but as Toren peered at him, any doubt was quashed. But once again his mind refused to tell him who it was and from where. It was years ago, but how far back?

The doors were sliding back, inches from closing, when Toren glanced down and hit the Open button. The two silver panels jerked to a stop, then lurched back open. Toren grabbed each door to open them faster and zeroed his gaze in on where the man sat. The seat was empty.

CHAPTER 6

Toren slept in the next morning — rest he desperately needed — but woke to a brutal image snaking through his mind from a dream he couldn't shake. He stood on a cliff, his back to it, the heels of his feet inches from the edge. Sloane was there, along with Colton and Callie. A bigger group stood behind them — fifteen, maybe twenty others, but he couldn't make out their faces, only the three in front.

None of them, not even Sloane, showed anger. Instead, their eyes, their mouths, everything about their countenance was painted with a kind of pity that wrapped Toren's mind in pain. Rage would have been better than seeing them stare at him like one would stare at a cow about to be slaughtered.

He rose up on his toes and reached out to them. He screamed till his throat felt raw, begging them to forgive him, but a wind that pounded into him like a juggernaut snuffed out his words. They fell to the ground at the tips of his shoes and were whisked over the edge of the cliff into blackness. Then in concert with each other, Sloane, Colton, and Callie strolled forward, no longer full of pity, but now full of laughter and joy.

It didn't seem as if they could see Toren, but when they reached him, their faces grew somber, and again in unison, each of them reached out a forefinger, pressed it against his chest, and pushed. He flailed, fighting to keep his balance, fighting to keep from falling backward over the cliff and into the darkness below.

Then, right at the moment Toren thought he would recover, Sloane came a half step closer by herself, and this time opened her palm and shoved him in the chest with a surprising strength. And he was over the edge and falling, screaming.

He woke covered with sweat, and after a few minutes of labored breathing, he headed for the bathroom. He took a shower. Cold. Drew the washcloth hard across his body as if he could scrub from his soul what he'd done to his family.

The scales had fallen from his eyes. He saw now, for the first time, what the past three years had been like for them. The explosions, the shouting, his temper raging like a fire, burning down his family, the fear in their eyes as his voice thundered at them again and again and again. He saw how the prayers of repentance, the promises not to lose it again only made the subsequent failings worse.

He ate breakfast in the hotel restaurant and made a sincere effort to taste the food and read the complimentary paper but didn't succeed in either pursuit. At just after eight he ambled through the wood-lined lobby and glanced at the front desk. Landry wasn't there. A good kid. If he ever made it back to the show, he'd find a way to get Landry season tickets.

Toren pushed open the front door of the lobby and stepped into the unseasonably cool May afternoon. Blue sky dominated the clouds jockeying to overtake it, but still, it seemed the rays of light refused to warm the earth this day. In a few minutes he reached the walking path he'd read about in the hotel's promotional materials the night before. He'd look for a spot along the way to call Quinn.

Quinn McPherson. Workout partner. Best friend. A man who had stood by him when the Seahawks blew him out because of his on-the-field anger issues and the rest of his teammates seemed to unanimously nominate him for Pariah of the Year. A friend who saw the good in Toren, a man who would fight for him till his last breath.

The trail brought him to a lush park five or six acres in size. Thick maple trees two goal posts tall ringed the dark-green lawn. A few picnic tables were scattered near a covered cooking area. A swing set and a small slide were the only other things in the park. No moms with small kids playing with abandon, no couples throwing Frisbees, no dads tossing baseballs into the worn mitts of their sons.

He wandered over to the west end, the farthest spot from the path, and settled down at the base of one of the largest maples. Toren lifted his cell phone and dialed Quinn. Would Quinn answer? Toren had little doubt. He was one of those with his phone stuck to his ear with Gorilla Glue when he wasn't working out or practicing, and he was also one of the few people who would answer his cell phone these days without the caller ID telling him who it was.

"Yeah, you reached Quinn, but you knew that, right?" A quick laugh. "But leave that message you're dying to leave and I'll get back to you as soon as I feel like it."

Toren didn't leave a message. Of course not. What would he say? *Sorry about being eight months late for our workout, but I finally woke up. You still at the gym?*

He got up and wandered back to the trail. Back to the hotel? Probably should, but his feet took him north, farther down the trail toward he didn't know what. After a few minutes a phrase rocketed into his mind: *To find true freedom, you must find true forgiveness.*

For a quarter second, maybe less, Toren saw a room with large windows, then the image was gone. He lunged forward in his mind to try to grab hold, but the picture melted like summer fog and all that remained was the phrase.

True freedom. True forgiveness. Forgive what? Forgive who? Forgive his dad, of course. Toren had known that all his life. But how?

Execute. Don't think, just execute. Isn't that what Coach had told him countless times from junior high all the way through his last game in college? *Let your game play flow from the deep places. Get your brain out of the way. Don't think. Execute. Do it so often, it's automatic.*

Execute. Simple. But this wasn't a game. It was life. Not simple to forgive.

Toren closed his eyes, but before he could make another futile attempt at letting go of his anger at his dad, the anger at himself, his cell buzzed. Toren glanced down and heat shot through his body. It was Quinn.

"Hello?"

"Hey, you called me about ten minutes ago. Sorry I missed it. Who is this?"

A shiver flew through Toren. He was about to give his friend a heart attack.

"It might be hard for you to believe who this is."

"Try me."

"Quinn?"

What a stupid question. Toren knew it was him, but any clever ideas for how to tell Quinn he'd come back from the dead were gone.

"Yeah, you got me. And now we're to the part where you tell me who you are. You sound like . . . Well, just tell me who this is."

"Are you sitting down? You probably should be."

"Who are you and what are you selling?" Quinn laughed, but the laughter wasn't true. There was nervousness in it, as if part of him recognized Toren's voice and didn't know what to do with the thought. "I'll warn you, whatever you're peddling, it better be good."

Quinn. The man who was everyone's friend. Who was far from naive, and yet chose the path of believing in a person till proven wrong multiple times.

Across the grass a bicyclist shouted, "On your left!" as she shot past a walker.

"You know me, Quinn."

"Okay, like I started to say, yeah, your voice sounds like an old friend of mine. Almost exactly like it, but since you can't be him, I can't pin the tail on the donkey on this one. So why don't you tell me and I won't hang up on you and get back to what I was doing, 'cause you're starting to irritate me."

"It's me, Quinn. Toren."

Quinn was silent for so long the only reason Toren knew he hadn't ended the call was because of the faint breathing coming through the phone.

"Quinn?" Toren finally said.

"Uh, listen, pal, I don't know how you were connected to Toren, or what kind of a warped mind is making you do this, but it's not funny."

"Listen to my voice, Quinn. This is real. It's me. Really. You know it. I'm back."

"Like I said, not funny, pal. It's sick." He paused and Toren thought he might hang up. But Quinn continued. "You're going to tell me who you are. And why you're doing that lame impersonation of my friend. And if you don't, I'm coming through this phone and I'm gonna bust you up, man. I'm gonna —"

"Quinn Bernhard McPherson!"

That stopped him. Few people knew Quinn's middle name, which his parents gave him after some distant relative he'd never met.

Quinn gasped. "How do you know that name?"

"You and I met the first day of middle school, sixth grade, and during Christmas break that year I hung with you and your parents. Almost every night we snuck out and hung raw eggs over telephone lines at windshield level and watched cars get slimed."

"No one knows about that. No one." Quinn stopped speaking and his breathing came through the phone in thick clumps of air. Then it stopped, and a few seconds later came out in a long *whoosh*.

"Toren? It really is you, isn't it?"

"Yeah, it's me, buddy. In the flesh. Alive and kicking."

"I don't understand . . . Toren?" He sucked in another breath and repeated his

56

name with disbelief hanging over its edges for the third time. "Toren. Toren. Toren."

"Yeah," Toren breathed out.

"This can't be happening —"

"I know. I know. I wasn't sure if I should just show up at your house or the gym, or if I should call you first, or if —"

Questions sputtered out of Quinn without giving Toren a chance to answer. "Where have you been? What happened to you? Why didn't you let me know what was going on!"

Toren let him go for a while before breaking in.

"I'm okay, Quinn. I am. But now I need to —"

"That's not what I asked. I mean, I'm glad you're okay, my mind is reeling, but I gotta know where you've been."

"I want to tell you everything. I *need* to tell you everything, but not on the phone. Can we get together?"

"Yeah, sure. I mean, of course . . . Sorry, I'm still having trouble wrapping my mind around this. When you vanished and then there was never any trace, any explanation, it tore me up. Tore up a lot of people. The church . . . Wow . . . It was brutal, Toren. People loved you. You should have seen the memorial, man. Must have been five hundred at least."

"Yeah."

He tried to think of what else to say but couldn't find the words. Five hundred? So Sloane must have let the illusion remain that he was a good man. No idea why, but it didn't matter. He was going to step out from behind the curtain. Expose who he'd truly been to the blinding rays of the truth.

"Yeah?" Quinn half laughed, half shouted into the phone. "That's it? 'Yeah'?"

"For now. But there's lots I want to talk about."

"Where are you? Right now, where are you? I'm coming over. Are you home?"

"No, I'm not."

"Are you kidding me? Why not? What's more important than being with your family?" Quinn blew out a hard breath. "Sloane and the kids had to have gone crazy when you showed up. Over the moon, over Jupiter with relief. She has to be planning a homecoming, a party, something. You have to have just made her the happiest woman in the world . . . and your kids . . . Oh my gosh . . . This is insane."

"Yeah, it is." Toren tried to say the words with enthusiasm, but he failed miserably.

"What's wrong with you?"

"Nothing, I'm good. I just need to talk."

"Yeah, of course. Sounds good. Honestly,

I probably won't believe it's true till I see you with my own eyes. Crazy. You've made my day, my month, my year. When do you want to connect?"

"As soon as you can."

"Right, right. Fine, fine, yeah, good." Quinn laughed again. "Insanely cool. It's really you. Okay, think, man! Think! I have a few things I can't get out of — have to shoot a stupid car dealer ad in an hour — but then I'm free. Where? Do you want to meet at your house?"

"No."

"What? You're not at home?"

"I already told you I'm not."

"And you'll explain why when we meet."

"Yes."

"No problem." Toren heard a smile come into his voice. "Then let's meet at my house. I still can't believe you're back. Carol will be thrilled to see you. I'll call her, make sure she's going to be there . . ."

"Quinn?"

"Or do you want to be stupid twelve-year-old boys and spring it on her, you know, have you come walking out from behind a door or something?"

"Quinn?"

"Nah, that'd be stupid, probably scare her half to death."

"Quinn?"

"Sorry. What?"

"I want to see her again too, definitely, but before that I need to talk to you first. Alone . . ." He trailed off, not sure how to say the next part. "There's a few things you need to know."

CHAPTER 7

At two thirty Toren entered Sassy's, a deli down near the shore of Lake Washington that had the best fruit smoothies he'd ever tasted. The place usually had no more than two or three customers at this time of day, and even when it was busy, people rarely sat in the booths at the back. Most people crammed into the tables at the front to listen to Sassy's innumerable stories about the days when she used to be in the roller derby, or to watch her truly baffling mind-reading trick.

Yeah, Sassy's was the perfect place for Toren to tell Quinn what little he knew about what was happening to him. A place of good memories, where he and Quinn had hung out during college and the summer days before they both headed for different training camps their rookie years in the NFL. Quinn had always chatted with Sassy, stayed to hear her stories even though he'd heard them all before. Toren? Not so much. He liked Sassy, but she reminded him too much of his dad's girlfriend. His dad had reappeared in Toren's life only after he'd become a standout on UW's defense.

But he still loved the place. And it was a good spot to kick off a new life. That's what he'd been handed, right? A fresh start. Nothing but a credit card, his driver's license, sweats, and a T-shirt. New clothes, new car soon, new cell, and most of all, new soul.

During the hours between calling Quinn and getting to Sassy's, Toren had spent time in silence, time in prayer, time in meditation, contemplating how his soul had been transformed. Transformed. The perfect word. Something revolutionary had changed in the deepest part of him. For the first time in his life, he felt like he could love Sloane the way she deserved to be loved. New man. Utterly.

Toren got there early. He wanted a chance to settle in, deal with the shock of Sassy recognizing him. He didn't think she would, but if she did, he wanted to get it over with before Quinn arrived. Toren glanced around the shop, then settled into a booth at the back.

Three minutes later the front door bells

jangled and Quinn stepped inside. He stood for a few seconds, his expression blank, but then it turned to wonder and then relief. He strode over to Toren so fast all he had time to do was slide out of the booth and get to his feet.

Quinn grabbed him in a fierce hug, which Toren returned with equal force. Still holding on, Quinn said, "I knew it was true, but not all the way till this moment. Insane."

"I know, that's exactly what it is."

"Shall we?" Quinn motioned to the booth.

They settled in, and seconds later Sassy sidled up to their table. "Hey, fellas, know what you're going to be having?"

"Hey, Sassy."

"Quinn McPherson?"

"Yeah, it's me."

"Oh my, skittle my brains with an extra dollop of butter. It's so fun to see you again."

"You too, Sassy." Quinn grinned, his blinding white teeth in perfect contrast to his dark skin.

"What's it been?"

"Probably four years. Maybe more."

Sassy whacked Quinn on the arm and he laughed.

She turned to Toren. "And you, I know you, don't I?"

63

"Hey, Sassy."

"Wait, wait, wait . . ." Sassy tapped her forehead with her order pad. "Toren!"

"You got it."

"Wait a minute." She frowned. "Didn't you disappear? Jumped on the outta-here bus for a year and no one knew where you'd gone? Or am I thinking of someone different?"

"I was gone for a while, yes."

"Well, welcome back."

"Thanks."

Sassy took their smoothie orders and shuffled off.

Quinn wiggled his forefinger at Toren. "You do realize you're going to have to do a press conference about your resurrection. Better to get it over with all at once. Get 'em all together, answer their questions, and it will die down in a week."

It was the first time Toren had considered the idea. But he said, "Yeah, I know. I'm going to get it set up. Just not looking forward to it."

"Why?"

"I'll only have one answer for all their questions: I don't know."

"Huh?"

Toren leaned forward, elbows on the table. "I have no memory of where I was, how I got there, what I was doing there, how I got back here . . . nothing."

"You're kidding."

"Eight months. Gone. I have no idea why I didn't call. No idea why I left. No idea why I came back."

"You don't remember writing a suicide note?"

"A suicide note! What are you talking about?" What Sloane had said in passing struck him with new meaning: *You wrote a note.*

"In blue Sharpie — your MO, my friend."

"What did it say?"

Quinn shrugged. "Only the police know, I guess. Maybe Sloane."

Toren shook his head.

"Eight months of amnesia. Is this for real?"

"Yeah, it's for real." Toren slumped back in the booth. "Which means if I didn't do it to myself, someone did it to me."

"And you're going to find out who."

"If it's the last thing I do."

Toren told Quinn the little he knew, and when he finished, Quinn stared at him.

"What a weird trip."

"Yeah."

"Give me anything. There have to be answers."

"I've given you everything I know."

A second later, Quinn blinked hard and whacked his palms on the table. "Hey, have you called Prinos?"

"No, not yet. I'm thinking about it."

"Thinking about it?" Quinn leaned forward. "What do you mean thinking about it? You need to. Like, today."

Quinn was dead right. He needed to call, wanted to call. Peter Prinos to most, just Coach to Toren. Brilliant. Motivating. Won the conference championship Toren's sophomore, junior, and senior years of high school. Almost took them to state their senior year. Then in a fluke of all glorious flukes, Coach got a shot at coaching the defense at the University of Washington. Guess where Toren got a scholarship? And guess who helped Toren get his shot in the pros by training him for the NFL combine?

Coach. One of the most significant men in Toren's life. From his freshman year of high school on, they'd had the classic, I-only-have-daughters-and-wanted-a-son-and-your-dad-wasn't-exactly-a-model-father-so-let-me-be-a-father-figure-to-you relationship. He'd been Toren's salvation on the field and off.

"It's been a long time since we talked."

"How long?"

"Since the day after the Seahawks released me. Coach was pretty disappointed in me."

"Well, so was I — so were a lot of people. So were *you.*"

"Said a lot of things to him I wish I hadn't. Lost it on the phone with him."

"Let it go, Tor. I guarantee he has. You know exactly what's under that eighty-grit sandpaper exterior. He never had a player he cared for more than you. Call him. You'll make his day almost as much as you made mine."

"Yeah, you're right. I'll get around to it."

Sassy returned with their smoothies and they each took a sip, then sat in silence for a few moments before Quinn sighed and said, "All right, you ready to tell me what's going on?"

"I just told you."

Quinn cocked an eyebrow. "Come on. You know what I'm asking."

"Yeah. Sure." Toren sat back in the booth. "Might as well."

"Tell me, Tor. All of it."

Tor. Quinn's nickname for him ever since they'd met, eons ago. The only person who called him that. The sound of him saying the name again made three truths rocket through Toren's brain, each one stacked atop the other. First, there was something special between the two of them. Always had been. A true friend. Second, he didn't want to confess what he'd done to Sloane and the kids, but he didn't really have a choice. Third, Quinn would stand by him. No matter what.

"I've been living a lie."

Quinn looked up from under his eyebrows, his voice a whisper. "I know."

"What?"

"I called Sloane on the way over here. Couldn't stop myself. She did a good job. Told me what a miracle it was. How happy she and the kids were. Faked it so well I almost believed her. But not quite good enough."

"Wow."

"Yeah."

Silence again. Toren's number was up. Time to trust his friend. Time to get authentic.

"The temper I showed on the field never showed up at home. Till I stopped playing. Then it took up residence there in full force. The only difference was I didn't hit anybody. But the language, the rage, the fuel that drove me on the field took over my home. And I couldn't stop it."

"Junior high school, college ball, the

pros . . . You always had an outlet on the field."

"Yeah." Toren squeezed his glass. "But when the pressure valve went away . . ."

"I'm sorry, Tor."

"Yeah, me too."

Toren stared at his friend, looking for understanding, seeing only challenge.

"What are you going to do about it?"

"That's the craziest part of this whole thing. I think that's what I've been doing all this time — dealing with it. I think my temper might be gone."

"What?" Quinn snapped his fingers and chuckled. "Poof! It disappears, huh?"

"I'm serious." Toren tapped his fingers on the table. "I think that's where I was."

"Anger management school?"

"More than that. What if I went to a place where they can fix things like an out-of-control temper on a deeper level — a spiritual level? Soul surgery."

Quinn rolled his eyes.

"I'm just saying, Q, what if it was possible? That would fix everything. I might be able to convince a team that my anger wouldn't be an issue, and if I could convince Sloane it was gone . . . she'd take me back. I'd get back the two most important things in my life." Toren reached into his pocket and pulled out the letter he'd received in the package.

Quinn read it with a skeptical expression before handing it back.

"I've got to find out where I was and what they did to me."

"If those are your two most important things, then yeah. But seriously, Tor, if it's not already gone, then you have to figure out a way to destroy that part of you." Quinn's eyes were full of grace and fire. "But my opinion? To make that happen, you have to figure out where your temper came from in the first place."

Quinn was wrong and right at the same time. Yes, he did have to make sure his temper had truly been annihilated, but he didn't have to figure out how his rage was born. That he knew already. He'd taken enough psychology classes in college to know precisely where his temper came from. It exploded into life the summer of his fourteenth year, but the detonator was constructed when he was only ten, on a September afternoon in the basement of the house Toren grew up in. As Toren stared into Quinn's eyes, the memory rushed in like a hurricane.

CHAPTER 8

"What're you doing, squirt?" Toren whispered to his brother. "Get away from those."

"I just want to pick them up. I'm not going to throw 'em or anything." Toren's younger brother, Brady, grinned as he stood on their dad's leather chair and peered into the glass case that sat on the shelf.

Their dad's prized collection of baseballs from the 1930s sat inside. Brady lifted the glass off the balls, set it down on the chair, then reached into the case and plucked up the ball in the middle, hit out of the park by Lou Gehrig, and tossed it up and down.

"I'm just going to look. I promise." He grinned. "Unless someone wants to play catch with me."

"Don't be an idiot. You know what's going to happen if Dad catches you? You won't make it to your ninth birthday."

"He's not going to catch me."

"And if he's been drinking, which is

ninety percent of the time, you'll *really* get it."

"He won't catch me!"

"Just put it back, Brady. Don't do this."

"Fine. Spoil the fun."

Brady set the Gehrig ball back in the carved-out indentation in the wood, then lifted the glass cover and started to set it back over the balls. But Brady missed the corner by a quarter inch. Then lost his balance on the chair. Toren watched as the glass case and the ball holder did a slow-motion flip and a half before shattering on the floor, the baseballs bouncing and scattering.

Ten seconds passed before the thunder of their dad's footsteps on the basement stairs sent both boys to the wall, their backs pressed against it as if they could part the molecules in the concrete and disappear.

An instant later, their dad flung the door open. His gaze swept the room, stopping for only an instant on the shattered glass case and the five baseballs now strewn around the room. He fixed his gaze on Brady and Toren, then spoke, his voice barely a whisper.

"Both of you? Or just one? Give me the truth."

Toren's voice came out like a rustling of

72

tissue paper. "Just one."

"Who?"

"Me. I did it," Toren sputtered.

Toren's father strode over and towered over him. "That right, huh?"

The smell of beer floated down on Toren.

"Yes. I'm so, so sorry, Dad. I didn't mean to, I was just —"

Toren's dad smacked him on the head and pain shot through Toren's skull. "You need to learn to be a better liar, kid."

His dad went to a cabinet on the other side of the chair and snatched out a thick belt, then advanced on Brady. "Bend over. Now."

After the third blow, Toren couldn't keep the words inside. "Stop! That's enough, Dad! You have to!"

"You stay here!" His dad thrust his finger at Brady. "Do not move."

His dad swaggered over to Toren. "What'd you say, boy?"

"Please stop. You need to stop!"

"You some tough guy, Toren? Huh? Telling me what to do? Is that what you are? Tough guy?" His dad smacked the belt against his own hand almost as hard as he had hit Brady with it.

"No, I just think . . . I just wish you'd . . . stop it! Please. Pretty please."

His dad pressed his heavy body into Toren's, pushing into him, and Toren staggered back a step.

"Did you say please? Yeah, I think you did. In fact, I think you just said pretty please. I got a word for you. *Pansy.* Can you say pansy, Toren? You should be able to — that's what you are right now. Little Pretty Please Pansy boy. Three little Ps."

Chunky laughter spewed out of his dad's mouth.

Toren whispered to his brother, "Get out of here."

"You think I'm deaf, pansy boy?"

"No, I just want you to —"

"Stop. Yeah, I get it. That's it, right? You want me to stop, huh?"

"Yes."

"Okay, I'll stop." His dad grinned at Toren and kept bumping his chest into Toren's head, pushing him back another step, then another. "Here's how that's going to work. You take the belt out of my hands and put me on my butt, and I'll stop. How's that for a deal. Huh? Ya like that? We got a deal?" His father's voice rose to a roar. "We got a deal?"

"No, that's not what I mean. That's not —"

"Oh, I get it. Sure. You want to yap at me

like a little dog, bark, bark, bark! But you don't really want to do anything about it, do ya, huh?"

"I don't know what you mean . . ."

"Sure you do. Take a swing at me. Come on." His dad slapped his stubbled cheek with the palm of his oversized hand. "Take a swipe at your old man. Feel real good."

The words seethed out of him, and the rage in his dad's eyes bordered on maniacal.

"No, Dad, all I want is —"

"You think you're up for it? Taking me down?"

"No, I just —"

"I'd love to have you take a poke at me. See what you got inside. See if it's anything more than squishy mush."

"That's not what I'm saying, Dad!" Tears forced their way to Toren's eyes.

"Come on, tough guy." His dad smacked his hand again with the belt so hard, Toren couldn't believe the look on his dad's face didn't change. "You want some of the leather here? Or wanna try to give me some? Yeah? That what you want? Then let's go. Right now, let's go, you and me. Be a man, you little pansy!"

"No . . . but . . . but . . ." Toren pointed at his brother. "He's bleeding. He's . . .

75

he's . . . You've really, really hurt him."

The tears in Toren's eyes welled up and he screamed at himself not to let it happen, not to let them pour over onto his cheeks. He lost the battle. But at least his dad wasn't beating his brother any longer.

"Oh, man, this is good. Turning on the waterworks for your little brother. Wow. Nice job. We oughta put you in the movies. Yeah? Should we? Little pansy actor boy?"

Another hard smack of the belt into his dad's palm.

"You think that doesn't hurt me? Yeah? Well, it does. But you gotta figure this out if you want to do what you just did, go and pretend you can be a man, stick up for people. To do that, you gotta figure out how to do something. You wanna know what it is? What you gotta do?"

Toren pulled in quick breaths as he wiped tears from his cheeks.

"Huh? Do you?"

"Ye . . . yeah."

"You gotta keep it under control. All of it. Rein it in. Your emotions. The exact opposite of what you're doing right now. Spilling your tears all over the world. Really? Really? What is wrong with you? You're almost eleven years old. Figure it out. Lock it down. Keep a lid on it."

What leaked out of Toren's mouth next were words he'd regretted saying every moment since. He didn't know where they'd come from. Why didn't he keep them bottled up? If only he'd stayed silent. If only he'd let the moment play out, just nodded and let his dad eventually walk away, like he had every other time. But that day he didn't stop.

"Keep a lid on it?" Toren balled his fists. "Like you keep a lid on *your* temper? Is that the kind of lid you're talking about, Dad?"

What happened next remained a blur in Toren's mind, even in the dreams he had about the Incident, as it came to be known. His dad shoving him onto the floor, his knee in Toren's back. Then his dad yanking Toren's jeans down and the belt striking him till he could no longer feel the shooting pain of each blow. And then darkness.

He awoke hours later, after the sun had relinquished her reign over the day to a dark night with no stars. His mom was beside his bed when the pain was too much, trying to explain why they couldn't go to the hospital. She was there when he fell back under, when he woke for the second time, and all during the days of Toren's recovery. There in the middle of the night when he woke, screaming, nightmares flooding his mind.

His dad shuffled into Toren's room eight days after the beating and stood in the doorway, leaning on the doorframe.

"How ya doing, champ?"

Toren glanced at his father, then to his bedcovers.

His dad pushed off the doorframe, an edge to his voice now. "I said, how are you doing?"

"Good."

"That's my kid." His dad ambled up to the edge of Toren's bed. For once, his breath didn't reek of alcohol. "Hey, things got a little out of hand there a few days back. Sometimes what I'm feeling inside just kinda gets . . . so, uh . . . I'm . . . I'm . . . you know."

Toren sank his teeth into his tongue and stared at the poster on the far wall of his bedroom. His grandpa had given it to him, a picture of Dick Butkus. A moment later the bed shook.

"Hey, kid, look at me."

Toren narrowed his eyes and looked at his dad.

"Don't give me that look, boy." A storm stirred inside his dad's eyes and they went black as he leaned in. Toren silently prayed for his mom to come in before his dad lost it again.

"You hear me?"

"Yes, Dad." Toren swallowed. "I'm sorry."

"Okay."

They sat in silence, Toren trying to hold his dad's gaze, the man's eyes expressing the exact opposite of his attempt at an apology. But after a few short seconds Toren dropped his gaze and fixed it once again on one of the greatest linebackers ever to play in the NFL.

"Hey, look at me."

Toren stared up into his dad's darkness as he said, "We're good, right?"

Toren nodded.

"And if your mom asks, I said what I needed to, and you're feeling good and I'm feeling good and it's all in the past, right?"

"Yes, Dad."

"All right." His dad patted Toren's shoulder and strode toward the door at the same moment his mom walked in.

"There." His dad sneered at her. "You happy now?"

Her hands trembled, but her face was blank. She'd learned not to show weakness, irritation, fear, anything that could be interpreted the wrong way — which it was most of the time.

"Thank you," she said.

"Yeah."

His dad walked out the door, but his mom stood frozen, her lips the only part of her body that moved, silently counting. If his dad didn't spin back in thirty seconds, history said he wouldn't return. They listened for the sound of the TV coming on in the living room, or of the front door slamming as he left for the rest of the night. Thirty seconds later, Toren heard the TV blare to life, the signal to his mom that it was safe to come talk to him.

She closed the door softly, then eased over to his bed and sat on the edge.

"How was that for you, Toren?"

"It was good."

"Because you can tell me if it wasn't. You know that, right?"

"Yeah, I know." He gave her a weak smile. "It was good."

"Really?" His mom rubbed his hand. "Your dad is sorry, he is so sorry. He's a good man and he loves you, but sometimes he gets . . . well, sometimes he . . ."

She trailed off and looked away, still believing that Toren couldn't see the lie in her eyes. The look that screamed with the force of a tempest that she wanted to leave his father. But she couldn't tell that story, couldn't tell about the countless times he'd lost it with her and slapped her so hard she slumped to the floor in a daze. He never hit her with a closed fist, but a slap was every bit as brutal. Toren and his brother heard them through the living room walls, down the hall, and into the upper and lower bunks they slept in.

When she married his dad, she'd vowed to keep her family together no matter what. She made a promise to stay with Toren's dad for better and for worse. So she told herself stories she made up in her head and told them to the neighbors and her sister and her mom and dad, and anyone else who wanted to know. Life was grand at the Daniels home. Always had been. Always would be.

She'd undoubtedly already made up a story about what happened to his brother's backside and his own backside, and too soon she'd believe the lie herself and convince herself that Toren and his brother believed it as well. But he wouldn't. He knew the truth.

"So you and your dad, you're okay now?"

"Yeah, it's okay."

"You mean that?" She scooted closer.

"Yes, Mom."

"Because you can tell me if it isn't."

"Yeah, Mom, I know. You just told me that!" Toren's gaze dropped to his hands.

"Sorry, I didn't —"

"No, Toren. It's fine. I know I already said it, but I wanted to make sure. Make sure you're really, truly okay."

When Toren went back to school a few days later, the other kids stared at him. A few asked where he'd been. He didn't give any of them a straight answer, not even his friends, until a kid new to the school plunked down next to him at lunch on Toren's third day back.

"So what happened to you?"

"Nothing."

"Yeah, right." The kid glanced around as if to make sure no one was listening. "You can tell me. I can keep a secret."

Toren had the odd feeling he could tell the truth to this complete stranger. Still, he didn't even know the kid's name.

"I was out back goofing around in my tree fort and fell and scraped my face and stuff and fell on my back and hurt it."

"You gotta come up with something better than that." The new kid took one of Toren's french fries, stuffed it into his mouth, and grinned as he chewed. "Want to try again?"

"What do you think happened to me?" Toren said.

"I *know* what happened. I can see it in

your eyes 'cause the same thing happens to me sometimes. Your dad loses it, even when it's not your fault, and beats the tar out of you. And then you gotta pretend it's okay, 'cause if you don't, your dad will beat on your mom a little. Sometimes more than a little, okay?"

Toren didn't answer, but his head gave a slight nod of agreement.

"I don't know what you're going to do about all that going on, but I can't take it going on like that without thinking about a way out. Now I have a way out. Now I have a plan."

Toren stared at the new kid. There was a strength in his eyes and a hint of danger. More than a hint maybe.

"You ever want to hit him back?"

"What?" Toren frowned at the kid.

"You heard me."

Toren turned back to his lunch and took a drink of milk.

"I'll tell you if you want me to." The kid leaned closer. "About my plan to take care of my dad. You can use it for your dad if you want to."

Toren nodded again.

"I'm going to get strong. Stronger than my dad. Start lifting weights soon. Maybe learn some karate too, or kung fu, and then

I'm going to get in my dad's face, stare him down, tell him I hate him. Then when he comes after me with the belt, I'm going to take it out of his hands and do to him what he did to me."

An anger boiled deep inside Toren as the kid spoke. "I don't hate my dad."

"Yeah, you do."

Toren poked at his cheeseburger, the churning in his stomach making him not so hungry. "What's your name?"

"Letto."

"You're new here."

"Yeah."

Toren gathered his lunch and got up. "I'll see you, Letto."

"Yeah, see ya around, Toren."

That was the day Toren made the vows. Just the way Letto had laid them out. First, he would get stronger than his dad. Whatever it took. Second, a day was coming when he'd stare his father down and take the belt out of his hand. And his father would never hit Toren's mom or Brady ever again.

"Toren?"

He pulled himself out of the memory and stared at Quinn. "I'm here."

"What else?" Quinn drummed his fingers

on the table. "With Sloane, I mean. Anything else you want to tell me?"

"I need you, Quinn."

"I'm here, man. But you have to get things fixed."

"I did. That's what I'm saying. I've changed. Radically. I'm a different guy."

"I hope so. If that's true, you might have a second chance with your kids. With Sloane. That's gonna take time."

"I know."

"So what are you going to do to stay occupied, keep from obsessing about it?"

"Work out with you."

"And the rest of each day?"

"Keep working with all that reclaimed wood, building tables, nightstands, keep doing custom jobs for people to keep a little money flowing in. Turn it into a business, I'm thinking. If I don't make it back to the field, I can't keep living off what I saved from my playing days forever."

"It's a good plan." Quinn downed the last of his smoothie. "So what happens next with Sloane and the kids?"

"It's already in motion."

CHAPTER 9

On Friday afternoon, Sloane went to her mailbox, grabbed the postcards promising thousands of points at luxury hotels, bills, and her fitness magazine along with a letter that doubled her heart rate. She knew the handwriting on the front of the square envelope as well as she knew her own, even though she hadn't seen it in months. Written in blue ink. Toren's.

Four months back she'd finished tossing out all his old letters to her, cards, anything and everything with his penmanship on it. It had been difficult at the time, but she'd done it to be free of him. Free of the pain, free of the memories of when she'd loved him.

A groan pressed its way out of her throat as she stuffed the white envelope into the middle of the mail and slogged back up the long driveway. No. She wouldn't read it. What would be the point? It would be full of how he'd gone away to figure out how to truly change and a miracle had happened, so now she needed to give him one more chance, and this time would be different, blah, blah, blah.

She should head for the garbage and shove it deep into the green can. But her feet didn't turn. Crazy. What was wrong with her? A feeling stirred deep down. She squashed it, but before she finished, a word formed in her mind: *hope.* No. Not possible. Toren was dead. Not physically. But in every other way he had perished from her life, and no resurrection was coming.

Sloane stumbled into the house and flung the mail to her right. She watched it separate as if in slow motion and flutter to the carpet, the couch, and what used to be Toren's favorite chair. She should have tossed that out alongside his old love letters.

She looked away, rubbed her palm over her eyes, and looked back at the mail. Come on. No question God had a sense of humor, but this wasn't funny. She shuffled toward Toren's old chair. His note had made a perfect landing, right side up, stuck between the back and the cushion, perpendicular to the ground. She reached for the envelope and stared at the writing, which eons ago made her heart pound in a good way, and now in the opposite way.

Sloane hesitated, then reached for the note and lifted it from the chair, her fingernails scraping the brown leather. She carried it at arm's length, staring at it as if it were infected with a virus. In a strange sense, it probably was. She'd slowly slipped into the illness his virus had caused for the past three years.

His anger on the field always bothered her, but she wasn't the only football wife whose husband transformed into a different man when he played. But he'd never brought his work home with him. Till he stopped playing. His anger wasn't much at first, but then it became more frequent and more intense. And then the final straw, and then a month later he disappeared. Ever since that day, life had continued to get better. Now? She pushed the future from her mind.

Sloane reached the kitchen, threw the note on the counter as if it were a Frisbee, and watched it slide across the speckled granite till it bumped into the backsplash, its lettering now upside down and unreadable from this distance. Sloane stared at it, arms crossed hard across her chest, her emotions doing battle inside. She glanced at Callie's school book — one of Shakespeare's plays rewritten for children — then back to Toren's note. She laughed bitterly at the irony. To read or not to read, apparently that was the question.

It wasn't truly a question. She would read it. Of course she would. Had to. If she didn't read it and didn't do whatever he wanted her to, he would keep sending notes until she did respond. Might as well get it over with. But not inside. Outside, where she could leave any emotions that might try to break out with the Douglas fir trees towering over her backyard.

Sloane strode around the end of the counter, snatched the note off the granite, and pushed through the door into her backyard. The waterfall they'd had built seven years ago was chortling away as if it didn't care that Toren had shown up and her life was now threatening to come unglued. She eased down the path that circled her acre-and-a-half backyard and didn't stop till she reached the gazebo at the far end of the property, which overlooked a lush greenbelt.

The gazebo roof was covered in moss half an inch thick, and leaves filled the edges of the floor. It looked like no one had stepped inside in months, which was precisely the case. She made her way to the table in the middle, brushed off one of the chairs, and sat. A robin landed on the railing on the far side of her and cocked its head.

"Would you like to take a look at Toren's stupid note and tell me whether I should read it or not?"

The bird responded by hopping a few inches closer, then cocking its head left and right, and finally turned and flew off.

"I'll take that as a no."

She held her breath and pulled a stiff square of paper out of the envelope. Handwritten in thick blue ink. She smiled in spite of herself. He was still using Sharpies to scrawl his notes. It was the only thing he'd written with since before the day they'd met. Sloane set the envelope on the table, lifted the note, and read the words of the man she thought she'd never see again.

Hello, Sloane,

Let me start by apologizing once again for appearing on your doorstep without warning. I was hoping to ease the shock of discovering I was still alive, not exacerbate it. I clearly did the latter, so I ask for your forgiveness as well as for Colton's and Callie's.

I of course have no way of knowing if

you're reading this note or simply tossed it in the garbage, but if you have chosen that path, I can't blame you. I don't want to upset your life or change it or even enter it again.

Actually, that's not true. I do want to be in your life again. I'm begging God every hour for that to happen. I want to be in Colton's and Callie's worlds again. But after seeing you and witnessing what my being alive did to you, I realize that's a long road that I might never get to go down.

All I want at this point is to see you once more, sit down with you one last time, and try to explain what I think has happened to me. I don't need much more than ten minutes or so, but I think it's important.

Will you consider it?

Yours,
Toren

Sloane snatched the envelope off the table and kicked at the chair next to her. She shoved the note back into its envelope and flicked it across the table. It came to rest hanging over the edge. What was she supposed to do? Easy. She'd write him back, tell him to say whatever he needed to say in a letter. They didn't need to sit down face-to-face.

The maddening part was the look in her kids' eyes. Not Colton's as much, but definitely in Callie's. She wanted a dad. Needed a dad. Not Toren, but the man Toren had been before he stopped playing ball. The dad who played Barbies and pushed her on the swing for hours. The dad who had never broken her heart with rage or words no little girl should hear.

Dinner started out quiet that night, as it had every meal since Toren had shown up on their doorstep. The memory of that horror had grown like a specter, becoming more solid every night till it hung over their table like fog.

Between the meal and frosting-covered brownies, Callie gave them all a reason to speak. She reached into her back pocket and pulled out a light-blue envelope. Square. Sloane didn't have to ask what was inside.

"I got a card today at school."

"From who?" Sloane said, even though she had no doubt it came from Toren.

"From Daddy."

"Oh?"

"Yeah." Callie put her finger on one of the corners and spun the note in a slow circle.

"Why would he make it come to me at school instead of having it sent here?"

"What did it say?" Sloane took another forkful of salad and tried to chew.

"That he loves me. And misses me. And wants to see me." Callie stopped the card from spinning and pulled it toward her. "Do you know why he sent it to school, Mommy?"

"Because he wanted you to read it." Colton tossed his fork onto his plate and it clanked with a dull sound.

"What does that mean?"

"It means he knows Mom would toss it in the garbage can if she found it first."

"Would you have?" Callie turned to Sloane.

"I don't . . ." She hesitated. "No, I wouldn't have, of course not, but yes, the thought would have crossed my mind."

"That wouldn't have been the honest thing to do."

"No, Callie. It wouldn't have been."

"I got one too." Colton pulled a brown envelope out of his pocket and waved it.

Sloane gave a tiny shake of her head as she stared at Colton's note, then Callie's, then picked at the remaining pieces of chicken dijon on her plate.

"What did your father have to say to you?"

Colton shoved the note back into his pocket and said, "Just that he was sorry. Asked me to forgive him. Said he finally understood what he'd done to me. What he did to you, did to Callie."

"That was it?"

"Yeah." Colton jabbed his fork into his potatoes. "Except . . ."

"Except what?"

"He said he was going to find a way to make it up to us. Show us he's changed."

"He hasn't changed. Trust me."

"How do you know, Mom?"

"Because he did change. Hundreds of times. I'd finally get so frustrated at all his broken promises to stop losing his temper that I'd scream as loud as he did, trying to get him to fix it."

Sloane ran her fingers down her forehead, over her eyes, and down her cheeks. Maybe this was a dream. Maybe she would wake up and Toren would still be missing. Sure. And maybe the Tooth Fairy really did put all those silver dollars under her kids' pillows when they were young.

"Mom? You there?"

"Yes, sorry."

"So you're saying Dad did change."

"Yes. He did change." She gave her kids a sad smile. "He'd count to ten when he started to get angry. He'd pin up Bible verses in the bathroom and on the dashboard of his car and memorize them, and he played worship music to try to calm his spirit, and he'd get up half an hour early to pray.

"But the rubber band always snapped back into place, and he'd start losing it again and then he'd . . ."

Sloane stopped herself. Her kids didn't need to hear this. They sat in the silence of great intentions and shattered promises till Colton sat forward and leaned toward Sloane.

"So what are you going to do, Mom?"

"What do you mean?"

"We're your kids."

"This I know. I was there both times."

"What I means is, we're not stupid." Colton gave her a lopsided smile.

"I'm still lost. Sorry."

"Callie got a card." Colton pointed at his sister, then at his pocket. "I got a letter. Which means the odds are really, really high that you got a letter or a card. And we're guessing what Dad wrote to you is that he wants to get together with you and talk and try to convince you that he should get to get back in our lives and that has to happen somehow because people are going to find out that he's back and it's going to cause a bunch of people we know to maybe find out he's not back here with us and that we didn't have the perfect family and that would really not be fun and I agree with that and so does Callie because we already talked about it and . . . well . . . I'm asking what are you going to do about all that?"

Sloane smiled as light laughter spilled out of her mouth.

"What's funny?" Colton said.

"First, you're much smarter than a ten-year-old should be, and second, I don't think you took a breath that whole sentence." She reached over and rubbed his arm. "What you said is exactly right. And, to answer your question, I don't know what I'm going to do. But we are not forsaken, and the wisdom of the ages is ours for the asking. So tonight, as I lie with my head on my pillow, I will be asking, and I suggest you two do the same."

Sloane stayed up late that night, as if not going to bed could save her from having to ask God to tell her what she should do. But eventually, after she'd binged on three episodes of a show that everyone had raved about but that turned out to be mediocre, she gave in to logic, dragged herself off the couch into what could be called a standing position, and started up the stairs to her bedroom. She stopped halfway up and looked down on the silence. So quiet. Peaceful even. But a storm was coming.

As she passed Callie's bedroom, Sloane glanced down. A faint glow escaped between the door and the carpet. Callie's light was still on at this hour?

Sloane gave a soft knock that was barely audible and opened the door a foot. Callie was looking her direction, the light on the nightstand bathing her face in a golden glow.

"Hi, sweetie."

"Hi, Mommy."

Sloane opened the door another foot and slid just inside the room. "You okay?"

"No."

"Do you want to talk about it?"

Callie nodded, and Sloane eased over to Callie's bed and sat on the edge.

"What's going on?"

"Can I say something that might hurt your feelings?" Callie pulled her pink blanket up tight to her chin.

"Of course."

"What about something I *know* could hurt your feelings?"

"That too."

"There's part of me way deep down, I

mean really, really deep down . . . that misses him."

The sensation of being shoved off a high cliff filled Sloane's mind, but just as quickly something pulled her back.

"Mommy? I'm sorry, but . . . I had to tell you."

"No, no, honey. I'm glad you did. I understand. He's your father. He loves you."

"He does?"

"Yes, I know he does. For sure, for sure."

"So what are we going to be doing about Daddy?"

"Our next steps are pretty simple. We're going to listen to God's Spirit and trust that the answers will come."

Sloane kissed Callie's forehead, switched off her light, then shuffled back across her carpet. Just before stepping into the hallway, she said, "I love you, Callie. So does the One who created you, more than you can possibly imagine."

She closed Callie's door and let a tightly bottled-up sigh slowly escape. Then she took a deep breath and resumed her slow trek to the end of the hall toward her bedroom. But before she could reach for her doorknob, her son's voice stopped her. Sloane turned. Colton stood with his door open five inches, half his face showing in the hallway light, his room dark behind him.

"Hey, Colton."

"Promise me something, okay?"

"Sure."

"Dad can be amazingly persuasive. At least he used to be."

"Yes."

"So if you do decide to go meet him, be strong. Fight, okay? Don't let him talk you into anything you don't want to be talked into, okay?"

She shuffled toward him, and as she did, he opened the door wider. His face was tough and scared, an old man's and a little boy's all in the same moment. Sloane wrapped her arms around him and pulled tight.

"I love you, Colton."

He squeezed back and gave her spine three quick pats before letting go. "Yeah, I hear you, Mom. Me too."

Sloane lay in bed, still awake as night crossed over into the first few seconds of two a.m., not asking for the wisdom she'd told her children she would seek. She wasn't refusing to ask. The need simply wasn't there. She already knew what she had to do. The Spirit had already spoken to her. She had prayed already and received a crystal-clear answer.

Still, she fought it. Life had settled. She had moved on. So had Colton and Callie. Things were going good. Better than good. After so many years of being out at sea with thirty-foot waves crashing over her, years in which Toren promised to change, she'd learned to find peace in the midst of the storm. She didn't need him to be her rescuer any longer.

Sleep continued to dodge her attempts to wrestle it down. Two Ambien didn't help. Finally she snatched up her cell phone, tapped in the cell number Toren had written on the bottom of the card, then wrote a quick text.

Tomorrow. 9am. Jana's coffee shop. Ten minutes for you to say whatever you need to say. Then i'm gone.

Three minutes later she was asleep.

CHAPTER 10

Toren was five minutes out from the coffee shop when his cell rang. Unknown number.

"Hello?"

"You moron, I thought I'd lost you to the great beyond."

The thick voice on the other end of the line raised a slew of competing emotions. Hope. Regret. Shame. Peace.

"Coach?"

"What were you thinking, disappearing for a year?" Coach swore. "I thought you were dead."

"I didn't know you were keeping track of me. Didn't know if we were still talking to each other."

"Don't be an idiot. I'd die for you, Toren."

The words stunned Toren. Coach had always been a rock for him, but more in actions than in what Coach would call sentimental babble.

"I, uh . . ."

"Where were you for eight months?"

Toren stumbled through the same essential facts he'd told Quinn. When he finished, Coach cleared his throat.

"That real? About your temper? Getting it handled?"

"Yeah."

"You keeping in shape?"

"As good as I've ever been."

"Listen to me, Torrent" — Torrent, precisely what he'd been on the field for Coach all those years — "don't give up on the dream. You'll play again. I believe it. You have to believe it too."

Before he hung up, Toren said he'd be in touch sooner than later, and Coach made him swear to it.

A flood of words poured from Sloane's lips as Jana's Coffee Shop loomed in front of her.

"You have me held tight in the midst of the hurricane. I'm safe, I'm in your arms, and I will be strong, because I carry inside me the strength of my Father, the strength of the Son, the strength of the Spirit. I am in you, and you are in me. I can do this. It's going to be okay."

Sloane repeated the prayer a second time, then a third as she pulled open the door of the shop and stepped inside. She glanced around the store. Toren wasn't seated at any of the tables. She stole a look at her phone. Five after the hour. No way he would be late for this.

She stood just inside the door and scanned the room again. A group of teens sat together, their cell phones piled in the middle of their table. Teens not glued to their phones — there was hope for the world. Three other people, their focus on their notepads or laptops. To Sloane's left, an older couple, a middle-aged couple, and a tweener, probably waiting for his mom to get her coffee. No Toren.

Sloane made to leave. Wait. In line, with his back to her, was that him? Yes. A strange mix of disappointment and relief washed through her. Disappointment that he showed. Relief that he showed. She refused to examine the second emotion.

A moment later he turned, the expression on his face one she knew yet didn't know. There was a kindness she hadn't seen in ages. Dare she say contrition? Yes, definitely. And pain.

By the time they settled at a table in the far corner of the coffee shop, her heartbeat had slowed and her emotions had settled. She would get through this. Nine minutes and twelve seconds left.

"I hope I got it right." Toren shrugged as he handed her a grande-size cup and sat.

"What is it?"

"Grande white-chocolate mocha with caramel drizzle."

Her eyes widened as she wrapped both hands around the cup.

"You're surprised?" he said.

"It's been a while. Surprised you remembered."

He shrugged a second time. "Just a good guess."

She stared at him, realizing the look of pain she'd seen earlier wasn't for himself, but for her. A second surprise. But it didn't matter. Let him say his piece, then leave. She looked down at her cup, then back up at Toren. He stared at something outside the shop, out on the street, his eyes flashing alarm.

"What?"

Toren leaped to his feet and sprinted out the door of the shop. He returned a few minutes later, frustration painted on his face.

"What is it?" Sloane said.

"Who works on the yard? Did you see who was there the other day? What's the name of the landscaping company you're using?"

"What I do with the yard or the house and who I hire isn't any of your business any longer, Toren."

"Just tell me."

"When I said I'd give you ten minutes, I wasn't kidding." She took a long sip of her coffee. He'd gotten it exactly right. "If you want to use them arguing about what I will and I won't tell you about my house, fine by me."

"I get it."

But he didn't speak. Simply sat there, hands wrapped around his coffee, each hand a mirror image of the other. His choice. She glanced at her watch. Finally he spoke, his voice soft.

"I'm not the same man. I've changed, Sloane."

"You said that in the letter."

"Yeah, I did. But it's true. Look." He pushed a handwritten letter across the table. She glanced at it. Something about a "life-altering eight months" and "significant changes," from someone who couldn't be bothered to sign his name. Or hers. Sloane thought the handwriting looked feminine. She pushed the letter back.

"Yes." Sloane gave a thin smile, lips pressed together. "I'm absolutely positive you have."

"Don't you want to know where I've been, what's been going on?"

"Not anymore."

He almost laughed. "I understand why you don't believe me, why those words mean nothing to you, but I have to say them anyway."

"Why?"

"Because they're true this time." He tapped the letter still lying on the table between them.

She didn't respond. "Anyone might have written that."

"Can I explain why they're true?"

"What do you want, Toren?"

"I want things I know I can't have. Things I will pray for every day till I die." He leaned back and glanced at the ceiling. "I want to be reunited with my family. To show them that something happened to me while I was gone that I can't explain, but every minute of every day makes me more and more certain I've gone through a transformation of everything I am.

"I want to be the daddy my daughter needs. I want to be the father my son needs as he gets ready to step into manhood. Most of all I want to be the husband I was up until three years ago. I guess by now it's been almost four years. I want you to know

106

the war you watched me fight with my anger is over, and I've won."

Toren paused, eyes pleading.

"I'm happy for you, Toren. Really. But you're right, those are dreams that are not going to come true." Her voice was quiet, but by the look on Toren's face, the words must have felt as loud as thunder. "Are we done?"

"No." He shook his head and studied the table. "I want you to forgive me for the man I was and what I put you through."

"Fine. You're forgiven. Now are we done?"

"Almost." He looked up, stared deep into Sloane's eyes with those deep blues that could no longer melt her heart, and laid his hands over the ridiculous letter. Then he gave her that half-cocked smile and said, "Just one more thing, okay?"

"What?"

"I want you to stop hating me."

Sloane settled both hands over his, pressed down gently, and ignored the shocked look on his face.

"I don't hate you, Toren. I never have. Never did. Never will."

"Then why —"

She patted his hands and pulled hers away. "Let me finish."

"Yes, of course." He touched his lips. "I'm sorry."

"What happened to me was worse than starting to hate you." She took a quick sip of her coffee, leaned toward him, and said, "I lost heart, Toren. It's gone and it's not coming back. I believed you so many times. I really, truly did. And then I didn't believe, but I still hoped. God, did I hope. And then the hope became too frayed, too thin to hang on to any longer, and it slipped from my hand. And one day when I looked for it, I discovered it had vanished, long before I even knew it had."

Tears formed in Toren's eyes and he pulled away from the table. His body seemed to shrink into his seat. "There has to be a small part of you that —"

"No. That hope sprinted away six weeks after you disappeared. After three months it was replaced by the hope that you were truly gone. I have a new life now."

"But if you truly knew what has ha —"

"I realize you need to have a relationship with your children. And as much as I don't like the idea of it, I'm going to get used to it. It's what is right. They need one with you as well. You're their father. Just take it slow, okay?"

Toren nodded and started to speak just as

Sloane raised her forefinger, making him go silent. She closed her eyes for a moment, nodded to herself, then opened them and spoke just above a whisper.

"But as far as you and me?" She sighed. "If you are truly admitting to who and what you were, then you understand why I've moved on. And you'll know why your coming back and trying to reinsert yourself into my life is not only a tremendous shock but proves you haven't really changed. Because if you had, you'd go back to wherever you've been."

Toren stared at her, several emotions flitting across his eyes in a matter of seconds. Surprise. Pain. Anger? No, not anger, frustration. And innocence. And then, resolve. He rubbed his eyes, forehead. His upper teeth bit into his lip as his head wagged back and forth, a pensive look settling on his face.

"You're right, Sloane." Toren shook his head. "You are absolutely right."

He stood and for a second she thought he would step over and kiss her on the head, but instead, his fist rose to his lips, he nodded once more, and he turned and walked out of the shop.

CHAPTER 11

Toren peeked out between the curtains at the Kirkland Performance Center, his gaze sweeping past at least twelve TV cameras and as many radio microphones as he tried to gear himself up for the onslaught of questions from the media. Nothing inside him wanted to be here. He'd never enjoyed the media during his playing days — most reporters passed him by for the stars, which was fine by him — but now he was the focus and he had to face them full on.

Quinn and he had agreed this was the best and fastest way to get the word out that he was back. Better to have one session with as many press as wanted to show than to have them come to him for interviews by ones and twos for months on end. Plus, Quinn was still a star in the NFL, and some of the pressure would be taken off Toren simply with Quinn's presence.

"You ready for this?" Quinn whispered

into Toren's ear.

"No."

"Good. Let's get it over with." Quinn winked and grabbed his shoulder. "It'll be fine. I promise."

Quinn pushed through the curtain, and the crowd noise faded into silence.

"Friends, thanks for coming. As you all know, my best friend and brother in arms since junior high, Toren Daniels, has just returned after an eight-month absence. He's going to make a short statement and then will be open to questions. We're going to keep the Q&A to fifteen minutes, and after that we're going to respect his privacy as he eases back into his life. In other words, he's not going to be doing any one-on-one interviews, so if you've got a question you're dying to ask, don't save it. This is your one shot to ask."

As Quinn continued, doling out Toren's background, Toren's attention shifted to a frazzled-looking young reporter who was working his way toward the front. He motioned toward the podium with a microphone as he whispered to another reporter. The other reporter wiggled his fingers at the podium, and the kid waddled up to where the other microphones lay and set his on top. He was nearly seated again when his mic fell off the podium and hit the table with a boom that filled the room. The kid's face went dark red.

Quinn looked down at him. "Well, tell me something, son, where you working tomorrow?"

The crowd erupted in laughter as the young man sank into his seat.

"Hey, just kidding, my man!" Quinn pointed at him. "You'll be telling this story for decades."

The kid smiled and gave Quinn a thumbs-up. The incident put Toren at ease, and his breathing slowed.

"All right, enough intro, please welcome my friend, Toren Daniels."

Toren stepped through the curtain and sat next to Quinn, then pulled out his written statement, cleared his throat, and began.

"Ladies and gentlemen, as you're well aware, I vanished eight months ago without a trace and showed up again a few days back without any fanfare. But as far as where I was, why I left, and why I didn't let anyone know what happened to me, I'm afraid I'm going to be a big disappointment to all of you, because I can't answer any of those questions."

Toren paused and took a drink of water.

"You don't know, or you can't say?" a

voice from the back called out.

"I don't know." Toren glanced at his notes and set them aside. "The truth is, I don't have any memory of where I was, how I got there, what I was doing for the past eight months, or how I got back home. I know it sounds crazy — believe me, I know how crazy it sounds 'cause I'm living it — but there's very little I can tell you.

"The last thing I remember is going to bed last September. Then I woke up in a hotel with nothing but some clothes, my credit card, and my driver's license inside a package that the hotel gave me, and they don't know where the package came from. That's it. Any questions?"

Instantly the room filled with voices climbing over each other, the roar intensifying until Quinn started directing traffic.

"Is it true you left a suicide note?"

"I have no memory of that."

"Did you try to take your own life?"

Toren hesitated. "Not that I recall."

"Do you want to kill yourself?"

Quinn leaned toward Toren's mic. "Next topic, thanks."

"Have you been examined by a doctor?"

"No, I haven't."

"Are you going to be?"

"I'm considering it."

"You don't have any guesses as to where you were?"

"No, I don't."

"What about hypnosis?"

"I'm considering all options."

"What does your family think about you showing up alive?"

"I think they like it better than me showing up dead. But just barely."

The crowd laughed, and Toren wished the joke was a lie.

"Are you still hoping a pro team will consider signing you?"

"That's my hope. I'm in great shape, I'm training daily, and for the first time I can promise you I have my temper under control. There was no excuse for how I let it drive my behavior, but if a team gives me a shot, I can promise them it will never be an issue again."

"Is that part of what happened to you while you were away? Some kind of anger management therapy?"

"Possibly, but like I said, I have no memory of where I was or what I did."

"Then how do you know you've changed?"

"You know how when you meet the person you want to marry, you just know? That's the feeling. That's how certain I am. Plus,

I've had some things happen since I've been back that normally would have set me off, but the rage simply isn't there anymore."

The questions continued for another five minutes, but when it became clear Toren's answers were going to be short and sweet with no real substance, the media packed up. In another five, the room was nearly empty.

"You survived," Quinn said.

"Thanks for the help."

As Toren stood and slipped into his blue jacket, a slender woman with Asian features strolled toward him. Quinn motioned at her with his head. "Looks like you have someone who wants to talk. I'm gonna jet if you're good here."

"Yeah, I am."

The woman stopped a few feet away and said, "Hello, Toren, it's good to finally meet you."

"Finally?"

"Yes." She smiled and her eyes almost disappeared. She stepped closer and offered her hand. "My name is Eden Lee."

She was beautiful, not skin-deep beautiful, but the kind that permeated every part of her. Black hair parted in the middle stopped two or three inches past her shoulders. Her intensely bright eyes reminded him of someone he couldn't place.

Toren shook her hand and said, "Are you a reporter?"

Eden smiled again. "How is Sloane doing?"

"You know my wife?"

"Sloane hired me to find you. Obviously I didn't succeed."

"Private detective?"

She nodded.

"How long did you look?"

"I gave Sloane updates for six months. Our contract said I would get paid when I found you or found proof of your death."

"So you didn't get any money."

"No." Eden pointed toward the door. "Do you mind if we chat while we walk to our cars? I need to get going."

As they moved toward the door, Toren said, "Everyone is convinced I had a death wish. What is that from?"

"Do you?"

Toren glared at her sideways. "Not at the moment. You find any evidence I did, once upon a time?"

Eden pulled out her phone and tapped up a photo. She held it out for him to see. A sheet of notebook paper torn from its binding was covered in Toren's large blue-ink scrawl. The letter was in a plastic bag labeled with an "Evidence" sticker.

Dearest Sloane,
   It won't go on like this, I promise. I
will end this mess I've created for you,
for the kids, for me. Torenado doesn't
deserve to exist anymore. He's only rip-
ping up your lives, hurting you all. I will
protect you. For your sake, I will kill him
if it's the last thing I do. I hope you will
forgive me.
Love you forever,
Toren

"I mailed that to her?"
"No. A flight attendant found it under a
seat on the plane."
"A flight I'd taken?"
"To Phoenix, apparently."
Phoenix? Toren was sure he hadn't been
to Phoenix since he stopped playing.
"The trail went cold at the airport," she
said.
"I have no desire to kill myself."
"Good to know."
"Would you like to have another shot at
the case?"
"How do you mean?"
"Help me track down where I was, what I
was doing there. I'll pay you whatever

Sloane offered you if we succeed."

"That's an intriguing idea."

"I'm going to find out, one way or another, but I'm guessing if we worked together it would go a lot faster."

"I'd need my expenses covered whether we get answers or not."

"Not a problem."

"I'll think about it."

"Fair enough."

They walked through the door that led into the parking lot and bright sunshine.

"Where are you parked?" Toren asked.

"Far end of the lot."

"Same." As they ambled toward their cars, Toren said, "If we do take on this mystery together, where would you start?"

Eden raised an eyebrow. "Trying to get free advice out of me?"

"Yeah, exactly."

Eden laughed and said, "You mentioned receiving a package. I'd suggest trying to find out who gave that to the hotel. Someone has to know something."

"I feel a little stupid for not thinking of that."

"Tell you what, I won't feel bad about not being able to play in the NFL if you don't feel bad for not thinking like a detective."

"Done."

As Toren's rental car came into view, he spotted a man leaning against it with a hat pulled down over his face. Toren stutter-stepped to a halt, and his heart ticked a few beats faster.

"Are you okay?" Eden said.

"That guy leaning against my car. I think he's been tracking me. I think I know him from somewhere in my past. And I think I'm about to find out if I'm right."

"You want company?"

"Sure."

Ten yards before they reached the man, he yanked his hat off his head, grinned at Toren, and opened his arms. Once again, Toren stopped. No wonder he hadn't recognized the guy. It had been at least fifteen years. But this close, there was little doubt. He was older, his hair cut shorter, but there was no question the person standing before him was Letto Kasper, the man who had helped him create his vows, the catalyst that thrust him into the NFL.

Letto took a few steps toward them, light on his feet. He looked lean but muscled. Toren had trained with a group of Navy SEALs one summer before training camp, and that's exactly what Letto reminded him of. It wouldn't surprise him to find out he'd been in some kind of Special Ops unit.

Maybe still was.

"Unbelievable."

Letto laughed, sauntered up to Toren, grabbed his shoulders, and shook them. "Look at you, man! You're even bigger in real life than on TV."

"And it looks like you never cracked the five-foot-eight barrier."

"Nope, never quite got there." Letto fixed his eyes on Eden. "Who's your friend?"

"This is Eden Lee. Eden, this is a classmate of mine from a long time ago, Letto Kasper."

Letto stared at Eden. "Back in those days, till the end, he would have called me more than a classmate. He would have called me a friend. But seasons change, don't they, Toren?"

Toren leaned down and whispered in Eden's ear, "I need to talk to him in private. Can I have a few minutes alone?"

"Take as much time as you need." Eden handed Toren a card. "Call me in the morning, I'll give you an answer then."

Eden turned and strode off.

Toren faced Letto. "It was you in the landscape truck. It was you at the hotel. Outside the coffee shop."

"I see after all these years you still enjoy stating the obvious." Letto grinned and pointed a finger at him. "It's been a long time. A long, lonely, lonely, lonely, lonely, lonely time."

"Led Zeppelin. Off their fourth album."

"Yeah, Toro, yeah! Nicely done. You still listening to classic rock like we used to do in days way gone by?"

"Not so much anymore."

"Pity. I have some CDs in my car. Thought we could take a drive and listen a bit."

"Your landscape company works on my home now?"

"Not my company. I just work for that schlup, but yeah, that's kind of crazy, don't you think? I mean, what are the odds of me showing up at your house?"

"I don't think you work for them. I think you were at my home for another reason."

"Don't get smart, Toren. Stick to the weights, okay?"

"Stay away from my family."

"What's your problem?"

"No problem. Unless you come onto my property again."

"Sure, okay. Whatever."

"Why are you stalking me?"

"Lighten up. Thought I'd have a little fun with you, play a little game, see if you could figure out it was me or not. Sounds like you didn't. So I'm up, one to zero."

"What do you want?"

"I don't want anything." Letto squinted up at the sky. "Well, I guess I do want something. I want to keep the promise I made to you."

"Promise?"

"Yes. The promise I made to you the day the music between us died."

"Don McLean. 'American Pie.' "

"Nailed it again." Letto slipped his Mariners hat back on over his thick blond hair. "Two for two."

"What promise?" Toren's hands went to fists.

"Hey, relax, Toro. You don't need to threaten me with your impressive-looking muscles, old friend. I'm just messing with you." Letto thrust out his chest and bumped up against Toren. "But I don't need to tell you what promise. You remember, don't ya? I think you do. If you don't, nothing to worry about, I'll be in touch in a few days anyway — give you a reminder if you need it."

"Why don't you remind me now?"

"She's really pretty, Toren. And you've got good-looking kids. Worth fighting for, I think."

Toren lunged for Letto, but the smaller man skittered out of the way faster than

122

Toren expected.

"Are you threatening my family?"

"Oh, Toren, come on, brother. Put some slack in the rope, you're all bound up. I'm just giving you a compliment. I mean it, nice-looking family! And I hope you get 'em back. That's all."

Letto yanked his cap down over his eyes and backed away, a grin splashed over his face that never reached his eyes.

CHAPTER 12

Sloane stood on Main Street on Saturday night, staring at Levi Greene through the window of Aleta Restaurant and Grill, feeling guilty and scolding herself for feeling even a shred of shame. There was no reason. Toren leaves a fake suicide note, shows up again after eight months, claims to have revolutionized his life, and she's supposed to be happy about it? Welcome him back? Sorry. She had been happy. Before he showed up. Happy with Levi, more than happy with him, in love. The past six months had made her believe she could give away her entire heart again — Levi already had more than a few pieces. And Colton and Callie seemed to really like him. She was so glad they hadn't said anything when Toren showed up at the house the other day. That would be the definition of awkward conversation.

She shrugged off the thoughts of remorse,

clipped across the street, and opened the front door of the restaurant. The scent of warm bread and olive oil spun around her, along with the clatter of knives and spoons and forks and cups. The place was busy. Typical. The mix of great atmosphere, great food, and an owner who cared was a potion richly rewarded.

Levi spotted her, and that zillion-dollar smile that had made her first notice him six months ago spread across his face. He stood as she approached, and she leaned in for a quick kiss.

"Hey, beautiful, tell me all about life since I last saw you." He slid her coat off her shoulders and draped it over her chair, then helped scoot her in close to their table.

How long had it been since they'd been together? Five days. That was all, but it felt like an age.

She settled, and he sat back down and frowned. "What's wrong?"

"Wrong? Why would anything be wrong?"

That smile again. And the eyes. Slightly green, always laughing even when he was concentrating on fixing her computer or phone or anything technical.

"I admit there isn't any lettering on your forehead saying something is wrong, but even someone not completely taken by you could tell something strange is going on."

"I need a glass of wine."

"I've already ordered you a glass of your favorite Syrah, but I'm guessing that's not what's wrong."

As if perfectly timed, their waiter appeared with two glasses of wine and showed them the bottle.

"Would you like me to pour?"

"No, thank you, we've got it," Levi said and the waiter glided off.

"Question." Sloane folded her hands on the table as he filled their glasses. "Can we not talk about what's wrong?"

"Sure." Levi waved his hand. "Gone."

"Thank you."

"I have something for you." Levi leaned over and picked something off the floor next to him. "Care to guess?"

"Flowers."

"Too typical. Strike one."

"Chocolate."

"Always enjoyable, but again, very cliché." Levi grinned. "Strike two."

"Good point, but it doesn't mean you can't bring me some."

"Noted. One more swing."

"A new bicycle."

"Home run." Levi pulled what was hidden on his lap up onto the table. A cardboard box. "Well, not really, but you were so close."

Sloane took a sip of her wine, and as she gazed at Levi, the tension of the past few days slipped away. She didn't think about Toren or the future or anything but the kind man sitting across the table. A man who adored her. This was exactly what she needed, a distraction, a night not to think about the man she had once loved with everything inside her showing up like a ghost on her front porch and stirring up feelings she thought had died out three years ago.

"Sloane? You with me?"

"Sorry." She gave her head a quick shake. "Just thinking."

Levi made the motion of zipping his lips closed.

"Right, not going to talk about it, so I'm not going to think about it either."

He handed her the box.

"Sorry I didn't wrap it." Levi shrugged. "But I did tape it shut, so I'm hoping that counts for at least half a point."

"Two pieces of tape, two points."

She smiled and opened the box. Inside was a pair of boots. The exact ones she'd spotted when they went into Seattle three weeks back. The ones she'd gushed over, but only inside her own head. She hadn't mentioned anything to him. Unbelievable.

"How did you know?"

"Lucky guess. They're okay?"

"I love them." She ran a finger over the soft leather, then lifted one out to check the size. "How did you get my size right?"

"Another lucky guess."

Two emotions exploded in her stomach simultaneously. The heady realization that she was falling deeply in love with this man, and a thick dread, knowing she had to tell him.

Their waiter strolled over and waited till they looked up.

"Have you folks had a chance to look at the menu?"

Levi motioned toward Sloane, who glanced at him, then at the waiter, then back to Levi. Then she reached into her purse, pulled out her wallet, and snatched her credit card.

"I am so sorry, but we have to leave," she said to the waiter and handed him her card. "Please let me pay for our wine and put a little extra on there for us taking up your table and not ordering dinner."

The waiter almost hid his frown, took the card, gave a slight bow, and shuffled off.

"I'm sorry." Sloane slid her hand across

the table, and Levi placed his hand on hers. "I have to talk to you about it right now, and that fact has kind of made my appetite disappear."

Sloane and Levi faced each other on the sparring matt at his dojo and bowed. This was where she'd met him when he opened the school six months ago. She'd enrolled the kids here because it was more conveniently located to home than where she'd earned her black belt. In less than a month she found herself training in Levi's advanced classes several times a week as well.

"Now this is my idea of a romantic date," Levi said with his sly smile.

Sloane attacked first with a roundhouse kick that put Levi on his back. She straightened her *gi* and tugged her *obi* tight again.

He looked at her from the ground with a rare look of surprise on his face. "Ready to tell me what's eating you?"

"Toren's back."

She wanted to watch Levi's face as she spoke the words but instead kept her eyes down. He didn't speak for a few seconds. Then he stood slowly and took her hand.

"I know."

"You do?" Sloane lifted her eyes. "How?"

"He held a press conference." Levi smiled,

a puzzled look on his face. "You didn't see it?"

"No," Sloane said as she shook her head.

Levi ran a hand through his hair. "So is this the moment where you tell me you're having second thoughts about us and want to have time to think about —"

"No." She took his other hand. "This is the moment where I tell you I'm in love with you and that, yes, there are going to be some complications now that weren't there before, but it does nothing to stop what we have going between us."

Levi leaned in and Sloane lost herself in a long, lingering kiss.

After starting her car, Sloane glanced at the passenger seat where her phone sat face-down. Whoops. She'd forgotten to take it into the dojo with her. If the babysitter had called . . . She picked it up, turned it over. Seven missed calls. All from Toren. She sighed, but before she could check to see if he'd left a voicemail, the phone buzzed.

Toren again.

She answered, feeling annoyed. "What?"

"Where were you?"

"Out."

"With who? Doing what?"

"I was out with Mr. None of Your Business and his friend I Don't Have to Tell You. They both say hi."

Toren sighed. "Sorry."

"What do you need, Toren?"

"I just want you to be careful."

"What are you talking about?"

"I don't want to scare you, but I bumped into an old friend and I saw him pulling out of our driveway the other day when I —"

"My driveway."

"Right. Yours." Toren paused. "And I wanted to ask about who is doing your landscaping —"

"You already asked that, remember?"

"Yeah, but this old friend of mine might be working with them, and I don't trust the guy."

"Toren, I've had the same landscaping company working on the yard for the past six months. There've never been any issues, nothing weird, okay? And if there ever was, I can handle myself. You know that."

"True. I just —"

"Anything else?"

"I could have watched the kids."

"I'll keep that in mind next time."

"Sloane?"

"What?"

"I love you."

"Good night, Toren."

CHAPTER 13

For the third time in as many minutes, Toren spun and glanced behind him. And for the third time he spotted no one staring at him from the vast expanse of grass in Farrel-McWhirter Farm Park as he trudged over its lush turf. No one lurking in the shadows behind the line of Douglas fir trees that stood where the lawn met the forest with their gaze fixed on his movements. He laughed at himself. At least tried to. What was his problem?

None of the dozen people spread out on the thick grass having picnics and throwing Frisbees seemed the least interested in him — unless he counted the golden lab that cocked his head and looked quizzically in his direction each time he spun.

He glanced at his cell phone. Four minutes after one. Eden was late. Why she wanted to meet outdoors he had no idea. But when he'd called her that morning just before eight and she said she would work with him, she insisted they meet outside. Fine. He didn't care how they got answers. He just needed to get them.

There it was again. The sensation of being watched tickled up and down his spine. He couldn't convince his gut the feeling was irrational even though anyone with a smattering of knowledge about psychology would know there was no reason to feel this way. The perception of being watched originates from a system in the brain devoted to detecting where others are looking. It's a kind of gaze-detection system especially sensitive to whether someone is looking directly at you or at something just over your shoulder. Yes, it even worked with peripheral vision. But a person directly behind you? Imagination only. Just fodder for those people who thrived on the paranormal and conspiracy theories. Not him.

But the feeling jabbed at the edges of his mind like an acupuncture needle, slipping past his logic. Toren concentrated, trying to picture in his mind the exact spot the feeling came from. Center of the park. No, a little left of center. Way back. It came from behind the tree line, past the swing set and near the trail that wound deep into the woods. He closed his eyes and laughed. This was ridiculous. Who had the ability to pinpoint the spot where a nonexistent person stared at him? It was all in his head. But the image of a person who stood two hundred yards behind him, shielded between two hemlock trees, stayed burned into his mind's eye.

Toren whirled and fixed his gaze on the spot he'd seen in his mind. Yes. There! Movement. Not shadow. A man's body and a strange flash of silver light — there for an instant, then gone as if he knew Toren had spotted him. He kept his eyes riveted on the spot as he broke into a sprint.

He thumped across the grass as fast as he could, a breeze shoving back his thick brown hair as he concentrated on the spot where he'd seen movement. Ten yards from the tree line he slowed and peered into the woods. Nothing moved. There was no otherworldly light. But he'd seen a man and a weird light. No doubt.

Toren stepped off the lawn into the forest and made his way to the tree where he'd seen the movement. He studied the ground where the man would have stood. No indication of footprints or broken underbrush or twigs, but then again, he probably couldn't have spotted anything even if the man weighed over four hundred pounds.

Toren had been in Boy Scouts before he was old enough to be a true scout. He'd been a Webelo but hadn't gone beyond that, so his tracking skills weren't exactly stellar.

Toren stepped around the back of the tree, then moved toward the next Douglas fir and immediately felt stupid. A yellow Frisbee with a silver and emerald *Green Dot Sub Shop* logo hung on a rusty nail embedded in the tree. A breeze moved it slightly and the sunlight flashed off of it. Next to it hung a beat-up black hoodie. Mystery solved.

Toren shuffled out onto the grass and glanced around the park, not expecting to see anything unusual, and his expectations were met. His imagination had once again sprinted away and carried him with it. In spite of the evidence, he still couldn't shake the feeling someone had been watching him.

A voice called out from his left.

"Toren!"

Eden strode toward him. Her black shoulder-length hair had been pulled back, exposing an intensity in her eyes he hadn't seen the day before.

"Hey."

"I'm sorry I'm late. I was held up on a phone call."

"No worries."

"Are you okay, Toren?"

"Why?"

"You look spooked."

"Nah, I just . . . I'm fine."

"Good." Eden motioned to a winding trail that led to the river. "Let's walk."

They strolled down the path, maple tree branches thick with new green leaves providing a canopy, silent for more than a few paces.

"What happened to you, Toren?"

"What happened to me?" Toren gave his head a shake. "Isn't that what we're going to find out?"

"I'm not asking what happened to you physically, but emotionally, spiritually, however you want to describe it. Are you different now? Have you noticed any changes in your outlook, your personality?"

"Yes."

"Tell me."

"I'm guessing you've read up on me. The NFL suspending me because of my temper. And then the Hawks cutting me loose because I couldn't get a handle on it."

"True."

"It's gone. Whatever happened to me while I was away flipped a switch. That part of me doesn't exist anymore."

Eden nodded as if that were the exact answer she'd expected. Silence again settled on them.

"Why did you want to meet here? Outside?"

"Because I pulled up old videos of you online. Studied them. Compared them to the man I met yesterday. I saw a difference. I see it in your eyes right now. And I know that finding out where you were and what was done to you is about far more than facts and figures. It's about connecting to the unseen, enabling you to connect to the unremembered inside your mind. I believe the memories of what happened are there, but we have to trigger them somehow. And I believe that trigger will come more easily in this kind of setting, created by God, than inside a sterile box like a coffee shop, created by man."

"Wow." Toren snorted a laugh. "I thought you were a detective, not a guru."

Eden smiled. "I can't be both?"

"No, I think there's a law against that."

Eden's smile faded. "Let's lay out our plan of attack. First, I'm going to talk to the management at the hotel, see if we can get anything out of them, a clue to who sent the package. Second, I'm going to tap a few friends and ask them to search for any retreat centers, educational centers, training programs that deal with personality issues like anger. Third, I want you to do research on memory loss. See if you can figure out any strategies that help with recall."

"All right," Toren said. "Anything else?"

"Yes."

Three joggers approached and Eden waited to speak till they passed.

"I'd like you to tell me about your friend Letto."

"What does he have to do with this?"

"When you talked to him in the parking lot, there was an intensity in your eyes. Not anger. But a fierceness. I want to know about that fierceness. I want to know everything. The more I know about you, the more I can put together a picture in my mind of where you were and why you would have gone there. I want to know about Letto and Quinn and Sloane, and your truncated NFL career, and anything and anyone else that's currently in your life."

"Letto is not in my life."

"No?"

"No, not at all. That was a chance meeting."

"Yes, of course it was. I could certainly tell by the way you reacted when you saw him." Eden drilled Toren with her eyes. "I have an idea. If we're going to do this, I'm thinking the fewer secrets between us, the more effective both of us can be at getting to the truth. What do you say?"

It wasn't truly a question. She wanted in, and even though he'd only known her a short time, he found it difficult not to trust her.

"Yeah, I get it."

Toren rubbed his eyes and began speaking. He told her the story of being beaten by his dad, and how he had met Letto a few days later and had vowed on that day to get stronger than his dad and someday take the belt out of his father's hand.

"Did you?"

Toren nodded.

"Want to tell me about it?"

"Someday."

"But you and Letto went different directions."

"There was always something twisted about Letto. It wasn't just the cigs and the pot, the drinking, the dirty jokes. It was deeper, darker." Toren chuckled. "My mom said kids like Letto were like eggs that didn't smell quite right when you cracked them open."

"Your mom met him?"

"No, Dad didn't like me bringing friends home. But I told her about him, what he was like, things he said, things he did."

"I see."

"We hung out all the time in seventh and eighth grade. We worked out together, talked about how we were going to take down our dads, how we were going to save our moms. And how I'd take care of my brother, and Letto would take care of his sister. But by my freshman year I was consumed with football year-round, and Letto didn't play, and he kept getting closer and closer to the edge. We had a pretty brutal falling-out."

"What happened?"

"God got ahold of me the summer of my sophomore year, and that drove a pretty big wedge into our relationship. I stopped drinking and just didn't want the friendship any longer. Didn't need it. So we drifted apart. I'd see him around school, but I was getting closer to God, and when I tried to talk to Letto about it, he didn't want anything to do with me. And then one day he kind of lost it."

Letto's words echoed in his mind as if they'd been spoken yesterday.

"I made you! Don't you get that?" Letto's eyes had narrowed into dark slits as he shoved Toren into a wall in the gym one fall day during their junior year. "You're getting all this attention from colleges, going to get a scholarship, go be a big football star, huh! How? Me, that's how. *I'm* the one who gave you the idea to get strong. *I* pushed you in the weight room, *I* taught you how to fight, *I* put the idea in your head when we were just kids. And now you go and get religion and dump our friendship? Don't need me anymore, huh? Toss me away like I'm rotting garbage?"

"You're a freak, Letto."

"I'm a freak? I'm a freak!"

Letto's voice grew till he screeched, and Toren glanced around the weight room to see if anyone was paying attention.

"Yeah, you are. So am I. Or I was. I went with you on that path, Letto. Yeah, a lot of good came out of it, but a lot of darkness too. Now I'm asking you to think about getting on a new path with me. You need it as bad as I do."

"I'm going to make you a promise." Letto bounced on his toes and pointed a finger of each hand at Toren. "Someday I'm coming for you, Toro. I'm going to take you down. Going to destroy you — light you on fire and watch you burn. I promise."

Letto backed away with the same smile Toren had seen in the parking lot after his press conference.

"After that, he must have moved away. I

141

never saw him again till last week."

Eden stayed quiet for at least a minute after Toren finished.

"Will he come after Sloane and your kids, or just you?"

"He's mentioned them, but everything inside tells me this is personal, just between us, that he'll only come after me. But how in the world can I know that for certain?"

"Have you talked to Sloane about it?"

"I tried."

Eden turned around, and they strolled back down the path toward the park. "I have to go out of town for a week. Sorry, but it's been scheduled for a while now, so work on the things we talked about and hang tight till I get back."

"I'm not good at hanging tight."

"Too bad. Work on it."

"Got it."

"And find something to do to take your mind off Letto."

"I'm going to find a house to rent, work out, and put together a surprise gift for my daughter."

"Good. And text me if your buddy shows up again."

"I'll be fine."

"Text me anyway."

"Why? You think I need quick access to

law enforcement?"

Eden raised her eyebrows. "Something like that."

CHAPTER 14

Six days later, early on Saturday night, Toren stepped into the garage of his rental house to put the finishing touches on his gift for Callie. It had turned out even better than he'd expected. A half day more and he'd be finished. He strolled toward the far side of the garage where he'd set up a work area and examined his simple creation.

A nightstand. A bookcase. Three shelves. And a dresser. All made from reclaimed wood that hadn't been put to any use in at least forty years. He'd found the wood in the middle of a deserted field the morning after his meeting with Eden in the park, during a long walk out in Duvall.

The wood was covered by years of growing and dying grass, not visible until he was almost right on top of it. A third of it was rotted, but the two-thirds on top? After a quick inspection Toren suspected he could turn the wood into something special.

144

He dug through online records till he found the owner of the field and fired off an e-mail, asking if he could purchase the wood. The owner replied forty-five minutes later and said he didn't know the wood was there, so he wouldn't miss it if Toren took it, and he could have the whole batch if he'd get rid of the rotted pieces too.

During the sanding process Toren got down to fresh wood in places, but he left the evidence of the years in the sun and rain and occasional snow swirling through each piece of wood. Heavy sandpaper, medium, fine, finer. Then a clear stain that would bring out the highlights and take the darker streaks darker. He decided on a semigloss stain to give the pieces that almost wet look, but not so glossy they would look overdone. The bedroom furniture was almost perfect, and he smiled at his creation.

The door from the garage to the house opened and broke Toren out of his musings. He spun to find Callie standing in the door-frame.

"Hi, Daddy."

"Callie, what are you doing here?"

"I hope it's okay that I used the key you gave Mommy a few days ago. I knocked, but you must not have heard it."

"That's why I gave it to you." He smiled

as he meandered over to her. "You're a wonderful surprise."

"Thanks." She stepped the rest of the way into the garage and let the door shut softly behind her. "I wanted to come see you, so Mommy dropped me off."

"She didn't want to come in?"

Callie shook her head. "She's running a quick errand and said I could come see you while she's doing that."

He nodded his understanding.

"I did ask her to come say hello, but she said another time maybe."

"Thanks, pumpkin." The endearment slipped out before Toren could stop it. Pumpkin was his nickname for her when she was younger, in the days before losing his temper had become a semi-regular occurrence. Before he'd lost it eighteen months ago and she screamed, "You never ever get to call me that ever, ever again!"

He'd never called her pumpkin again, until now. They looked at each other across the garage floor for a few seconds before he said, "I'm sorry, Callie. That slipped out before I could —"

"It's okay."

Another few seconds passed before he tried to smile and motioned her toward him. "Come in, come in. I want to show you what I'm working on."

He could tell by the look on her face that she'd spotted the furniture.

"What're you making?"

"It's a bookcase, or whatever the owner wants it to be. And a dresser, and a nightstand."

"They're really, really pretty."

"They're turning out okay, I think."

"Okay?" Callie smiled, a genuine smile that yanked on his heart. "Way more than okay. They're really super pretty."

"Thanks."

Callie stepped up to the bookcase and ran her fingers along its surface, then moved to the nightstand and finally to the set of drawers. "I bet you're going to get a lot of money from whoever you're making these for."

"I'm building this collection for free." He smiled as she raised her eyebrows.

"Really? You could probably sell this for way a lot of money. Like millions!"

Toren laughed. "Probably not millions, but yes, for a lot."

"So who gets to have it when it's done?"

"To answer that, I'd need to tell you a story. That okay?"

She nodded. Toren shuffled over to the workbench he'd set up, leaned against it, and folded his arms across his sweatshirt.

"Once upon a time, there was a princess who was the most beautiful princess the world has ever known. Her father, the king, was captivated with her, as was her mother, the queen. But as she grew from a little girl into a young woman, her dad, the king, started to get upset at things that didn't used to upset him. He let his fierceness in battle with other kingdoms spill over into life in the castle.

"As time went on, the king realized he had a temper he could not control, and often he would lose this temper in front of the princess. He hated himself for this and promised to change, but he didn't have the power to do so. Then one day he left his kingdom for a long, long time — no one knew where he had gone — but when he returned, he was different. He had changed. His temper was gone. And it came into his mind that long, long ago, his princess daughter asked him to build her the prettiest set of furniture ever for her room, and he said he would. For he used to tell her she was the prettiest girl in all the land, and the prettiest girl in all the land needed furniture almost as beautiful as she, and she believed him.

"So the king built a bookcase with shelves, and a nightstand and a set of drawers. And he hoped beyond hope that his princess would forgive him for his anger, and that maybe she and he could be friends again."

"I love it." Callie stared up at Toren as the hint of tears formed in her eyes.

Toren closed his eyes and dropped his hands to his sides, took the risk, and opened his arms. Two seconds. Three. At seven he opened them to see a look on his daughter's face that broke his heart — not for him, but for her.

"I'm not ready for that, Daddy."

He answered her in a way that surprised himself. He wasn't hurt, wasn't offended as the old him would have been. He was good. Really, really good.

"That's okay, sweetheart." And Toren meant it. "It's completely okay."

The hint of hope came into her eyes, and she stared at him as her top teeth massaged her lower lip.

"When will you be finished? When can we move all of it up to my room?"

"Twenty-four hours."

"Can't it be done right now?"

He laughed. "I'd love it if it could be, but I need to do one more sanding, one more coat of stain, and then give it time to dry all the way."

She ran her fingers over the nightstand.

"This is so pretty. How did you get the wood to look this way?"

He looked at her in mock horror. "Are you asking me to reveal my secret sauce, the secret formula that no one else in the world knows — just because you're my daughter?"

She smiled that shy smile that had shot to the deep places in his heart ever since she was a toddler.

"If you want to tell me." Callie laughed and rubbed her fingers again on the surface of the nightstand.

"I can teach you if you want. We can work together on something."

"Okay."

Toren let the silence between them linger. After a time he knelt down and brought his face close to hers.

"I'm really sorry, Callie."

"It's okay."

"No, not okay." He took Callie's hand lightly in his. "And more than anything I wish I could go back and change what I did to you, and take away the words and the countless times I yelled at you for no good reason . . . But the past has withered away like flowers in the hot sun, and I can't do anything to help them. But I can say there are new flowers, and those flowers I can water."

"You sound like a storybook."

"Yeah, a lame version of one maybe." He chuckled.

Callie released his hand and once again placed her fingers on the golden surface of the nightstand, then looked back at him.

"I'm going to be a good daddy from now on."

"Really?"

Toren put two fingers between her hands on the nightstand, bent close to her ear, and whispered, "Really."

She stared up at him for an eternity, her eyes shifting from hesitancy to hope. Then she slipped around the edge of the night-stand and barreled into him, and Toren wrapped his arms around her. After far too short a time she pulled away, her eyes damp as his had become.

A shuffle of feet near the door leading into the house whipped his gaze from his daughter to Sloane, who stood in the frame just as Callie had ten minutes earlier. The message in Sloane's eyes — the eyes he thought he knew so well — was hidden from him, but it was okay.

"Hi," Toren said and took a few hesitant steps toward her.

She glanced at him and bounced her eyebrows once, then turned her gaze to Callie. "We have to go."

"Okay," Callie said to Sloane, then turned and looked up at him, her brown eyes full of anticipation. "We'll really work on something together? Soon?"

"Yes. Very." He took her hand and gave it a quick squeeze. "Is tomorrow too soon?"

"No, that's perfect." For the second time, she released his hand, but this time she gave a return squeeze before she let go.

Callie eased over to her mom, who gave her a quick sideways hug. She looked up at Sloane and said, "Daddy's going to teach me how to do woodworking like he does."

"That's great, honey." Sloane gave Callie a fake smile. "Can you go wait inside the house for a few minutes, sweetheart?"

Callie glanced back and forth between the two of them and finally gave Toren a tiny wave, turned, and walked through the garage door into the house. Sloane watched the doorknob for a moment, then turned back toward him and strode to the middle of the garage floor.

"What are you doing?"

"I'm trying to —"

"It was a rhetorical question." Sloane jabbed a finger at Toren. "You're worming your way back into her heart just like you did so many times before you disappeared. And like so many times before, you're going to let her down and break her heart once again."

"No, this time —"

"This time it's different? Really? How is it different than the other times you promised not to lose your temper?"

"Wait a second." Toren frowned. "You said you were okay with this, with me having a chance with the kids. Did I miss something?"

Sloane sighed heavily and rubbed her forehead. "No. It's just . . . This is a lot . . . and fast." She turned and looked at the furniture. "Who are those for?" He could tell by the look in her eyes she knew they were for Callie.

"I'm trying, Sloane."

"I don't want her getting hurt again. You have no idea —"

"I know. I won't."

She turned to go. "You did a wonderful job. Good-bye, Toren."

After they left he went into the family room — empty except for a sofa, a small coffee table, and a TV — and celebrated his time with Callie, but it couldn't erase the pain he'd seen on Sloane's face. Toren tried to lose himself in a show, but his mind kept spinning between images of Sloane and Colton and Callie and Eden and Quinn and Letto.

His cell rang. No caller ID.

"Hello?"

"Hey, pal, didja have a good talk with your new friend Eden the other day? Looked like you did. She's cute." Laughter. "You gonna give up on Sloane and go for her instead?"

"Let's get together and talk about it."

Letto's laughter was high pitched. "No, no, I don't think so. I might make you mad enough to awaken the sleeping giant inside, and we wouldn't want that to happen, would we?"

"I'm going to find you and —"

"And do what, ol' pal?" That laughter again. "Kill me? Nah, that won't work. Take me down to the police and tell them a buddy from high school who is six inches shorter and seventy pounds lighter is threatening you? Told you he was going to keep a promise? That won't work either. Don't be an idiot, Toren."

"Let's get together."

"Let me lay it out for you, Toro. As long as you don't go crazy and stir things up, I'll stay away from you. But you start mucking around in stuff that's dead and gone and buried, and I'll have to come out and play. With you. With Sloane. With your kids. Got it?"

Toren blinked. "Are you talking about me finding out where I was for eight months and what was done to me?"

"I shouldn't have called you an idiot. See how smart you are?"

Toren's heart hammered. "What do you know about that?"

"Nothing, really. Nothing important."

"Are you part of it?"

Silence.

"What do you know!"

The line went dead. Toren set down his cell and wiped his damp palms on his legs. Letto knew something. What? How much? And why, after all these years, would the psychopath suddenly decide it was time to even the score?

He groaned. Nice. He'd just hit the trifecta. Trying to win Sloane back. Trying to figure out what had happened to him. And now, trying to deal with a man who was probably truly insane.

CHAPTER 15

"That's the bizarre thing, the reason I know I've truly changed," Toren told Quinn the next morning at the gym. "I'm ticked off, but I'm not out of control. I'm actually quite calm. I'm simply going to track the guy down, grab him around the neck if needed, and give him an extremely detailed description of what I'm going to do to him if he gets anywhere near my family."

Quinn added another forty-five-pound plate to each side of the barbell and slid onto the bench.

"That's good." He lifted the bar off the rack and started his reps. "Maybe you really have crushed your temper. You're turning into the Hulk, or getting control of the Hulk, or figuring out how to keep Bruce Banner in charge, you know?"

"What?" Toren staggered back as if he'd been shot.

"Hey, you spotting me here, brother?"

Quinn grunted out another rep. "Gonna need you for the last three, and I'm almost there."

"Yeah, sure." Toren moved back to the bar, his head in a daze. "I'm here."

Toren helped Quinn gut through his final three reps, but the moment the bar lodged back into place on the rack, he tilted his head back and clutched for the shard of memory that had cut into his mind the second Quinn had mentioned the Hulk. A memory from his time away.

Quinn sat up, a puzzled look on his face as he peered at Toren. "You okay, man?"

"What do you mean, getting control?"

"In the *Avengers* movie, you know. The first one with Robert Downey Jr. and Mark Ruffalo . . . You saw it, right?"

"Yeah . . . but what about the control part?"

"At the end of the first movie, Dr. Banner gets control of the Hulk's rage. So he can use him to tear up the Chitauri at the end."

"Tell me about the Hulk, Q."

"You're getting a memory."

"Yeah, for a second I did, but now it's gone. Help me get it back." Toren sat next to Quinn on the bench, his heart hammering harder than it had at any point during the workout. "Tell me everything you know."

Quinn flexed his arms and waggled his fists on either side of his stomach. "Hulk smash puny human!"

"I'm serious, Q."

"I know, just had to set the stage."

"Stage set."

"*The Incredible Hulk* is a brilliant interpretation of two classics of nineteenth-century literature."

"What?" Toren said. "You're saying the Hulk came from classic novels?"

"Yeah." Quinn smiled. "You don't know where the story came from?"

"That's why I'm asking, Professor. Not everyone is a geek like you."

"Stan Lee says the Hulk is a combo of Frankenstein's monster plus Dr. Jekyll and Mr. Hyde. You know, the monster within all of us. In the Hulk, the monster is the alter ego of Dr. Bruce Banner. And he escapes the doctor."

Toren's gut twisted. More shards of memory stabbed at him, but they faded even more quickly than they appeared.

"I think the story resonated with people because, if we're willing to admit it, we all have a monster inside us, and we're fighting to stop it from taking over our lives. In *Dr. Jekyll and Mr. Hyde,* a potion caused the transformation. With the Hulk, it's gamma radiation from a bomb plus stress that causes the change. And when the Hulk is ticked off, wow, look out. Serious anger issues. Just like most humans walking around this planet."

Something snapped in Toren's mind, something like a piece of wood being broken off a door panel, allowing him to peek into a room long boarded up.

Toren put his eye up to the door in his mind and peered into the room. Short bursts of light illuminated memories for too short a time to figure out what they were. But Toren refused to let go. Inside his mind he grabbed the doorknob and tried to turn it, but it was as fixed as rusted iron. He had to get in, and he willed the flashes of light to last longer, but they refused. As he continued to peer through the opening, Quinn's monologue seemed muted. Toren yanked himself away from the images and spun toward Quinn.

"What else, Quinn? Tell me more."

"I am. You just interrupted."

"Where did the story came from? How did Stan Lee develop the idea for the comic book?"

"You mean the Jekyll and Hyde thing."

"Yes. In detail. Please."

Quinn frowned . . . apparently seeing

something in Toren's face that bothered him. Little doubt it was his desperate yanking on the door inside his mind.

"In *Frankenstein,* Victor Frankenstein creates a grotesque creature during a science experiment. But he's not the monster most people think of when we think of the movies. In the novel the monster has times of self-reflection. He ponders why he was given his horrible fate. Wonders why he was created and then hated and hunted down and tortured by society.

"That theme is in the early Hulk issues big-time. He doesn't even understand who he is — back then the Hulk's IQ didn't make it past sixty — and all he wants to do is be a hermit, run off, and find peace. But he can't control himself when he gets mad, so he ends up giving in to his rage and destroying a lot of things.

"That contrast led Stan Lee to *Dr. Jekyll and Mr. Hyde.* Essentially it's a novella that explores the idea of a split personality. Or in terms psychiatrists would use, dissociative identity disorder, meaning more than one personality exists within the same body."

Toren shook his head. "I thought it was just about a monster that was incredibly strong. Had no clue about Jekyll and Hyde."

"But do you see now why the story of Jekyll and Hyde is so relevant to the Hulk?"

"Pretend I don't," Toren said.

"Because in Jekyll and Hyde, Robert Louis Stevenson portrays one distinctly good personality and one distinctly evil personality. Henry Jekyll ends up in an all-out war with his dark half, Edward Hyde. Jekyll says that he and every other man and woman is 'not truly one, but truly two,' and he sees the human soul as the ultimate battleground of our lives — one part of us an angel, the other a demon, both struggling for mastery and destruction of the other."

The door inside Toren's mind burst open, and the flashes of light began lasting longer and coming faster. A man holding a book. A white T-shirt one day, then a black T-shirt the next. Every other day. Black. White. Black. White. Others around Toren. A memory of the air being dry. Dark wood on the walls. Floor-to-ceiling windows framing red rocks outside.

More images flooded his mind: of exercises for body and mind, of memorized disciplines and texts, of deprivation and resolve. Then, without a shred of warning, the door slammed shut, the light went dark, and the spray of memories was cut off as if a great fire hose had been stomped on by a foot the size of the Hulk's.

Toren fought to hold on to the memories that had swirled in his mind moments earlier, but they melted away amid a voice growing steadily louder somewhere above him.

"Hey, Toren, my man, you okay? You okay?"

He felt a hand on his shoulder and opened his eyes to find himself slumped on the gym's floor mats, Quinn kneeling beside him, deep concern reflected in his eyes.

"Yeah." Toren shook his head as if to rid himself of the frustration of being so close to answers and seeing them slip away like water sinking into sand. "I'm good."

"No, you're not."

"Yeah, I am. They're starting to come back. Memories. I think I was someplace down in the Southwest."

"That's good, man. That's really good." Quinn motioned to the barbell. "We done?"

"No, let's finish. I'm fired up." He nodded at Quinn. "Answers are coming, and I'm not going to give up till I get 'em all."

As Toren walked to his car an hour later, his cell phone vibrated. A text from Eden:

I've returned. Can you meet tomorrow?

10am at the Starbucks just off main?

Toren texted back:

Thought you didn't like coffee shops.

Yes or no, Toren?

Yes, I'll see you in the morning. I've had a breakthrough.

CHAPTER 16

Toren stepped through the doors of Starbucks the next morning at nine thirty, needing to get out of his house, which was too quiet, too empty. He'd called Sloane a few times, but she hadn't called back. She only texted, and her responses were as short as possible. She'd left minutes before he'd arrived to move Callie's furniture in — no surprise — and he racked his brain thinking of how he could get to her heart. Plus, there was Colton, who wasn't hostile toward Toren but wasn't exactly warm either. He had to give it time.

He cleaned out his e-mail — there wasn't much these days — and had almost finished pulling up the research he wanted to show Eden when the same feeling of being watched that he'd had at the park grabbed him around the throat and clamped down tight. Maybe it was his imagination working overtime, but the sense was palpable. Whoever it was felt close. Letto?

The hairs on the back of his neck stood at attention like little soldiers. Someone stalking him in a coffee shop? Why? There were no reasons. Not true. There were two hundred and forty-two days of them, the lost days when he could have done things, said things, that didn't please any number of people. The days when he could have made friends or enemies.

The place was crowded. If someone was watching him, they would see him turn and avert their eyes too fast for him to be sure of which gaze had been locked onto the back of his head. A second later a possibility struck him. If he had a mirror, he could look behind him without turning around. But how? If he asked one of the female customers for a makeup mirror, he stood a good chance of scaring the watcher off — not to mention the strange looks he'd get from the woman.

Toren glanced at his laptop screen. Bingo. He had a fifteen-inch mirror right in front of him. Easy to make it work. Create a black background that filled his screen and it would act like a mirror. He pulled up his graphics editor, then tilted his screen down so the person behind him would have to be on their knees to see what he was working on. Then he created a new file, made a box that filled the borders of the program, and colored it black. In less than ten seconds it was done. He turned down the brightness on his screen to its lowest setting and studied his reflection. Excellent. It offered a clear mirror of his shirt and the table.

Toren tilted his screen slightly and five people came into the reflection. Two elderly gentlemen sat at a table close behind and to his left. To his right, three women were gathered, the one in the center noticeably tall. Farther back, a woman sat by herself. Next to her, another woman alone was staring at her cell phone, and a man nearby held a newspaper. None of them looked his direction. He stayed focused on his screen.

Over the next three or four minutes, two of the women from the group of three looked up, as did one of the men to the left. Then one by one the rest of them did, except for one of the women sitting by herself. It was impossible to tell if they were looking at him or simply glancing around the shop. He needed a way to zero in on the one who was watching him in their peripheral vision as well.

Toren reached for his cup of coffee, and as he did, he nudged a stack of three napkins off the table. They fluttered to the tile floor.

Perfect. In a few seconds he would make the cup take a similar leap to land right on top of the napkins.

If his aim were true, the sound of the cup hitting the floor would be muffled by the napkins. No one would notice unless they were focused on him. And if they were, it would be tough for them not to be distracted by the cup falling off the table and at least glance down at the floor. The slightest movement of their head — when the rest of those behind him didn't move — was all he needed to see. The problem was, he didn't have much hope this little experiment of his would help. If it didn't reveal anything, he'd still believe someone was following him. Didn't matter. He had to try something.

Toren adjusted the screen again and stared into his make-shift mirror.

He slid his drink to the edge of the table, then leaned back. Was the feeling of being watched still there? Yes, as intense as ever. No reason to wait any longer. Toren counted down from three . . . two . . . one, then pushed his cup over. The instant it hit the napkins, he stared at the reflection of the shop behind him.

Yes! His heart rate spiked. The tall woman who was part of the trio glanced for an instant at the cup, then jerked her gaze back up. Her eyes were riveted on the back of his head. An instant later they caught sight of the computer screen and went wide — she had to have realized what he'd done.

Toren twisted in his seat, but not quickly enough. The woman was gone. He leaped to his feet and scanned both directions. There! He spotted the back of her head disappearing through a door at the back of the coffee shop. Toren sprinted toward it. He reached the door, yanked down on the handle, and growled. No! She'd locked it. He slammed his shoulder into the door. It shuddered, but the lock refused to give way, even with his full 235 pounds behind it.

One of the baristas looked his direction and frowned. Toren held up his hands and grinned. "Sorry! It's all good."

The employee glared as his gaze raked Toren up and down. Then he motioned with his head to get away from the door. Toren complied by shuffling away, but the instant the barista turned back to serving up coffee, he sprinted for the front door.

Had to find her. In less than ten seconds he was around the back of the building whipping his gaze back and forth in all directions. How had she slipped away so fast? Easy. Any of the doors across the alley could have been her corridor of escape. Or she could have backtracked and still be inside the shop. If he went in asking to search their back rooms, he doubted they'd comply.

Toren pounded his fist into his palm. A flash of emotion tried to surface. The rage he knew so well was about to erupt. No. *Had* known. He did not know that rage anymore. That was not him any longer. The old man was dead. Toren shifted his focus to trying to wrap his brain around the reality of what had just happened.

A shudder went through him, and he felt cold even though the morning was rapidly warming. Until now he'd thought Letto was working alone. Unsettling.

As he staggered back inside, he was accompanied by curious glances from four or five customers. Apparently they'd never seen a lunatic jump up and race out of a coffee shop like their hair was on fire. He offered a sheepish grin, which they didn't seem to accept.

Toren eased over to the two women still at the table. He guessed they were in their midtwenties, one blonde, one red-haired.

"Excuse me."

They looked up, guilt splashed on both their faces.

"You want to tell me about your friend with the lightning-fast reflexes?"

He didn't hold out much hope, but it was worth asking.

"She wasn't our friend," the blonde on the left said.

Exactly the answer he'd expected. "She wasn't?"

"We didn't even know her."

"No?" Toren motioned to the now-empty seat the lady had occupied and sat in it. "Do you mind?"

"Uh-uh," the blonde said. She explained, "She came in, sat down, and whispered, 'Do you mind if I sit with you for a while, and you do me a really big favor and pretend like we're friends?' As she says it, she slides a twenty in front of each of us."

The blonde took a drink and the redhead continued the story.

"So I think that's kind of weird. I can tell by the look on Stacy's face she does too, but she doesn't look like a psycho and twenty bucks is twenty bucks, so I say yes and so does Stacy. We play along for five or ten minutes — and we can tell she's crushing on you — and then she jumps up and sprints to the back, and so do you, and here we are."

"I'm guessing she didn't give you a name."

"No."

"Did she say anything about herself, did she have an accent, is there anything you can tell me about her that stood out?"

"She was super tall," Stacy said.

Toren took a calming breath.

The redhead frowned and said, "She wasn't here very long, but she did say, 'Thanks for doing this, and don't worry, I'm not stalking this man and have no ill intent toward him, but it's important for me to observe him.' "

"Anything else?"

The redhead shook her head. Toren stood, thanked them, and walked back to his table. For the first time he noticed Eden seated there, her hands folded across her lap.

"Hello, Toren. Having fun today?"

"Almost more than I can stand."

Toren sat and told her about his call from Letto and about the woman who had been stalking him just before she arrived. Eden didn't seem concerned about either.

"That doesn't bother you?"

"Which one?"

"Either."

"No. What I'd like to hear about is your breakthrough."

He stared at her, but her only response was slightly raised eyebrows.

"I think I know the area of the country I was in. I think it's pretty obvious now what was done to me, and I think I know why I can't remember anything."

Eden took a quick sip of her coffee. "Let's hear it."

Chapter 17

After Toren filled Eden in on learning about the Hulk and the few memories he still held from his flashback in the gym, she said, "So you think you were in the Southwest?"

"Yes. I was hiking, red dust kicking up from the trail. I breathed hard, but in a good way, like during a strong workout or when I used to be on the field, chasing down a quarterback. I was looking down, but there were other people around me, I'm sure of it. Not exactly friends, but still, people I trusted. And then we reached the top of somewhere. I can't see it in my mind, but something tells me the view from up top was spectacular. That's all."

"And the feeling?"

"Exhilaration. Not from getting to the top or seeing the view. The feeling of elation came later that day, but I can't tell you what from."

"Was there anything else?"

Toren hesitated for a moment. Rubbed his thumb against his coffee cup.

"Nothing. But more is coming. I know it is. This is a good start. Red rocks, heat . . . has to be New Mexico, Arizona, maybe Utah."

"Yes, possibly." Eden took notes on her laptop. "Why do you think you have so few memories of that time? And how could anyone have wiped your memory?"

"I don't know — but it turns out, memories are surprisingly easy to manipulate."

"It seems you used your time wisely while I was gone."

Toren spread his palms on the table and said, "Our memories are fluid. Every time we bring one to mind, we change it. Slightly, but it's altered. Think about that old game everyone's played at one time or another, Telephone, where there's a circle of people and one person whispers a phrase to the person next to them, and they whisper it to the person next to them until it goes around the whole circle and winds up with the person who started, usually a completely different phrase. Psychologists believe that's what happens with our memories, and the game of Telephone keeps going till we die.

"Each of our memories is constantly evolving. We add or change details. That time when you broke your leg on the sledding hill. Was it cloudy? Sunny? Snowing? Did you change that part of the memory, or maybe someone else who was there suggested it? Did they remember it right?"

Eden was nodding.

"What about being told a story of something that happened when you were a kid and hearing it so much from your mom and dad over the years that now you think you remember it happening, when all you really are recalling is the story? And it rewrites, or overwrites, the old memory.

"Now scientists have figured out how to take advantage of our fragile memories and can neutralize them — and in turn the feelings associated with them — of sadness, fear, or joy."

"How do they neutralize them?"

"By shutting down a chemical called norepinephrine. They've figured out that norepinephrine is associated with our fight-or-flight response to a frightening situation. And they've developed a method of blocking it when the memory is trigged. Then, when we put the memory back in the files of our brain, it's changed. Scientists call the process reconsolidation."

"Go on."

"They've tested it. Researchers in the

175

Netherlands stuck people scared of spiders into a cage with live tarantulas, which not surprisingly freaked them out. Then they gave these people beta blockers, which restrict norepinephrine levels. Guess what happened?"

"No longer scared of spiders." Eden flicked her fingers. "Those memories were obliterated."

"Yes!" Toren leaned forward. "A few days afterward, they not only had no problem being with the tarantulas, they had no problem letting the spiders crawl on them!"

"I would think most people would need a megadose of those beta blockers."

"In severe cases of PTSD, scientists have experimented with a therapy that involves xenon gas, which targets certain brain receptors that are closely related to learning and memory. When xenon is inhaled during a bad memory, it strips out all negative feelings associated with it, rendering it neutral."

Eden spread her palms on the table and leaned in. "But we're not talking about getting rid of a specific memory. We need to know how someone wiped out months of your life. That sort of thing is still just a fantasy, right? Like the thing that was done to Jim Carrey's character in that movie, what was it?"

"Eternal Sunshine of the Spotless Mind."

"Yes."

"That's a perfect example," Toren said. "In the movie, an electric brain scanner targets and zaps the man's painful memories while he sleeps. Turns out, scientists can accomplish something similar with mice by 'incepting' their brains while they're asleep."

"Fascinating."

"Yeah. So I guess we have to throw Christopher Nolan's movie *Inception* into the mix." Toren blew out a slow breath. "You want to hear how they're doing this?"

"Of course."

"Essentially it involves mapping a mouse's brain — identifying the cells that are activated by certain activities or locations — then manipulating those particular cells while they're sleeping using an electrode to link them to a reward signal whenever they fire. The scientists were able to engineer positive associations with particular places so successfully that when the mice awoke, they headed straight toward the locations that were linked to the reward signal."

Toren glanced over Eden's head and out the window of the shop and gave an amazed chuckle.

"I've always believed scientific knowledge is far more advanced than we're told. I think it's possible that right now scientists are able to alter memories while we sleep. To target unwanted memories and zap them out of existence. Scientists are already doing it with mice, so if science is always ten to twelve years ahead of what the average man believes can be done, who's to say this wasn't done to me? With my full knowledge and consent?"

"For what purpose?" Eden leaned in, both hands around her cup.

"Ah, yes, finally we get down to the reason for all this." Toren glanced around the coffee shop. "At least this is my theory on what happened and why it happened."

Eden narrowed her eyes.

"I've changed, Eden. What's happened to me went beyond getting control of my temper. I love my family far more than I did before. I'm praying for my kids like crazy. Praying for Sloane. My relationship with God is better than it's ever been. I feel more free even with this mystery hanging over my head and some wacko friend from a hundred years ago stalking me.

"I'm kind now, not because it will get me anything, but because I want to be kind. I'm giving without any expectation of return. I'm patient like I've never been. I'm not offended by the things that used to tick me off. I could go on, but I think you get the point."

"So they wiped out the bad and implanted you with the good."

"Sounds like science fiction."

"Or . . ." Eden trailed off as her forefinger circled a small stain on their table.

"Or what?"

"God."

"What?"

"Isn't that the point of your faith, Toren? You said you were a Christian — didn't I hear you say that?"

"Yeah."

"According to your inspired writings, when you surrender to God, you die. You're eliminated — *crucified,* to use the Bible's word — and from then on, it's Christ living in you. God's Spirit comes into your heart and changes everything from the inside out." Eden tapped her collarbone. "The old man is gone."

"I've never thought of it like that."

Eden turned to her laptop. "Do you want to hear what I found out?"

"About retreat centers?"

"Yes." Eden slid her laptop over so Toren could see. "All the red dots on this map are retreat centers, spiritual awakening places, gathering spots. The good news is if we narrow our search to the Southwest, we cut down the number considerably. The bad news is if you did go to a place in the Southwest, we don't know that it's necessarily listed here, or is even registered as a retreat center."

"Where do we go from here?"

"I'd love to say we jump in a plane and check these places out, but it's going to be a lot more boring for a while longer. I want you to start pulling up all seventy-five of the centers in Arizona, New Mexico, and Utah and see if any of the pictures on their websites jogs a memory. When you finish, text me."

Eden gathered her things and stood. "You're going to figure this out, Toren. You have my word."

CHAPTER 18

Toren arrived at the baseball field just as Colton's team gathered for practice. He headed toward a cluster of trees across from the far corner of left field — far enough away that Colton wouldn't spot him, but close enough that he could watch Colton play the hot corner, third base, the same position Toren had played ages back in a vain attempt to capture his dad's attention before he'd walked out on their family.

As he settled into a spot next to the tree and Colton jogged onto the field, a feeling urged him to turn and look behind him. His heart skipped. One hundred yards away, on the edge of the four sets of diamonds, Letto loitered in a black sweatshirt, dark-gray jeans, face shrouded by a baseball hat. Toren didn't need to see his face to know it was him. As Toren watched, Letto lifted his forefinger and pointed it at Colton like a gun, took a pretend shot, then turned to

Toren and grinned.

Toren sprinted toward Letto without thought.

Letto spun and rocketed away. Toren was spent from the workout he'd done after meeting Eden, but nothing was going to stop him from catching this psychopath. Letto wove between the trees quicker than a lot of the backs Toren used to chase down on the field. A clouded memory of Letto running the 100 meters in school flashed through his mind. Obviously he hadn't lost even a step since those days.

Toren's spirit was more than willing, but his flesh was more than weak. His workout had sapped his wind. Didn't matter. Toren forced his body to move faster. For a few agonizing moments the distance between them stayed the same, but then he started closing the distance. Ten yards. Nine. Seven.

"I feel you back there, Toren," Letto rasped out between breaths. "Come on, a little faster, don't fail me now. Prove it. Prove to me you belong back in the pros."

Toren gritted his teeth and pressed hard. Yes! Now five yards. Fire in his lungs. A low branch clipped his shoulder. *Stay with it.* Four more seconds and he'd nail Letto. He ignored the burning in his legs. Three yards. Two. Toren reached out for the man's jacket. Inches!

An instant before Toren's fingers closed down, Letto darted to his left around a Douglas fir. Toren planted his right foot to make the cut. But an instant later Toren's foot was sliding on dry needles. He went down hard on his left hip and shoulder. His momentum dragged him across the ground and slammed him into the trunk of a maple tree. He staggered quickly to his feet, but it was a futile gesture. Letto was thirty yards out and not slowing.

Toren checked his shoulder and hip. He'd deal with a bruise for a few days, but nothing broken. By the time he got back to the field, his breathing was almost back to normal.

His fear for Sloane and his kids, on the other hand, was through the roof.

The practice went well for Colton, and when it was over, Toren smiled at the back of his son's head as he huddled up with his teammates around the coach, likely to get a few more pointers about their game the next day. He'd wait until he knew Colton was safely headed for home with a friend before leaving. No telling where Letto was right now.

They broke up a few minutes later with a cheer. Colton and his buddy Tim started strolling toward their ride — Tim's dad — when for no reason, Colton stopped, spun, and stared right at Toren. He turned to go, but Colton began to lope toward him, then ran. Toren moved toward his son, his steps hesitant, hands jammed in his pockets.

"Hey, Colton!" his coach called out. "Where are you going?"

Colton stopped and turned back. "It's okay. It's my dad."

Toren waved at the coach.

When Colton reached him, he said, "What are you doing here, Dad?"

With the sun streaming into his eyes and Colton's cap pulled down over his face, Toren couldn't tell if it was good or bad that he'd come.

"I came to watch you practice."

"Oh, okay."

Colton looked up at him now, his curly dark hair poking out from under his hat, the expression in his eyes a mix of nervousness and irritation.

Toren let a few seconds pass before saying, "How did you know I was here?"

Even in profile, he saw Colton's eyes twitch under his furrowed brow as if he were trying to figure out one of the math problems he was so good at.

"Lyle says to me, 'There's some big guy

standing out next to left field watching the whole practice. Did you see him?' So I looked over and I could pretty much tell it was you."

"I thought I did a good job of hiding behind the tree."

"No, not really." A hint of a smile formed in the corner of Colton's mouth, but it shifted into a frown. "I wasn't going to let you know I saw you, but then I decided I'd come over."

"Glad you did."

"Why'd you come today?"

"I've come to every one of your practices since the day I got back. So I guess I'm not the worst in the world at hiding."

Almost a smile now on Colton's face.

"Why did you want to hide?"

"Not sure." Toren looked up at the clouds gathering as if they had permission to start dumping rain now that practice had finished. He searched for words that refused to form in his mind.

"You looked good out there today. Your swing is getting solid. For a kid your age, you're really pounding the ball. And your anticipation at third? Fast. And your arm is strong. Looks like you're almost comfortable having those line drives hit your direction."

"It's feeling better, I guess."

Toren leaned forward and rested his hands on his knees. "You keep playing like this, you could be a star." He looked into Colton's eyes before turning his gaze back to the diamond. "Seeing you out there, going for it with all your talent, it's a treat, Colton."

Colton turned back and matched Toren's posture, maybe his father's son in this way only. "Why did you want to keep me from knowing you're coming to my practices?"

"Because I want it to be real."

"Why wouldn't it be real if you told me?"

"Because if you knew, you might suspect I was doing it to make you feel good about me, make you want to be my son again."

"I didn't ever want to stop being your son deep down. I just wanted you to be . . ."

"A better dad?"

Colton glanced at Toren for less than a second. But it was enough. And then he ripped into Toren's heart in the best way possible. "And I never wanted you and Mom to stop being married."

Toren threw his arm around Colton's neck, and they walked back toward the diamond together.

CHAPTER 19

The next day Toren couldn't concentrate on his research into Southwestern retreat centers. He was far too distracted by the image of Letto taking aim at Colton. Finally he pushed away from his laptop and texted Sloane. She needed to know. Had to know.

Can we have coffee again? It's imperative we talk.

Toren returned to his laptop to go over the websites of every retreat center again but only got through three before his phone buzzed.

I don't think that's a good idea.

How to respond without scaring her? No idea. Toren held his phone in both hands, begging his mind to come up with something clever and truthful that would convince her to meet. But before he could, his phone buzzed again.

I'll see you. I probably need to. 2pm same place.

Yes! Hope surged through him. A chance to warn her. He smiled. A chance to connect again. As long as Colton and Callie were safe.

What about the kids? I don't want to take any

Sloane's text came in before he could finish typing the sentence. She always dictated her texts, so she was always faster — something she used to tease him about.

The kids will be in school.

In school. Good. Toren turned back to his laptop to study the photos he'd pulled up of the retreat centers.

Toren arrived at the same time Sloane did, and for the first time since he'd woken up in that hotel room, he knew everything would turn out all right, especially when he did his Johnny Cash impression, a few bars of "I Walk the Line" with the voice and everything. There was no warning; it just popped out of him as they waited to place their orders.

Sloane tried not to smile, and no, her mouth didn't move, but her eyes lit up like they had in the old days, the first seven years of their marriage before the beast inside him had grown strong and shown up uninvited too many times.

Her hair was pulled up, and as he scooted along toward the cash register, he gazed at the back of her neck, at the spot he used to nuzzle on fall nights when the air was crisp but still carried a hint of summer. Wait. What was that? A thin white line ran through that area. Toren peered closer. A scar.

"Where did you get that?"

"Get what?"

"On the back of your neck. It looks like a tiny scar."

She turned on him, eyes cold. "You've got to be kidding."

"What?"

"You think that's funny?"

"What's funny?"

She turned back and shuffled forward in line.

"Sloane, I —"

She didn't turn, and her voice was almost too soft to hear. "If you don't want me to walk out of here this second, you'll shut up about the scar and I'll pretend you didn't ask. Okay?"

"Sure."

She turned around. "What happened to you while you were gone? Where were you?"

"I don't know."

Sloane frowned and shook her head. "What do you mean you don't know?"

"I've gotten back only fragments of memories of where I was. Nothing more. I don't remember being gone. Where. What was done to me."

"You're serious."

"I wouldn't have put you through the agony of not knowing what happened to me. Wouldn't have put the kids through that. Are you kidding? Never."

She stared at him before saying, "I almost believe you."

"I'm trying to find out what happened to me, Sloane. I am. I have to know what was done so I never turn back into the man I was before I left. If there's any kind of shot for you and me —"

"There's no shot, Toren, so don't do it for anyone but yourself."

The barista interrupted to ask for their order. "Why don't you go sit down and I'll get the drinks," Toren said softly.

After he got their coffee and they settled at a table at the back of the shop, some of Sloane's ice had thawed, but Toren's optimism was gone. They made a few minutes of small talk about Colton's baseball team and Callie's wanting to try swim team this summer. She continued to glance at him with guarded eyes. More than understandable.

"What did you need to talk about?" she finally asked. "What's so important that you couldn't just call?"

Toren glanced around the shop. "A long time ago, do you remember me telling you about a kid from junior high and high school named Letto Kasper?"

"Vaguely." Sloane frowned as if trying to remember. "He wasn't the one who inspired you to start lifting weights, was he?"

"That's him."

"What does he want?"

Toren sighed, balled his fists, and set them on the table.

"He showed up at my press conference. He's gotten even weirder than he used to be back in school. Told me he was going to keep his promise to me."

"What promise?"

"That he'd take me down for abandoning him. For backing out of our friendship.

Before we graduated from high school, I told him if he didn't change, I didn't want to hang out much anymore."

"People drift away from each other all the time, especially at that age. Is this guy a little crazy?"

"A lot crazy." Toren leaned in, clenching and unclenching his hands. "I'm not telling you this to freak you out, just so you know this is serious, but for some reason he doesn't want me looking into the last eight months."

"So?" Sloane's eyes narrowed. "That's all?"

"He's threatened you."

"He doesn't know who he's dealing with," Sloane said, her eyes dark.

"I'm going to find this guy, Sloane. He thinks he's going to take me out? It's going to be just the opposite. I will not let anything happen to you or the kids."

"The kids? He's threatened the kids?"

Toren closed his eyes for a moment. "I probably can't believe anything he says. Or does. He talks a lot. He was always over the top. But yes, I want you to think about taking the kids away for a while. Maybe to your mom and dad's."

"I can't do that, Toren. The school year is almost over. Callie has her play, and Colton's team is in the playoffs."

"What if this guy is not playing around, Sloane?" He couldn't bring himself to say Letto had been at Colton's baseball practice.

"Has he done anything other than make threats?"

"Not yet."

"I can handle myself, you know that."

"This feels different."

"I can still handle myself."

Toren sighed. There was no way he could talk her into going. "At least let the school know — give them a description of Letto. He's five feet eight, short blond hair, in decent shape."

"Okay, I'll tell the school. And you'll keep me updated on the wacko."

"Absolutely." He leaned forward. "I just want to make sure you're safe, the kids are safe. I love you."

Sloane looked down at her cup.

"I got you something," he said.

"Oh?"

Toren pulled a small, flat, rectangular bundle out of his back pocket and placed it in front of Sloane.

"What is it?"

"Take a look."

She tentatively pulled off the tissue paper

and stared at the object. A petite wood frame around a pressed four-leaf clover. Her symbol for God's love, his promise to take care of her. She'd found one the day after losing her grandma when she was seventeen, and ever since then had found them at difficult moments in life.

"I don't know how you do it. You find them in minutes. It took me three and a half hours to find that one."

Sloane placed a finger on the edge of the frame and whispered, "Thank you. It's perfect."

She pushed her cup around the table, and for the first time since they'd sat down, he realized she hadn't taken a drink. Time stretched on. Finally Sloane spoke.

"I also need to tell something."

"Okay."

"It will likely sting."

"I don't think anything will sting like the reception I got when I first showed up on the porch."

"I think this might be worse." She pursed her lips.

Toren swallowed. "Tell me."

"We were not in a good place when you left."

"I know."

"And that's putting it mildly."

"I get it, Sloane."

"No. You don't get it. You think you do, but you don't."

"What are you trying to say?"

"Plus, I thought you were dead. And like I said before, my heart left us a long time ago. So even if you hadn't disappeared —"

"And you're bringing all this up because . . ."

Sloane sat back in her chair and folded her arms. "I'm dating someone, Toren."

The words hit him in the gut like a sledgehammer. Toren's hand slid off his cup and he clasped both sides of the table.

"What?"

Sloane stared at him, her eyes distant. Toren bit his upper lip and tried to block his mouth from speaking but lost the battle.

"You cannot be dating someone. No. You are not. That cannot happen. You cannot do this to me."

She didn't respond.

"How long have you been dating him? Who is it? Are you kidding me? Are you kidding me!"

His fingers dug into the table so hard he wondered that it didn't break. Deep inside, a sliver of darkness appeared. Behind it, specks of the rage he'd banished forever. He took a quick breath and pushed back, and instantly the peace he'd known since coming back flooded him.

Her eyes iced over. Then she turned and gazed out the window overlooking the street for at least twenty seconds before she shot the bullet that shattered his heart.

"It's more than dating." She glanced at him, then looked away. "I'm in love."

She said it as she continued to stare out the window, steel in her voice, as if to defend herself from an onslaught of words that would convince her she wasn't. That the real part of her still loved Toren. He sat back as heat flashed through his body. Breathing came with difficulty.

"No. Please no."

Her words didn't truly register. This couldn't be true. Her eyes had lit up when they'd stood in line. That was real! She finally turned her head back toward him and smiled a sad, exhausted smile, the type she'd given him in the years before he vanished.

"I'm sorry. I imagine that has to be difficult to hear. But if you're going to be in the kids' lives again, and we're going to work together as their parents, you need to be aware of it. You'll need to deal with it. We'll need to figure it out."

"I want to be in your life again too." The

words sputtered out before he could stop them. "I can't lose you again."

"You didn't lose me, Toren. You left without a word. You went away on a beautiful late-summer day in September and never came back."

"I'm back now."

"It was the best and the worst fall we've ever had." She rubbed the side of her cup, still as full of coffee as when they'd sat down. "I told the kids that night that you'd be back. But then the darkness of the evening turned itself over to the new light of morning and you still weren't home. The light of the day left and came again, but still there was nothing. Nothing from the police who investigated. Nothing from the lady I hired — the private detective — to find you.

"I convinced myself I still loved you, convinced myself I missed you, and part of me did. Really did. But as the days melted into weeks and then months and there was no sign of you, I began to let you go. Let us go. Let go of the hope that you'd return and somehow magic would have happened and you would have gotten rid of whatever demons haunted you after your dream died."

She looked up with fire in her eyes, a challenge she was convinced he could never answer.

"Don't you understand, Sloane? That's exactly what happened to me. I've changed. I am that man again. I'm that father, that husband, that friend I was before I stopped playing football. Give me a chance to continue to show you it's true!"

"The kids are open to that, but me? Not so much. For family things, yes. I want you to be in their lives. They need it, and from what I've seen so far, it will be good for them. It means a lot to Colton . . . the whole coming-to-his-practices thing."

"I've changed, Sloane, far more than you've seen. Far more than you can imagine."

For less than an instant, light filled her eyes and he saw past her wounds into her soul and saw that she believed it was possible. Wherever he'd been, whatever had happened to him, he'd been utterly transformed.

"Like I said —"

"Don't say it, Sloane. Give us a shot. Please."

"I'm sorry, Toren. Truly. For you. For the kids. For us."

Sloane stood, paused for an instant, then walked out of his life.

CHAPTER 20

That night, Toren stood in the middle of a crowd celebrating the birthday of Quinn's lawyer, a man Toren had only met twice. But Quinn had convinced him to come to the overpriced restaurant on the top floor of an expensive building in downtown Bellevue — something about Toren never having a social life ever again if he didn't get out and get social.

In his head it made sense — the only thing he'd be doing right now otherwise would be torturing himself over the conversation with Sloane — but in his heart the party was a 250-pound stack he couldn't lift from his chest. Smile. Make small talk. Pretend he didn't feel awkward and alone.

He'd just accepted a welcome back to the land of the living from an old friend of Quinn's when his heart rate kicked into third gear. Letto was standing in the corner of the room sipping a drink. Toren glanced at the exits, then eased toward him. No easy escape this time. When he was thirty feet away, Letto slid to Toren's left, a smattering of people between them. Toren matched his move, eyes never leaving Letto.

Letto set his drink on a small table and half jogged along the back wall till he reached a set of double glass doors framed in brushed nickel that led onto a balcony overlooking the city. He pushed through them. Seconds later, Toren shoved open the same doors and whipped his gaze around the sizable balcony, searching for Letto. Not there. Not possible. Wait. In the far corner, there he was, leaning against the railing, mostly blocked from view by two couples who laughed too loudly.

A breeze kicked in as Toren moved to his right a few feet to gain a clear view of Letto, bringing back the smells of fresh rain from an hour or so ago and Thai food being cooked somewhere hundreds of feet below. Toren approached slowly. Letto shifted his elbows on the railing, but his head stayed steady, staring out over the city.

Toren reached out his hand, expecting Letto's evasion. But the man was a statue. One foot away. He clamped his hand down on Letto's neck hard, his thumb and fingers digging into the smaller man's skin as he shook his neck back and forth. It felt good.

"Hey, ol' pal, I have no idea what you're doing at Quinn's party, but I'm glad you came so we can have a little chat."

Letto squeezed his eyes shut. "That hurts."

"Good to know." Toren squeezed harder.

"Do you mind letting go?"

"Do you mind staying away from my family?"

Letto coughed and motioned behind them with his thumb. "I'm wondering if those people mind what you're doing."

Toren glanced behind him at the two couples who had stopped laughing and were staring at him, concerned looks on their faces. He released Letto's neck and nodded at them.

"We're good. Just two old friends messing around."

They continued to stare, one whispered something to her companions, and all four moved away.

"That's exactly right, Toren. Just messing around. That's all I've been doing with you. Well, maybe there was more to it, but that was mostly all it was."

"I'm not into having fun with you anymore."

"Again you've nailed it, my old friend. I

understand now. It's why I came tonight, to apologize."

"What?"

"I would never, ever go after Sloane or your kids. Are you kidding? Anything I have against you is between you and me. That's where it stays. Besides, you really think I want to try to take on your wife, with her black belt in karate? Uh-uh."

"If that's true, then I think we're done here. But if you even breathe in their direction, I will crush you."

Letto nodded and glanced up at Toren, blinking, then turned his gaze back to the lights of the city.

"My childhood was like walking through Hades every day. Think back, Toren. Did I have a lot of friends other than you? No."

Toren pulled up his memories of those days. It was true.

"Only child, no cousins, few friends other than you, I wasn't good at school, and yeah, too much pot took me running down the skid-row fast track. And then on top of all that, you leave me when you get religion. Self-righteous bastard. Yes, it made me mad. Yes, there was part of me that vowed to make you suffer for abandoning me. But look, I'm not going to stalk you or your family. I wanted to scare you, hurt you inside, and it was wrong, but I couldn't help myself. You hurt me; I hurt you. A little civil war between us, but one that should end."

Letto turned back and stared at Toren. "All I wanted, the only reason I showed up again after all these years, is I want to be friends again."

Toren peered into Letto's eyes. The words, the tone of his voice, his face, everything about the man oozed sincerity. Except his eyes. There was a laughter in Letto's eyes that didn't fit, and it brought Toren back to their days in school when Toren had pushed him away.

"I don't want to be friends. Our friendship was a long time ago. We had some good times. Let's keep them there."

The laughter in Letto's eyes sharpened, then vanished, instantly replaced by a manic intensity that made Toren blink. A second later it winked out. "Okay, I get it, really I do. But I had to ask."

"Why is it that I don't believe a word you've said?"

"You don't have to. After a day goes by, then a week, then a month, a year, a decade, you'll realize this moment, right now, is the last time you'll see me for the rest of your days." Letto patted Toren on the shoulder. "Good-bye, old friend. I wish you well."

Toren watched Letto stroll off, wanting to believe the man's promise, but knowing he would still keep an eye open every moment of every day.

He turned to head back into the party when he was stopped cold by a woman strolling toward him. The tall stalker who'd run away from him at the coffee shop.

CHAPTER 21

Tonight the woman wore black slacks and a dark-green blouse. In her heels she was almost as tall as Toren. She gave a thin smile and motioned out over the city.

"Beautiful, even if they're man-made, don't you think?" Her voice came out silky smooth. "The lights."

Toren didn't turn, kept his eyes locked on her face. "I agree."

She slid a few inches closer to him, near enough to chat discreetly, not so close as to be inappropriate.

"Hello, Toren."

"You've been following me."

"I can certainly see how you would think that."

"I don't think it's a matter of debate."

"I prefer to describe it as observing."

"Is that so?"

"Yes."

Her voice was soothing, but with steel

underneath it. She didn't speak as if to defend herself or to convince him, but simply to state facts.

"So you're not following me, just observing, when you happen to show up at the same place I am."

"Yes. Curious, isn't it?"

"You want to explain to me how that works?" He turned to face her, but she still gazed out over the lights, her hands resting like two delicate birds on the railing.

"I believe there are forces operating in this world that are far beyond us, and my preference is simply to have faith that I am where I am supposed to be when I am supposed to be there."

"Then explain why you sprinted off when I saw you."

She turned and laughed, a lyrical sound that made him think of days on the lake at a childhood friend's cabin.

"You certainly have a severe desire to have things explained."

"Will you tell me?"

Her eyes narrowed. "I believe in going where the river wants to take me. I also believe I am given choice in every moment as to what part of the river I will experience. I have the choice to float, to swim away. To go to the shore. Even to go back upstream."

"Am I supposed to understand what that means?"

"It means you can let go of trying to understand everything."

An earlier image of the woman's face flashed into his mind — before the coffee shop — but it vanished as quickly as it had come. It wasn't from years ago; it was from months ago. Which meant . . .

Her hair was shorter then and streaked with dark-brown highlights. She'd been wearing jeans and a sky-blue T-shirt. An image of red rocks and the desert flashed into his head. The same images that had appeared in his mind a few days back. Toren shook his head. The woman peered at him with the hint of a smile as if she knew what he'd just seen.

"We've met before," he said.

She patted his hand lightly with warm, dry fingers. "Yes, my dear Toren."

"Where?"

"It is good to chat with you again."

"Again? Do you want to explain that to me?"

"You truly love that word, don't you?" She laughed for the second time.

"If it gets me what I need to know."

"Why do you need to know so badly?"

Before he could stop himself, Toren blurted out, "Because I'm concerned about something."

"About what?"

It didn't make sense, but he immediately began to spill everything that had happened to him since his return. He went quickly, hitting only the highlights, and finished by telling her about the anger he felt trying to rise in him during Sloane's recent revelation.

Her expression didn't change an iota during the telling, but the second he finished, she smiled wide and said, "Well done, Toren. I think you have a fine handle on things."

"You think I have a handle on things?" He slammed his hand down on the railing so hard it shook. "I have a handle on nothing!"

Toren put his other hand on the railing, closed his eyes, and took three slow breaths. *Control. Do not lose it.* Where had that come from? It was gone as fast as it had appeared, but this time the anger was more than a sliver.

When he looked up, the woman was peering at him, calm still spread across her porcelain skin, no shock in her eyes from the outburst.

"It's okay, Toren. Really. It is all okay. All will come in time."

"What do I have to do to make sure things stay the way they are?"

Her beautiful laugh illuminated her eyes. "Do you truly want to know?"

"Yes."

"I thought you knew this, Toren."

"I don't." He opened his palms. "Tell me. Please."

"Why, you have to accept your death, of course. And then destroy him once and for all."

CHAPTER 22

Toren met Eden early the next afternoon at the park, and she got down to business the instant he sat down.

"Give me an update on what you've learned and anyone you've talked to." She readied her fingers over her tablet.

"Good to see you too."

"Thanks." All she offered was the briefest hint of a smile.

Toren described his lack of progress in looking at retreat centers. He told her of his encounter at the party with the woman who had been stalking him.

"That's all she said? That you have to die?"

"And destroy him once and for all."

"Who do you think 'him' is?"

"I don't know." Toren bit his lower lip. "Yet." His mind went to the letter it seemed he had written. *Torenado doesn't deserve to exist anymore.*

"Anything from Letto? Any contact?"

"Big-time contact."

"Tell me."

After Toren finished describing his confrontation with Letto on the balcony, he sighed and said, "And my concern about that wacko is only slightly ahead of the other issue pounding at my mind."

"Which is?"

Toren glanced around the park.

"I can trust you, can't I?"

"I hope so."

"I'm starting to lose it."

"Lose what?"

"It's wearing off. Whatever was done to me is wearing off."

"I'm not sure I understand."

He told Eden about the rage he'd felt over the news of Sloane's boyfriend, then again with Letto at the party.

"I see."

As Toren studied her almond-shaped eyes, he truly believed she did.

"I *have* to find out where I was, because I have to get back, get more training, get refreshed, whatever it takes."

"If it's wearing off, it's wearing off fast."

"True."

"There was nothing inside the package to guide you. No instructions."

"Not true." Toren shook his head. "There

was a thin booklet. Things they said I should do."

"Why aren't you doing them?"

"I've been a little preoccupied."

"Sounds like you might need to make time for the exercises. Do you remember what they were?"

"No, I barely glanced at it." Toren sighed. "Meditation . . . prayers to read and memorize, and . . . I don't remember."

They slipped into silence. Toren stared at the towering fir trees, fighting the despair smothering his mind.

"Where do I go from here?"

Eden didn't respond right away. "To uncover where you were and what was done to you, you must realize this struggle is more about your heart than your mind."

"What do you mean?"

"Back in the early sixties there was a man who became exceedingly wealthy. The only thing that surpassed his wealth was the great fervor with which he served God. He gave away close to 250 million dollars during his lifetime to missions and churches and to feed the hungry, to clothe the needy — but he did more than give money; he gave away his time as well.

"Many months each year were devoted to reaching the lost, serving them, teaching them, empowering others to do the same. His library full of sermons, commentaries, and classic teachings from the first age of the church to the present was a wonder. But perhaps more startling, these books were not just a collection. No, this man had read nearly all of them. Studied them. Debated the ideas in the books with others more learned than him.

"But his study of these books did not come close to his study of Scripture and doctrine. Few were known who had memorized more of the Bible than he had. But what he is most remembered for is the day he gave up his life for the gospel."

"Really," Toren said. "How?"

"He was burned, Toren," Eden said. "He was on a mission trip, and he refused to deny Christ. So they burned his body."

"When this man died and slipped off his mortality, he stood before God, proud of what he had accomplished during his time on earth."

"Not a true story, then," Toren said.

Eden continued as if she hadn't heard him.

"God said to him, 'Welcome, son. But what you did on earth meant nothing.' The man realized in that moment that the apostle Paul spoke the truth. All his vast generosity, his wisdom, his precise knowledge of doctrine and dogma and the Bible, even his willingness to be martyred for his faith in the end amounted to nothing. *Nothing.* Not a microcosm of significance or eternal value. For he did not have love.

"Only love matters in the end. So only love matters in the present." Eden gave Toren's hand a quick squeeze.

"As I said a few minutes ago, I do not believe you will solve this mystery with your mind, Toren. It must be with your heart. The only possible way must be by discovering the way of love. Love is the greatest weapon you will ever wield. Right now, I suggest the best use of your time is to pursue understanding that weapon with everything you are."

CHAPTER 23

After leaving Eden, Toren headed north up I-5 till he reached La Conner. He rented a small boat and made his way over to Hope Island State Park. He had to get away, ponder what Eden had said about love and what it meant to pursue the way of love, clear his head, beg God to open Sloane's heart, beg him to tell Toren where he'd been. After tying up the skiff, he stared at the undulating waters of North Puget Sound for an age.

Finally he made his way over the rocks, over the driftwood, and onto the sand. He shuffled over its grains for an hour, then two, trying to come up with a deal to convince God to re-create Toren's life the way it had been before he stopped playing. A life in which Sloane loved him. But that wasn't how God worked. Toren knew it, but he had to find answers. Whatever it cost, he would pay the price to get them. He had to.

Toren would not give up till he'd figured out what had happened to him. And he would not stop till Sloane believed the darkness inside him was gone, till he convinced her how much he loved her. He would not give up on them. Ever. He had changed and would spend the rest of his life convincing her it was true.

Toren pulled out the booklet that had been in the package when he woke up in the hotel. If love was his ultimate weapon, then going through the exercises in the booklet was the only way to make himself strong. Had to do it. Fast. For the next two and a half hours he prayed, forced himself to memorize ten of the Scriptures in the booklet, sang every worship song he could remember, meditated on the truths of the faith. When he finished he felt better. A little. It would take time, he knew that, but time was slipping into the future too quickly.

He made his way back to the mainland and ate dinner at a small bar a few miles west, then drove back to the sound to watch the sunset. After he was out of prayers and almost out of hope, he got into his car and headed south.

The road slid by in darkness except for his headlights as he headed back to his rental house. A light summer rain fell. He flipped on the radio, and a voice broke into Toren's darkness like a lightning bolt.

". . . most scientists have a difficult time admitting how limited our knowledge is. Each generation believes they are at a kind of pinnacle of scientific knowledge, and yet the reality is that one hundred years from now scientists will look back on our beliefs and smile at how quaint and archaic and ill-informed they were."

By the time the woman finished the first sentence, Toren was more awake than he'd been all day. He knew that voice. Without question it had been part of his vanished 240 days. Not once, or a few times, but frequently. Images of women's faces floated through his mind's eye like vapors, but he couldn't be certain any of them were her.

". . . push back on you a little bit there . . ."

The host's voice brought Toren back to the interview. Yes. More of her voice. More memories.

"You're saying we'll look back and describe what we believed as quaint. Really? You're saying everything we believe is wrong?"

"No, no, not at all. *Wrong* is the not the word to describe it. *Ill-informed* is better. It's not that everything we believe is erroneous, it's that it is so woefully limited. Our vision is tragically narrow."

"Explain."

"Let's use an extremely simple analogy: If we were children and one day we walked by a fence and heard cheering on the other side of that fence, we might want to know what is on the other side. But the fence is too tall. So we search for a hole to look through, and we discover a tiny one in the fence. Each of us in turn looks through the hole and sees grass and a man in unusual clothing, maybe two or three men. And we might even see some breaks in the grass of light brown dirt.

"But that's all we see. Have we seen correctly? Yes. But let's say a year from then, we get to step inside the fence and take a seat in that baseball stadium. Will we see more than we did before? Will our narrow view become broader?"

Toren slowed to navigate a sharp curve in the road.

"Okay, now explain how that applies to science."

"Once upon a time, we believed the world was flat, and that driving above thirty miles an hour would kill a man, and that going to the moon would never happen except in science-fiction novels. The first belief comes from eons ago, but the last two come from less than 150 years ago. Until we believed those things could happen, those things could *not* happen. From a scientific viewpoint, perception is everything."

"You're saying you believe that old motivational cliché, 'Perception is reality'?"

"It's not a matter of choosing to believe it or not choosing to believe it. It is fact. Without question, perception is reality. More than most people can possibly imagine."

"All right, help us out. Give our imaginations a shot in the arm. Help us go beyond believing or not believing — give us proof."

The woman laughed, and even more than her voice, that laugh cemented in Toren's mind the belief that he'd not only listened extensively to this woman but interacted with her on multiple occasions.

Toren needed her name.

Come on, tell me the name of your guest.

Toren grabbed his cell phone and started to search for the show, then thought better of it, driving in the dark. It was okay — eventually they'd take a break and he'd discover who it was. He set down his phone and concentrated on her voice.

"At the end of the seventeenth century, the scientific community was enamored with the findings of a brilliant physicist named Isaac Newton. From his discoveries, we developed Newtonian physics. Finally, humankind gained understanding of the world we lived in. We were able to explain everything, we thought.

"Then, a relative few years later, along came a gentleman who turned Newtonian physics on its proverbial head. His name was Albert Einstein. This time we'd done it. Unlocked the mysteries of the universe beyond us, and the one smaller than we can imagine. And for decades we were convinced we'd found the equation, the formula to once again explain the way the world worked."

"E equals MC squared."

"Yes. But as time went on, we discovered a problem with Einstein's theories. Though they explained much on the atomic level, it didn't sync with what we were learning on the quantum level. Quantum mechanics once again turned science on its head."

"How so?"

"Quantum mechanics proves that one thing can be in two different places at the same time. Quantum mechanics says that our observation, our perception of an action, can cause the action to change. At the quantum level, observation of the activity changes it."

"You're serious."

"Deadly. And now we are on the brink of admitting that many of the mystics throughout the ages were right: faith can move mountains."

"Gotta say, you definitely are the right guest for this show, because you are on the fringe of the fringe, scientifically speaking."

"I have to disagree."

Toren heard a smile in the woman's voice.

"I'm not on the fringe at all. What I've just told you has been proven thousands of times."

The host laughed. "We're going to take a break, my fellow travelers, who are with me on the road to a destination we're not sure of . . . yet. But we wouldn't have it any other way now, would we? When we come back, we're going to hear from a man who says all of Houdini's magic tricks and escapes were done with the power of his mind. You won't want to miss it.

"As always, my intrepid explorers of the fringes of the scientific world — boldly going where people have probably gone before but haven't taken the time to tell us about — thank you for joining me, thank you for your e-mails and questions and suggestions. Thank you for making this show such a delight to host, and of course thank you to my wonderful guests, not the least of which is the wonderful scientist, philosopher, and change agent for the human psyche, Dr. Ilsa Weber.

"You're listening to *Breakthrough: The Weird and Wonderful World of Fringe Science* on SiriusXM."

Ilsa Weber. Toren racked his brain, trying to attach the name to the fragments of memories he was collecting from his lost months, but her name stirred nothing like her voice had. Didn't matter. He could find her. Figure out exactly who she was, where she'd been, and what part she'd played in his time away. She would bring answers.

He faced heavy traffic the rest of the way back down I-5, but the 405 to Kirkland was clear and he pulled into his driveway at one fifteen in the morning. By the time he propped himself up on his bed and pulled out his laptop, exhaustion had taken over. The last thing he remembered before sleep took him was typing Dr. Ilsa Weber's name into his computer.

CHAPTER 24

Ilsa Weber didn't exist. At least according to Google, Bing, Dogpile and three other search engines. Toren sat in the backyard of his rental house, sipping on strong coffee and trying to keep a tight seal on his frustration. How could she not exist? She'd been on the show the night before. Fine. He'd go to the show. Ten minutes later he reached the producer of *Breakthrough: The Weird and Wonderful World of Fringe Science.*

"Is this Tawny?"

"Yeah? Can I help?"

"My name is Toren Daniels, and I was listening to Carl Rodger's show last night, *Breakthrough: The Weird and Wonderful World of Fringe Science.* It's on Sirius and —"

"Yeah, I know the show." The woman slurred her words as if on purpose. "I produce it. Get to your point, please."

Toren didn't think it would have been possible for her to say "please" more sarcastically, but with more than a bit of focus he kept the fuse of his temper long.

"I want to find a way to reach Dr. Ilsa Weber, one of last night's guests."

"Got it."

She didn't continue. All Toren heard was what sounded like chewing. Then a long slurp. He waited till all that came through the phone was low static.

"Can you tell me?"

"Tell you what?"

He pressed his lips together. *Be the new Toren. The old does not exist.* He could do it. *Stay calm.*

"How I can reach Dr. Ilsa Weber. A website, e-mail address, social media page . . ."

"It's a pseudee."

"A what?"

"A pseudee, you know, a pseudee. Lots of people have them."

Stay calm.

"Sorry, what's a pseudee?"

"Her name is."

Toren finally got it and counted to five. "In other words, Ilsa Weber is not her real name. It's a pseudonym."

"Uh, hello, that's what I've been saying, yeah?"

Toren tried to stay kind, and he did, sort

of, but he also raised his voice and got to the point. "Give me her real name. And the shortest way to reach her. Right now."

Surprisingly, Little Miss Sunshine didn't seem upset when she responded. She actually got nicer.

"You know, I'd have no problem giving you that info if I could. But I can't. Sorry."

"Why can't you give it to me?"

"The doc doesn't want anyone to contact her. Doesn't want to be known. Weird. All these people get on the show and ask me to make sure we pump their websites and books, la, la, la . . . and here this woman gets on only if we promise to use a fake name and sign some stupid deal that we'll never reveal who she really is or where she lives, blah, blah, blah . . . so like I said, sorry, she's a ghost."

"Would a financial incentive help?"

"A bribe?"

"An incentive."

She laughed. "Nah, I really do like this job and they pay me enough, so I have to say no."

Toren hung up and jammed his upper teeth into his lower lip. His first truly solid clue. He was certain that Ilsa Weber was a cog in the machine that transformed him during his eight months away.

He had to get back there, to where he'd been for eight months, to the red rocks, to the classroom, to wherever *there* was. Had to have faith. Had to believe the woman at the birthday party was right and answers would come. Had to believe Eden that the way to the truth was down the path of love.

Toren set his phone on the wooden table on the back patio. He snatched the booklet out of his back pocket and riffled through its pages. Stopped and worked on more memorizing of Scripture. Focused on the principles of a godly life. Repeated them out loud three times, four times, six times. Then meditation. And singing even though the sound only seemed to flutter to the ground. He shoved a deep sigh through his teeth. It wasn't working. Deep inside, he felt anger stirring.

Finally, after half an hour more of futility, he prayed. For Colton and Callie and then for Sloane till tears came, over what he'd done to her. He begged God's forgiveness, begged Sloane's forgiveness, placed her in the center of his mind's eye, went over every moment with her since he'd been back, savoring the time even though it cut him to the marrow of his soul.

He thought of seeing her framed by their front door, seeing her in the coffee shop the first time, seeing her there the second time, discovering a tiny scar on the back of her neck and —

Toren's eyes flew open and he gasped. "No!"

Sloane's scar. He remembered where it came from.

CHAPTER 25

How could he have forgotten? It had happened in August, around a month before he'd left. They'd planned to watch a movie, and he'd been sitting in their media room waiting for her to come in. He was agitated from a less-than-stellar workout earlier in the day and a call from his barely available agent, who had told him no team would talk about Toren getting a tryout, even if someone got hurt in preseason or early in the schedule.

After ten minutes he got up to find out what was keeping her. He found her in the kitchen at the sink, staring out the window into the darkness.

"What are you doing? I thought we were going to watch a movie."

"We were." She didn't turn. Her voice was slow. "But then it happened."

"What happened?"

"It surprised me. I didn't expect it." She

turned, her eyes somber, a little puff of resigned laughter on her lips. "I thought it would come in a wave, along with a flurry of emotions, but it settled on me like a feather, without emotion, just a few minutes ago."

"Am I supposed to understand that?"

"No. But I do, and that's enough."

"You're not going to tell me."

"You wouldn't understand."

"Try me."

"It's okay." She tossed him a sad smile and turned back to stare out into the darkness.

"You're going to refuse to tell me."

"Yes." Sloane gripped the edge of the sink with both hands.

"But you're okay."

"I'm fine."

"Then can we go watch the movie?"

"No, Toren. I'm not going to be watching movies with you anymore."

"Okay, let's do a slice and dice on the fog and get some clarity. What is going on with you? What happened?"

Sloane raised her chin, eyes toward the ceiling, and took a long breath in and out before answering.

"The camel has been carrying an extremely heavy load for a long time. And today, the final straw, barely heavier than a daffodil, was placed on top."

"What are you talking about?"

"You. You placed the straw. And my back broke once and for all."

Her voice dropped in volume, slower now, almost gentle. Not good. It meant she had been thinking about this conversation for a long time. There was little emotion behind her words. Just logic. And conviction.

"What did I do? Just get it out. What is the major screwup that I accomplished that has sent you over the edge into the abyss?"

"I haven't gone over any edge." Sloane's voice grew even calmer. "I actually just pulled myself back from the edge, where I've been living for a long, long time."

"Are you going to tell me?" Toren stepped toward her. "Tell me what I've done?"

"I'm sorry." She turned toward him and slumped back against the kitchen counter. "But I'm finished. There's nothing left. I can't do this any longer."

"Do what?"

"Us."

"What do you mean you can't do us?" Toren jammed his fists into his hips. "Divorce? Is that it, huh? Is that what you're driving at? Go ahead, say it."

"Divorce? Probably. Maybe not. I don't

know yet. All I know is I can't live with you under the same roof anymore. You're going to move out. If you won't, then I'll move out. Because I will no longer pretend things are well between us. I'll no longer pretend you haven't broken my heart a thousand times when you vowed to stop losing it in front of the kids and in front of me."

Sloane turned on the water and ran it over her hands, massaging them slowly.

"I know you mean well. I know in your heart you love me. But your anger has shouted another message for years now."

Toren rocked his head back as he tried to quell the rage stirring inside. Heat simmered, then boiled in his head. No. He had to get control. Bolt down the lid. Fight! He jammed his hands into his front pockets and found his keys there and squeezed them, their jagged edges digging into his fingers.

"Sloane? Let's figure this out. Just tell me what I did and I promise I will fix it. Whatever it is, I'll take care of it."

"Don't you understand what I'm saying? I have figured it out. I've lost heart. My heart. I tried and tried and tried, but I can't get it back. It's gone."

"Knock it off. I get it. Just tell me what I did." He ground out each word. "Then we'll fix it. What was it? What did I do? What was this catastrophic daffodil?"

She turned off the water, wiped her hands on a towel, then squeezed her eyes shut. She leaned back against the counter, hands out to her sides, bracing herself.

"Just tell me."

Sloane didn't open her eyes. "I was here, in the kitchen earlier today, washing out the frying pan from breakfast. I glanced out to the left. You were out there. So was Colton."

"Yeah, what about it?"

"He was practicing throwing and missed the net and hit you in the leg."

Toren rubbed the back of his neck. "Yeah, I got a little hot . . ."

"A little? You screamed at him for a full minute."

"But I got it together." Toren opened his palms. "Did you see that part? I told him I was sorry."

Sloane just shook her head, then opened her eyes and peered straight at him. "You still don't get it."

"That's your big cataclysmic straw? That I yelled at Colton?"

"No." Sad smile. "Like I said, it was just a daffodil. A feather."

"You cannot be serious."

She didn't respond.

"Come on, Sloane. That's crazy. I apologized. Told him I was wrong. Asked his forgiveness."

"And promised and promised and promised and promised it wouldn't ever happen again? Did you do that part? Huh, Toren? Did you? Did Daddy kiss it and make it all better?"

Sloane's eyes seethed.

"Don't mock me, Sloane."

"You mean like you mock me or the kids when you lose it? When you lose it all the time?" She pushed off the kitchen counter and moved toward him. "Is it the king of mocking you're talking about, or is there another version you're thinking of?"

The dull simmer of anger in his gut grew stronger. This was insane. The rage pressed up out of his stomach into his brain, where it pounded at his temples.

"Guess what, superstar?" Sloane's shouting ramped up another thirty decibels, and she strode to him and popped him in the chest with both fists so hard he staggered back a step. "Other people in this house can yell too. Not as good as you, no way. You're the champ, but I'm a contender, and you're teaching your son and your daughter to follow in your footsteps. Well done, pro! Well done!"

"You have got to be kidding me. Really?"

Toren yanked his hands from his pockets and slammed his fist into his upturned palm. "We're finished. Do I have it right?"

"Yes. You have it right." She shook her head, all emotion drained from her face. "We're done."

The rage inside Toren broke through to the surface. He stepped back from Sloane and grabbed a plate off the kitchen counter. He pulled his arm back, but it wasn't his arm, was it? It was someone else's. Had to be, because he was now deep inside himself, watching another part of him lose control. He shouted out to himself to stop, but the other part of Toren squashed the command, and in that moment a realization swept through him. There were two of him. A Toren speaking logic and truth, a Toren of morals, the one who desired to do the right thing; and another Toren, who only wanted to let the frenzy inside him explode.

Time slowed, and from inside himself, Toren watched his arm move forward, heard a guttural cry surge out of his mouth, then watched the plate rocket toward their glass cabinets. Competing thoughts flashed through his mind in milliseconds.

What have I done?

Touchdown, Toro. You're out of control. You'll never rein me in.

No. Please, no. This will destroy me and Sloane once and for all.

Feels so good, yeah? Let it out, baby, let it all out.

The plate smashed into the cabinets, and the glass shattered like a star exploding. Time slowed as Sloane ducked and covered the back of her head and fell to her knees. Toren staggered back, his lungs reaching for air that seemed to have been sucked from the room.

He stared at Sloane as she slumped back against the dishwasher, moved her fingers over the back of her neck, then lifted them and brought them around to her face. She peered at the smear of blood on them and turned to stare at Toren. Her eyes met his with a mix of wonder and horror.

"No!" Toren collapsed next to her and reached out, but she blocked his arm as if she were sparring with a partner in her dojo.

"Get away from me."

Toren fell back, shame and remorse burying him. He'd never thrown anything. Never come even close. Never allowed his anger to spill over with this much force before. The sight of Sloan on the floor, blood on the back of her neck, shattered him. This wasn't him, he wouldn't do this to her — but of course it was and he had.

"I'm sorry. I'm so sorry. Please forgive me. Please."

Her head was down now, her hair covering her face. Should he stay? Leave? Speak? Stay silent?

Thank God the kids were spending the night with friends.

Time and silence stretched out like a blade. Sloane shifted forward, hair draped out in front of her, then sat up and pulled her hair back, eyes locked on his. She didn't speak. No fear crossed her eyes. Steel came over them, and she didn't look away as she moved her head to the right, then back to the left one time, so slow he could barely discern the movement.

"Enough."

She titled her head back toward the cabinet above and behind her, eyes still fixed on his as her hand went to the back of her neck and returned, now covered in blood.

Toren stood, glanced at the counter, found a napkin, and turned on the water at the sink.

He moistened the napkin, then again knelt at her side. "Here, here, let me —"

"No." She grabbed his forearm and sank her nails deep into his skin.

"Please, I —"

"No." Sloane flung his arm down and

slipped into silence.

"Talk to me. Please. Yell at me, scream how much you hate me, anything."

All he could hear for the next three minutes was the tick of the kitchen clock and the rhythmic stream of air flowing in and out of Sloane's nostrils. Finally she spoke.

"What you did just now? That wasn't a straw landing on the camel's back, Toren. It was an iron beam."

He knelt by her side for twenty, maybe thirty seconds more, begging God to fix this, begging God to fix him, knowing there would be no answer to either plea. Finally he rose, looked at his wife, and stumbled away, knowing he had to find a way to destroy the anger inside.

Just before he turned the corner out of the kitchen, the whisper of Sloane's voice floated toward him.

"You want to make it back to the NFL? That's your big problem, right? Have to fix your anger issue to do it, yes? Well, now you have a bigger problem, Toren. You and me? We're over. And there's nothing you can do that will ever be enough to fix us."

He stepped back toward her. "Please, Sloane. I'll do anything."

"Go away, Toren. Far away."

■ ■ ■ ■

Toren pulled himself out of the memory from so many months ago, his brain reeling and his body numb. The scar had come from him.

All he'd wanted after that was to change. He admitted all his promises were platitudes, vain attempts to keep his family placated. Toren didn't run from the truth, but faced it and determined to do anything necessary to become the man he knew he could be. The husband, the dad he'd dreamed of being.

He went to a counselor five days in a row, trying to face the darkness. He confessed and faced more truth, but they seemed to be getting nowhere. It was all too clinical. Toren asked his counselor how he could do more than understand. His counselor, a slim woman in her late fifties with blonde hair starting to gray . . . Toren couldn't recall her name. But he remembered with crystal clarity what the woman said.

"How badly do you want the change?"

"With everything in me."

"How badly?"

"With everything."

"How badly?"

"With everything!"

"Good."

With that she nodded and told Toren what it would cost. The fee was high, but he didn't care. He truly was willing to do anything. The next day he wired the money into an account number she gave him for a bank in . . .

"Sedona!"

That's why he'd left. He'd gone to Sedona, Arizona, to fix himself for good.

His next move was obvious. He'd be on the first flight out in the morning.

CHAPTER 26

At six forty-five a.m., Toren hurtled through the air at thirty-five thousand feet on his way to Phoenix. An hour and a half after the Boeing 737 hit the tarmac, he raced along a highway with a smattering of cars on it, then turned onto a road that he doubted carried more than a few cars every day. A road he remembered. He didn't know the exact route. Didn't matter. He believed he'd know when to turn when he needed to turn. So far it had worked perfectly.

He tried to conjure images of what he'd find at the end of his journey, but nothing surfaced. He didn't mind. Toren knew he'd been on *this* road. Once going in, once coming out.

Thirty minutes later he pulled up to a large white stucco building with a small parking lot. There were only two cars in it and no signage identifying the place. Slivers of memory flashed though his mind. It was enough. This was the place. Toren looked at his watch. His kids would be in school. Sloane would be finished with her morning routine. He plucked his phone from the passenger seat and dialed.

"Hello, Toren."

"Sloane, I —"

"I only have a few minutes."

"This will only take a few."

"Fine."

"I . . . uh . . . a bunch of memories have come back."

"Okay." Her voice was impatient.

"When I asked you about the scar in the coffee shop? I didn't remember. Now I do."

Sloane didn't respond. A western meadowlark landed on the parking sign ten feet to Toren's left and seemed to peer at him.

"Anything else, Toren?" she finally said.

"I'm so sorry, Sloane."

"I know you are." She paused. "It's okay. You're forgiven."

"No. Not okay. Horrible. I . . . Maybe that's why they wiped my memory, so I could have a fresh start."

"How wonderful for you to forget when I get to remember every day."

"I'm sorry."

"Like I said, I'm over it."

With that, she hung up, and Toren

watched the meadowlark give him a last look and fly off.

"Can I get you water while you wait?"

The woman smiled at Toren as he sat in the lobby of the massive building. No name on the outside. Nothing on the inside. No literature to give him a clue to what this place was, and all the woman standing in front of him would say is that someone would be with him shortly. But he knew this was where he'd been. And when he'd asked to see the person in charge, the woman hadn't seemed surprised or asked for a reason.

"No thanks, I'm fine."

Another fifteen minutes went by before she showed him into a large room. Nothing about it stirred memories. Not a problem. He would get them from whomever they sent to talk to him. After another ten minutes, a door at the far end of the room opened and a man passed through with a walk that made it seem like he was floating above the dark acacia wood floor.

He glanced at Toren and smiled gently, then fixed his eyes on something above Toren's head. Toren knew this man, didn't he? His thick dark hair was streaked with gray, his eyes gentle and piercing at the same time. He walked past Toren and went to the floor-to-ceiling windows looking out at the massive land bridge a quarter mile away.

"Hello, Toren."

Toren stood and took a few steps toward the man. Toren knew him, was certain of it, but that certainty was the only thought he could hold.

"I know you, don't I?"

The man turned, his hands clasped behind his back, his voice soft as he lifted one hand and held out his palm as if caressing the view beyond them.

"Do you know that this land bridge is the foundation of my work? At least metaphorically speaking. It is the perfect symbol of the bridge between the old man and the new man. Simple. Iconic. Yes?"

Toren looked at the formation.

"Can you see how the rocks on the left are harsh, unforgiving, a vertical face that would be difficult to climb? And then we see the rocks on the right. Beautiful, the slope easily accessible if you want to reach the top, and smooth. One side the good Dr. Jekyll, the other so clearly the nefarious Mr. Hyde. Inspiring the way nature would give us this image, don't you think? Certainly a gift for those seeking true change."

"Who are you?"

He turned and strolled toward Toren, his hands clasped in front of him now, his gaze like that of an adult extending compassion to a child.

"In complete honesty, I'm delighted to see you, friend. But also surprised."

"Why? What is this place?" Toren motioned with his hands. "And again, who are you?"

The man extended his hand to the chair Toren had been sitting in. The woman who'd greeted Toren reappeared with a tray bearing a water pitcher and two glasses. She set it on a nearby table and left them.

Toren sat down, and the man sat beside him so they both faced the view of the land bridge. One minute stretched into two, and still he stayed silent.

"I need answers," Toren said.

"Do you?"

"Yes."

"Why?"

"Because this is where all my questions have led me."

"And what are those questions, Toren?"

All the questions he'd been so desperate to ask competed for the pole position, but the man's earlier statement drove all other questions into the shadows.

"Why are you surprised to see me?"

A hint of a smile appeared at the corners of his mouth. "That truly is a question more pertinent than the obvious ones, like 'Who are you?' and 'What is this place?'"

He sat back and studied Toren.

"I'm glad you like the question." Toren frowned. "Are you going to answer it?"

The man's smile grew. "There is fire inside you. For the truth. Not the religious truth, not the way that seems right to a man, but truth for the narrow path. I saw it in you, but now the fire has been tested in the real world and it has not diminished; it has grown. Wonderful."

"So you're not going to answer me."

The man leaned forward and patted Toren's forearm.

"The effect of your training here is wearing off, from what I understand. You were focused. Determined. But as your temper began to reemerge, you didn't give up, give in, and hurl yourself over the cliff into the bottomless Mr. Hyde pit.

"No." He clapped his hands once. "You have decided to fight, to claw your way back to the source and unlock the mystery of what happened to you. Let me assure you, not many go on that journey of discovery. Well done."

As he spoke, more shards of memory sliced into Toren's mind — of being in Arizona, getting on a plane, but it was like a jigsaw puzzle made of light, and too many pieces were still shrouded in darkness.

"I was here."

It was halfway between a question and a statement. Of course he'd been here. The man had just said it, and Toren already knew it to be true, but he had no recollection of the experience.

"But you don't remember."

"No."

The man extended his hand with his palm up, as a parent might invite a child to take it. Without thinking, Toren placed his hand in the man's warm, dry palm. He held Toren's hand gently and smiled wide, his amber eyes brilliant, then squeezed three times. Then he let go and leaned in, his mouth centimeters from Toren's ear.

"Remember, Toren, remember. Not with your mind, but with your heart. And when the memories come, hold on to the truth you've learned. It will serve you well."

"What truth? Remember what?"

The man glanced at the empty water glasses, picked up the pitcher next to them, and filled them both halfway. He handed one to Toren and lifted the other in a toast.

246

"To truth. To remembering."

Toren lifted his glass halfheartedly and drank.

The moment they both set down their glasses, Toren realized how stupid he had been. Maybe it was the soft blanket of internal warmth that was the first clue, his eyelids dropping along with the feeling. Or simply a guess based on all the cryptic responses. The man had drugged him. But hadn't he drunk water from the same pitcher? Toren slumped back in his chair as his eyelids won the war and closed.

"Who are you?" he muttered, his mind teetering on the edge of darkness.

"We'll talk again someday, Toren. Don't worry. Trust. Only trust."

CHAPTER 27

Toren dreamed, and the dream seemed to last for weeks.

He sat in a semicircle of chairs that were too soft with thirteen others — six men and seven women who looked like he must have looked. Broken. Desperate for change. Willing to do anything. In front of them, the man with gray-streaked hair glided back and forth over the lush wood floor, a small paperback in his hand, his fingers covering the title.

Clavin Sorken. The man was Clavin Sorken, and this was The Center. His Center.

Sorken was speaking.

"A son once asked his father, 'How can I be a good man, a moral man, when I grow up? One who does good for others, one who loves well, one who cares deeply for the others around him?'

"The father answered, 'Once, my son,

there were two dogs, one dark as midnight, the other whiter than Christmas morning snow. The dark dog held nothing but evil in its heart; the white dog held nothing that was not pure.'

"The man stopped speaking till his son said, 'That's not all, is it, Father?'

" 'No,' he said, 'there is more, but you already know the answer to the question you want to ask me, yes?'

" 'I want to ask you what the white and the dark dog represent.'

"The father nodded.

" 'But I don't need to ask you, because I already know,' the boy said.

"The father nodded again at his son and with his eyes invited the boy to speak.

" 'The dark dog represents the evil inside me, and the white dog represents the good.'

" 'Go on,' the father said.

" 'And the two dogs — if one is evil and the other good — must hate each other.'

" 'This is truth.'

" 'Each trying to win the battle against the other.'

" 'Yes.'

" 'So if I want to be a moral man, I must learn to control the dark dog.'

"The father shook his head and said, 'No. This seems right, but it cannot be done.

You will never be able to control the dog inside you. It is a feat no man can accomplish.'

" 'Then what can I do?' The boy's face grew pensive. 'There must be another way, for there are moral men, good men who live among us, like you, Father.'

" 'Yes, there is another way.'

" 'What is it?' the boy wanted to know.

"The father only smiled, waiting till the answer landed in the stillness of the young man's mind.

" 'Whichever dog is stronger will win,' the boy said.

"The father smiled and said once more, 'Go on.'

" 'And whichever dog is fed the most, that one will be the strongest.'

"The father grabbed the boy up in his arms and hugged him close.

" 'Yes.' He placed the boy back down and cradled his face in his hands. 'So we must learn to feed the white dog well, and do everything we can to starve the dark one.' "

The whole time Sorken spoke, he rapped the paperback against his palm in slow but continual movement. Toren couldn't make out the white-lettered title. But now Sorken stopped and held the book out for each of them to see. Toren squinted. *The Curious*

Case of Dr. Jekyll and Mr. Hyde.

"You all know this book, I'm quite certain, but how many of you have read it?"

No one responded, except for a nod from a woman who looked to be in her mid-thirties. She had peroxide-blonde hair and a runner's figure.

"It is not a rhetorical question, my dear apprentices. Might I see a show of hands, please?"

Toren glanced to his right and left, but no hands went up except the blonde's.

Sorken raised his eyebrows, but it seemed mock surprise.

"Then allow me a reminder of the story, for it will be at the core of your study and transformation here at The Center."

The thick-waisted, middle-aged man sitting to Toren's immediate right set a beautiful wood clipboard with notepaper on it onto his lap. He clicked a pen to the ready position and looked up at Sorken, eyes bright.

"Mr. Harris?"

"Yes?"

"I'd prefer you don't take notes. Don't fret. The message all of you will learn here will be repeated till its truth is as familiar to you as your own name. We will immerse ourselves in these truths till they *are* you."

Mr. Harris hesitantly set his clipboard on the floor at his feet.

"Thank you, Mr. Harris."

Mr. Harris nodded, his eyes now dull.

"Now, where were we?"

It seemed to Toren that Sorken knew exactly where they were, and only spoke the words to produce some kind of effect on all of them.

"Ah, yes, I was about to give you a quick summary of Stevenson's novella."

He held out the book and flashed a thin smile.

"Stevenson apparently wrote the book in a torrent." Sorken glanced at a sheet of paper tucked in the back of the book. "His stepson wrote, 'Louis stumbled down the stairs in a fever; read nearly half the book aloud to us; and then, while we were still gasping over the tale he'd created, he slipped away, back upstairs, and continued to write. I doubt if the first draft took so long as three days.'

"The novella is set in late 1880s London. It starts with Mr. Hyde trampling a young woman and being confronted by a man named Enfield. Enfield is repulsed by Hyde, his disdain for the man intensified when Hyde shows no remorse for his actions. Instead of going to the police, Enfield forces

Hyde to give the girl's family money. Hyde agrees, leaves, then returns with a check endorsed with the name of the respected Dr. Henry Jekyll.

"A year later, Hyde murders Sir Danvers Carew with a cane. Jekyll's lawyer confronts him for having any kind of association with such a man as Hyde. Dr. Jekyll promises he will have nothing to do with Hyde ever again. Hyde seems to vanish. However, not many weeks later, Jekyll's lawyer hears of a mutual friend who has died of shock, and then the doctor secludes himself. His lawyer receives a letter with instructions to open it only in the event of Dr. Jekyll's death or disappearance.

"Soon after, Jekyll's butler reports that the doctor has locked himself in a room and strange sounds are emanating from behind the door. Jekyll's lawyer and butler break down the door to find Hyde's dead body. They assume he committed suicide. Neither Jekyll's body nor evidence of his death are anywhere to be found.

"The letter explains that Henry Jekyll saw the good and the bad that resided inside his soul and sought to find a way to separate the virtuous side of himself from the darker impulses that often threatened to overtake him. His potions accomplished this and transformed him into a monster — a being free of the restraints of conscience or remorse, pity or feelings, a man consumed only with his own needs and desires.

"At first, Jekyll delighted in becoming Hyde. He rejoiced in the moral freedom that the creature afforded him. He was free from the laws of the land and free of the moral law that raged against him. As time passed, however, he found himself turning into Hyde involuntarily in his sleep, even without taking the potion. He knew the unfettered evil residing in Hyde would cause untold damage to himself and his friends.

"So Jekyll resolved to cease becoming Hyde. For a time this tenacious resolution worked. But soon he could no longer keep his raging malevolence at bay.

"This was when the murder of Sir Danvers Carew occurred. Horrified, Jekyll steeled his mind against Hyde, vowing to construct an impenetrable wall of moral resolve. Jekyll believed with soul and spirit that he had accomplished his mission, and as time passed, it seemed his goodness had triumphed over his darker side.

"But one day not long after he had convinced himself that Hyde had been vanquished for good, while sitting in a state of rest and solitude in a park, without warning of thought or emotion, he suddenly turned into Hyde. It was the first time an involuntary metamorphosis had happened during Jekyll's waking hours."

Sorken again glanced around the room, as did Toren. He imagined the look on his face was the same as his companions'. Fear, revulsion, shame — mostly shame for what they had been — and hope that they could succeed where Jekyll had not.

Sorken closed his eyes for a moment, then opened them and paced from one side of the group to the other as he finished the tale.

"Eventually, perhaps inevitably, the good doctor's potion ran low. His ability to change from Hyde back into Jekyll slowly ebbed away like an outgoing tide. With horrifying clarity, Jekyll accepted the reality that he would soon become Hyde permanently, and the good residing in his soul would vanish forever. In the end, Jekyll killed himself, ending the war with neither side winning."

Toren didn't care for the glint in Sorken's eye. The man took a drink of water from a thin glass bottle before resuming.

"My fellow travelers? I realize this tale took a fair while to recount. Are you still with me?"

A few looked ill — as if they'd never admitted the truth that they had a Hyde living inside them. Others looked angry, and they twitched as if ready to bolt for the door. Not Toren. He felt abject despair and exhilarating hope in equal measure. He knew Hyde lived inside him. He had admitted it after he'd injured Sloane, when for the first time his anger had turned physical. It was why he was here: to seek a solution, an answer, a magic potion like Jekyll's, one that worked in the real world. A way to eradicate Hyde forever.

"My brothers and sisters of the journey, how does this story make you feel? What rises up in you?"

None of the men or women around the circle responded. Sorken gave only a cursory pause before continuing.

"Why does this story resonate and reverberate within us with such viscosity? Why does it settle in our souls with such weight?" Sorken tilted his head and spoke the answer in a whisper. "Because we know it to be true. Absolutely, unequivocally true.

"Why has this story been remade and retold hundreds of times in numerous ways — including more than 120 stage and film versions alone? Because in the darkest moments of the night, when not even the wind whispers against the silence, and the shadows seem to have overcome the light, a voice inside speaks and tells us that Hyde is alive and well in the fragmented, dark pieces of our soul.

"We see it in those around us, don't we? We see it on a cruise ship, where the people are having the time of their lives, with every pleasure they can think of attended to, and then when the ship breaks down, it's only a matter of hours before their darker sides emerge. They turn to raging and stealing and hoarding — this from people we would hold up as bastions of societal grace and kindness. We could find these people capable of great compassion and sacrifice, I imagine. Don't you?

"And yet they also show themselves capable of despicable acts. So which person are they? The good man, the good woman, or the evil?

"If honest — which is a victory in itself — even the most forthright man, the most virtuous woman, would admit to thoughts that echo the persona of Mr. Hyde. He was a man of small stature, slight of build, in want of physical strength, and yet his power to subjugate the light? Unparalleled. He is the dark dog. And though appearing gaunt and weak, the truth is that he can tear the white dog to pieces if left unchecked."

Again Sorken paused and closed his eyes. Again a few of Toren's fellow seekers of light appeared agitated, and again no one answered when Sorken opened his eyes and riveted his question on all of them.

"Would you like to be free? Would you like to drink the potion that will render Hyde impotent? Destroy the dark dog inside you?"

A few of them murmured their assent.

"Good, good." Sorken spread his arms and hands wide. "Of course you would. It's the reason you're here. We are in a civil war, my dear apprentices, the same civil war that Stevenson explored in his novella, the same civil war that Paul of Tarsus addresses in his letter to his friends in Rome, which is contained in the New Testament portion of the Bible.

"So the news is indeed dire. You are at war with your two selves, each vying for power and position — each on a quest to conquer the other and become the victor. But the news is also good, for here at The Center, you will be equipped to win that war every minute, every hour, every day of your life. The good and holy and true woman or man within you will emerge victorious.

"You will train your mind as an elite

athlete trains his body. You will eventually begin to respond in the ways of love and compassion without thinking. You will learn to put others first, to truly love your neighbor as yourself."

Toren's forehead broke out in a cold sweat as the dream morphed into hours of training, the relentless training. Hours melted into days, into weeks, months as he trained his mind to be calm, to use the mantras about surrendering to Christ. He mastered the spiritual disciplines of silence and meditation and fasting and memorizing Scripture and extending acts of kindness to the other students. Sorken taught him how to mold his soul into one who could step outside himself into light, into love. One who could conquer the dark man inside him. One who could banish his anger forever.

CHAPTER 28

Toren's lungs groped for air as he woke to his own shout, and memories rained down on him too fast to assimilate. A brilliant sliver of light from the cresting of the sun over the mountains to the east pulled Toren from the dream, and he shielded his eyes from the brightness. He was in his rental car in a large parking lot. The Phoenix airport. He'd been here overnight?

Sorken had given him hope. Promised that The Center had the secret, a potion Toren could take that would last. That would eliminate Hyde forever. But it hadn't worked. Here he was, slowly turning back into Hyde. The potion was wearing off.

He sat in the car for more than ten minutes before he saw the corner of a black package sticking out from under the passenger-side seat. Toren reached for it, but something stopped his fingers before they closed on the thick envelope. It would be from The Center. It would speak in cryptic language about why he'd failed.

All Toren knew was that he had to go back and repeat the training. Do it again. Fix whatever he'd done wrong the first time. Keep it from slipping away. Keep the walls from crumbling. Keep Hyde from rising again. More than keep him from rising, he had to kill Hyde. His hatred for his dark self filled his mind. He'd won Colton's and Callie's hearts back, still believed there was hope for Sloane and him, but here was Hyde, ready to steal any chance away. He had to go back to The Center. He didn't know what else to do.

Toren finally took the package between thumb and forefinger and lifted it to his lap. He stared down at it as if he had X-ray vision and could see the contents without having to rip into the coal-black paper. As he opened the envelope and pulled out the enclosed letter, he begged God for it to contain good news.

Dear Toren,

Regretfully, I didn't have a choice but to sedate you and leave you where you are at this moment. I don't believe you would have left of your own accord. Quite simply, where you are on this journey is the place you are supposed to be, so please accept this truth. This next sentence will be hard to read; consequently, I do not write these words lightly, nor do I take lightly the impact they will have on your mind and soul.

The reality we must face, and now you must face, is that sometimes Hyde wins. Sometimes, despite all our grasps for triumph, we must accept defeat. Understandably, we don't speak of this at The Center during the training phase. Having that lingering doubt floating in the air and in the mind would not enhance the chances of the training succeeding.

Does it help to know the trainee reverts back to the way they were two times out of every ten? I would not think so, and I only say it so you might find some sliver of comfort in the fact that you are not alone.

I would imagine the idea that Hyde wins — thus the Hyde inside you, Toren — is anathema to you. I imagine you loathe him more than ever before, but take heart. You are not fully Hyde, just as our successful students are not fully the good doctor. There is good in you as well. Great good. You are made in the likeness and image of God. How can that part of you not be good? And that good will remain.

Our wish for you from all of us at The Center is that you find another path that we were unable to provide for you, one that leads you to the transformation you are so desperately seeking. I say desperately, because that passion should show you that you still possess the deep desire to change, to become the man you know you can be.

To your eternal change,
Clavin Sorken

Toren let the note fall from his fingers as all emotion seeped away, replaced by a numbness that felt permanent. There was no fix. No redoing everything that had been done at The Center. His hope of a life with Sloane was gone. Same with playing in the NFL again. Both were over.

A rap on the window of his rental car ripped him from the thought, and he lurched forward in his seat.

CHAPTER 29

"Hello, Toren. It's good to see you again."

He rolled down the window for the woman in her late fifties wearing a yellow blouse and tan slacks. The smile on her face was both warm and sympathetic, as if she knew secrets about him that even he hadn't realized. Toren didn't ask her name. He knew exactly who she was.

How badly do you want the change?
With everything in me.

"Dr. Ilsa Weber." The counselor who had helped him find The Center in the weeks following the crisis. The reason he'd recognized her voice on the radio.

Her smile grew, and the laugh lines made her beautiful in the way only age can do for a woman. Something about her reminded him of the image he had of his mom, from those cloudy days before his father left and his mom sank into a depression she never climbed out of.

Toren started to get out of the car, but Ilsa, or whatever her real name was, waved him off and motioned toward the passenger-side door.

"May I?"

"If you didn't, I would get out and follow you till I convinced you to do exactly that." Toren chuckled as leaned over and opened the door.

Ilsa got in and said, "I don't doubt you would have."

She settled into the seat and clasped her hands on her lap. "Where would you like to start?"

"Who are you, really? And what do I do now? Why didn't it work for me? Can you help me get back there, go through the training again? And why did you make yourself impossible to find?"

She gave a quick wink and said again, "Where would you like to start?"

She laughed, not at him, but with him, even though he didn't join the laughter. Ilsa took his right hand and laid her hands over and under his own. Her touch was warm, and for a moment he was that little boy who had Christmases with his grandparents and was loved by them without reservation.

"I suppose I want to start with your name. The real one."

"Yes, of course. A good place to start certainly."

She patted his hand three times, then pulled away and held out her hand in a strikingly formal way. As he took her hand, she shook his, chin raised, eyelids half closed, and announced as if at a formal dinner, "I, Collette Engleton, am honored to be with you again, Toren Daniels."

With that she dropped her hand and laughed at her own jocular introduction. He couldn't help but return her smile as well as try to imitate her ceremonial delivery.

"It is with great pleasure I receive your name and the beginning of our association, although we both have already acknowledged this is not the beginning for you and merely a continuation of a relationship already begun, but I am at the disadvantage of not recalling with as much detail as you retain."

Toren finished with a mock bow of his head and short wave of his hand. When he looked up, a thin smile played at the corners of Collette's mouth, but her eyes were as intense as if she were in the heart of a battle she wasn't sure she could win.

"Yes. That right there. Hang on to that. That is your first lesson."

"What?"

"You were playing just now. You joined my play and became something you have not been for a long, long time."

"What was I?"

If possible, her eyes grew more focused, like gray steel forged in fire. "Don't think for the answer, feel it. Here." She rapped on her chest twice, her eyes never leaving his.

"I don't . . . I can't —"

"Stop thinking and tell me!" Her voice didn't rise more than a few decibels, but it felt like thunder.

"I was a boy." For a moment he let go of his mind, only a moment, but it was enough. "And like all children before their joy is stolen by life, I loved to play."

"Yes!" The intensity melted from her gaze, replaced by a delight that mesmerized him. "Yes, yes, yes, dear Toren, that's exactly what you were. And exactly what you must become for longer and longer moments in time. We must come to our Father like a child. Well done, yes, well done."

He stared at her, at once drawn to her like a magnet yet frightened at how deeply she saw into him. What secrets did she know about him? How much had he revealed over the months she was part of his life?

"Who are you?"

"I am one of many who want to bring

truth to people like yourself."

"Like myself?"

"Yes. Those who have been deceived."

"By The Center? Were you a plant there? Trying to help me? I wasn't deceived by them. What Sorken offered me worked. I just need it to work better. Become more complete. And now I have to do it on my own."

"And we are here to help you."

"Who is *we*?"

Collette opened her door.

"Wait!"

"Yes, Toren?" Her eyes had gone dark, not cruel, but rigid.

"I have so many more questions."

Collette patted her chest as she had before. "In here. Listen."

"I still don't —"

"Trust, Toren. Answers are coming. I promise."

With that, Collette stepped into the parking lot and strode off, leaving Toren full of hope and even more saturated in despair.

CHAPTER 30

Inside the terminal, Toren called Eden and filled her in on everything that had happened in Arizona. She didn't comment much other than to ask how he felt.

"I thought once I found out where I'd been, I'd get relief, understanding. It would be over."

"It's not?"

"You know it's not over." Toren scowled. "Where do I start?"

"You go back to where it began."

"What's that mean?"

"I think you need to go back to the day you took the belt out of your dad's hand."

Toren rubbed his eyes and squinted into the high-desert sun outside the large airport window.

It happened on the fourteenth of June. Six minutes past six in the evening. A date branded on Toren's mind like few other memories. He'd been working out down at

269

the gym and pushed into the family room at the exact moment his dad's palm met his mom's cheek with the speed and strength of a whip. She stumbled back and crumpled into a lamp next to their couch, then dropped to her knees.

Toren's dad stared at her for a moment before turning his eyes to Toren. Then he snatched the remote out of his recliner and plopped down in his chair, pointed the remote at the TV, changed the channel, and snatched his beer off the table next to his chair.

"Sorry you had to see that, son. She was out of line." His dad fixed his gaze on the boxing match on-screen as if he were alone in the room.

Toren lifted his workout bag to his full arm's length over his head, then released it. It thumped down on the carpet six inches from his dad's feet. His dad's head whipped around and he glared at Toren.

"What is your problem?"

Toren went to his mom, who waved him off. But he knelt next to her and helped her to her feet.

"This has to stop, Mom," Toren whispered as he led her out of the family room into the kitchen.

"I know. I know."

"Stay here a second." Toren held his palm up. "Don't move, okay?"

She nodded as her hand went to her cheek. Toren returned with a plastic bag of ice and lifted it gently to her face. She took it from him and whispered, "Thank you."

"When, Mom? When is it going to stop?"

"Soon."

"You've told me that too many times. When, Mom?"

"I don't know."

Toren sat at the kitchen table next to his mom, helpless. But that wasn't true. He wasn't helpless. Not anymore.

"I'll be right back." Toren shifted in his chair and lowered his voice. "There's something I have to do, Mom."

His mom grabbed his hands, held tight. "No. Please, no."

"I love you, Mom."

Toren pulled his hands out of hers, marched back into the family room, and stood glaring down at his dad till the man felt the stare and glanced up at him.

"Turn off the TV, Dad. I need to talk to you."

"Oh yeah?" His dad scowled at Toren, then turned back to his show.

"Yeah."

"Maybe when my show is done."

271

"No. Now."

"This better be good, 'cause I'm right in the middle of this match." His dad took a long slurp from his beer.

"It's good, really good, what I want to talk to you about." Toren eased closer to his father. "I think you'll like it. A lot."

"Yeah?"

"Yes." Toren moved to stand between his dad and the TV. "You'll definitely like it. You told me you would."

"You're really starting to tick me off, kid." His dad slammed his beer down on the table next to him, then lurched forward in his Barcalounger and gritted his teeth.

"Five and a half years ago you said you'd love to have me take a poke at you. See what I had inside. See if there was anything more than squishy mush. Do you remember that, Dad? Huh? Do ya?"

"Don't be an idiot, kid."

"I'm about to give you your wish. It's time to take the belt out of your hand."

"Oh really?" His dad got up from his chair and tossed the remote down, his eyes black. "Right here? Right now?"

Toren didn't speak. Simply gave a slow nod. His dad took a step forward, stuck out his chin, and tapped it.

"Go for it. Let's see what's inside you,

you little snot-nosed punk."

Toren reared back and swung at his dad with all his strength, but his dad was too quick. He blocked Toren's arm and, faster than Toren thought possible, hammered his fist into Toren's gut. He buckled over as pain shot through him. An instant later, his dad shoved him to the ground, then stood over him, grinning.

"Nice try, punk."

Toren struggled to his knees, his eyes fixed on his dad's legs. Another few seconds to catch his breath, then he surged up and forward, wrapped his arms around his dad's thighs like he was making an open-field tackle, and slammed his dad into the fireplace. His dad grunted, but a half second later brought both fists down on Toren's back like a jackhammer.

The sound of his back cracking barely registered in Toren's mind as he crumpled to the ground a second time. He was exhausted. The workout he'd just finished at the gym was maximum reps, fighting with the steel to the point of failure. The strength he'd labored to build for football and for this moment wasn't there.

His dad's foot slammed into his ribs. "How's that feel?"

Another kick. Ribs felt cracked.

"Thanks for the workout, kid." His dad put his foot on Toren's head. "I think maybe I'll get in a few more reps with your mom. Maybe Brady too when he gets home."

Something inside Toren snapped and a river of adrenaline shot through him, but it was far more than adrenaline. This was raw energy like he'd never known. Wild. Full of power. Rage burned every thought from his mind except the man he'd called Dad towering over him, gloating, threatening to hurt his mom and his brother again.

The rage lifted him, making him stronger than he'd ever been in the weight room. Like a wild stallion being ridden for the first time. Toren's heart hammered with exhilaration. He pushed to his knees a second time, then stood and stared into his father's eyes with the intensity of an inferno. It felt good. Toren embraced it with his entire soul.

"Before you go after Mom and Brady, I'd like one more shot." The words sputtered out of him, boiling rage.

Toren was a bull at the gate, straining to get out. His dad tried to grin, but something in Toren's eyes must have shaken him, because his dad hesitated, and Toren spotted a look of trepidation he'd never seen before.

His dad swung for Toren's gut again, but

Toren had anticipated the move, blocked the punch, and countered with his own, a direct shot to his dad's ribs. Air whooshed out of his dad's lungs, but Toren didn't hesitate. He pounded the other side of his dad's rib cage, then back to the exact spot of his first blow. Then another. And another, each shot accompanied by the dull sound of fist on flesh, and Toren had no doubt he'd cracked his dad's ribs in multiple places. The rage inside him swelled, more powerful than he'd imagined it could be, and he screamed with a guttural cry.

"You like that!" Toren shoved his dad to the floor and launched his foot into the man's stomach. "How am I doing now, Dad? What do you think I have inside? Is it more than squishy mush?"

Little bubbles of blood appeared around his dad's mouth. His eyes were closed, and deep groans emanated from him.

"Is this what you were going to give Mom? Give to Brady? I'll bet it is. So let me help you out, let me show you what it feels like before you give it to them."

Another strike, his foot landing in his dad's ribs.

"Toren!"

The cry settled on Toren as if it had come from a great distance. An instant later he realized someone had been calling his name.

He spun and found his mom standing at the edge of the family room, tears streaking her cheeks, horror in her eyes. "Stop! Please. You're going to kill him."

The waves of anger pounding at the shore of his mind started to recede into the ocean of rage, and he sucked in deep draughts of air. He glanced from his dad to his mom, back to his dad. Then Toren knelt next to his dad and whispered in his ear.

"If you ever lay a finger on my mom or my brother ever again, I *will* kill you. I promise."

His dad moaned as he tried to lift his head, but it thumped back onto the beige carpet.

"You hear me, Dad?"

His dad moaned again.

"I need to know you understand me, Dad."

"Understand."

Toren stood, moved slowly to his mom, and said, "I'm sorry, Mom. I'm sorry you had to see that. But I'm not sorry about what I did to him."

Toren pulled himself out of the memory and glanced around the terminal, his breathing rapid.

"What I'd like to know, Toren," Eden said,

her voice soft, "is what happened after that."

"It worked." Toren adjusted his sunglasses. "He never hit my mom or went after my brother again."

"No, I mean what happened to you."

"Crazy power."

"So your friend was right."

"Friend?"

"Letto."

Toren gave a weak sigh. "All that rage. It fueled me on the field. Drove me. And there's a part of me that liked it. Fed on it. After that day it was there whenever I needed it. Junior high, high school, college, the NFL. I went after every running back, every quarterback, every receiver on the other team as if they were my dad. The darkness inside gave me purpose."

"I see," Eden said.

"The field was my outlet. The place to let the dark side crusade. But it got worse and worse. I had a hard time controlling it when I got to the pros, and you already know it got me kicked out of the league. And since I couldn't relieve the pressure on the field once I stopped playing, I brought it home."

Toren glanced out the terminal window. "So I went to The Center. And it worked, I got fixed, but that fix is wearing off. And now I'm here, flying away from the only solution I can think of. I got Hyde into a cage, but he's breaking the bars and finding a way out."

"What will you do now?"

"I'll find a way. If it's not at The Center, fine. I won't give up. Not an option. There has to be a way to destroy Hyde, and I won't stop till I figure it out and stand over the slain body of my dark side."

"I see," Eden said again. "To that end, might I make a suggestion?"

"Yes. Please."

"Clear your head. Get away from this. If only just for a day."

"Where?"

"Someplace that holds good memories. Someplace that takes you back to when the days were bright and you and Sloane had life all figured out."

"Pretty good idea." Toren nodded to himself. "I guess we're done then."

"How so?"

"You said you'd help me track down where I was. You did. Thank you."

"You're welcome."

"I'd like to stay in touch."

"I think that will happen."

"Take care, Eden."

"I believe in you, Toren."

"Thanks."

Toren ended the call, knowing exactly where he'd be going sometime in the next few days.

CHAPTER 31

Friday Harbor rose out of the sea at eleven forty-three the next morning, and everything inside Toren shouted that this was the right choice. Friday Harbor, in the San Juan Islands, where he and Sloane had spent a magical weekend eleven years back. Not only because the weather had been magnificent, the crabbing had been spectacular, and their exploration of the remote parts of the island had been deeply invigorating, but because it was the place Sloane had revealed a secret she'd kept from him for three days. She was pregnant. It had been a weekend of celebration in every sense of the word. Eden wanted him to go to a place where he'd had life all figured out? Toren could think of few other locations.

He drove his car to a few of the spots they'd investigated more than a decade back, and walked, thought about everything, didn't think about anything, and stared out over the water, praying, asking for answers. After lunch at the Rocky Bay Cafe, Toren poked around a bookstore, then a bakery where he bought an oversized chocolate éclair, convincing himself the sugar-filled concoction wouldn't count against his training.

He'd almost settled into the belief that he would survive the coming days when the sensation of being watched danced along the back of his spine stronger than it had at any time since he'd returned from The Center. He glanced in the direction he felt it coming from and instantly spotted the tall woman from the party standing in the shadows of a building thirty yards away. She stared directly at him as she stepped forward onto the sidewalk.

She nodded at him. Yes. This time he would get the answers he desperately needed. He strode toward her, four steps, seven, and still she stayed motionless, like a boulder in a river as people flowed around her.

Was that a smile on her face? He couldn't be sure from this distance, but it looked like it. She turned and walked away. After two steps, she glanced over her shoulder, and saw Toren trotting toward her. She smiled — he was sure of it now — and upped her stride to just shy of running. Toren broke into a full-out sprint.

She rounded the corner of a building, but he would be there in seconds. There was nowhere for her to hide. He skidded around the corner just in time to see half of her disappearing around the building at the end of the block, fifty yards away. Impressive. She was fast.

Toren plowed down the street as if he were back on the field and reached the corner in no more than six seconds, but when he came around the next corner, she was gone. Saying she had nowhere to hide was an exaggeration. She could have slipped into any of three shops within fifteen feet of the corner. Or if she truly was lightning fast, she could have ducked into one of the two shops on the other side of the street. But no one was that fast. He would have seen her.

Now what? Which shop? The first? Too close, the obvious choice, and the last shop would have been too big a risk. She had to think if he was quick he'd get around the corner and at least spot the shop door closing. So Toren chose door number two. He didn't win the prize.

After he yanked the door open and strode inside, he did a quick, barely controlled spin through the shop. Nothing. She wasn't there. He took one more look and spun 360 degrees on his heel before approaching the counter and answering the question seeping out of the eyes of the woman standing behind it.

"I'm looking for a lady, tall, slender. Did she just come in here?"

"No." The manager, or owner, drilled Toren with her eyes.

For the first time, he took in the merchandise in the shop. Definitely for ladies only.

"Sorry, I don't mean to disturb. It's just important I find her."

The woman didn't answer except to jab her finger at the front door and glare at him. Toren made for the exit. He turned just before pushing through the shop door back onto the street to apologize again. The woman's ramrod-straight arm and finger hadn't moved a centimeter, and Toren thought it best not to offer a second lame apology.

He got the same result in shops number one and three, a small book shop and a marine supply.

"No, no one came in . . ." And the third shop: "There hasn't been anyone in the store most of the day."

He didn't think they were lying, exactly, but the woman couldn't have vanished into the floor or walls. She had to have come into one of the three shops. He turned to head back to his car when on impulse he decided to venture into the two shops across the street. He had no illusions the woman had stepped into one of them, but he was here and maybe she did have the speed and reflexes of Wonder Woman.

The first shop, a consignment clothing store, gave him the same response. Toren pushed through the door back onto the sidewalk and glanced up at the sign of the only remaining shop. *Mementos and Memories — A Safe Place to Find Your Authentic Self.*

"This ought to be good," he muttered to himself.

New Age pablum in the heart of the San Juan Islands. The shop was new since he'd last been to Friday Harbor five years ago. He pushed through the door and was greeted by a loud jangle of bells, but the woman behind the counter at the back of the store didn't look up.

Large sea-green glass floats lined one wall. Smaller ones sat on the thick gray wood windowsill. The sun streaming through the window lit them up and drew attention to their imperfections, which only made them more appealing.

Two shelves filled with old hardback books and brand-new paperbacks sat to his left. Down the middle of the store ran two rough-hewn tables full of carved eagles, sea otters, and whales. Some were wood but most looked to be sandstone.

He liked the place immediately, although he couldn't put into words as to why. The atmosphere of the place almost made him forget why he'd come in. Toren strode toward the employee in the back. If the tall woman had come in here, she'd be long gone by now, but still, there was no harm in asking.

He made his way to the woman, and when she still didn't look up after Toren reached her, he said, "Excuse me, may I ask you something?"

As the last word left his mouth, she raised her gaze to him, eyes alight, a gentle smile on her face.

"Thank you for coming in, Toren. We've been expecting you."

"So she did come in here." A wave of heat shot through him. "And you're part of all this."

"All what?"

"This crazy journey I'm on."

The woman simply cocked her head and smiled. Toren guessed she was in her late thirties. Straight, long dark hair and bronze skin coloring indicated she was Native American.

"What do I do now?"

"Please, take all the time to browse that you would like." The light in her eyes grew brighter as she motioned around the shop. "I truly hope you enjoy your visit to the store today, and of course I hope you take a step further to uncovering the authentic you."

It was clear she wasn't going to give any clue about what to do next. Toren figured he should be used to that by now.

"But she did come in here, didn't she? Tall, five nine, maybe five ten, slender, wearing jeans, dark-green coat. Ash-blonde hair with highlights."

The woman glided out from behind the counter as if she were on skates and gave him that kind smile again, as if he were a child she was quite fond of.

"Yes, Toren, a woman matching that description did come in here, oh, maybe five minutes ago."

"I need to talk to her."

He glanced around the store even though he knew it was a worthless exercise, and the woman answered his question before he could ask it.

"She's no longer here. But you knew that already, yes?"

He nodded. "Will you tell me where she went?"

"Why do you want to know?"

"She's been stalking me."

"Really?" The woman winked. "Has she threatened you? Verbally or physically?"

"No, but —"

"So what has she done that makes you say you're being stalked?"

"She's been following me around. She said some very weird things to me at a party, and now I see her again, miles from where I live, in a little town out in the middle of nowhere. And there she is, staring right at me."

The words sounded stupid even before they came out of his mouth.

"So a man over six feet tall, who certainly appears to be in good condition and no older than his early thirties, spots a woman he's met staring right at him in a town he considers to be out in the middle of nowhere."

"Something like that," he muttered. "Sounds ridiculous."

She leaned toward him, unsuccessfully trying to keep a smile from reaching the corners of her mouth. "I'm sorry. I missed that. What did you say?"

"I said it sounds ridiculous."

Her eyes continued to smile, but the rest of her face grew serious. "Why are you so desperate to find out who this lady is, and what is it that tells you in here" — she patted her chest as Collette Engleton had done — "that she is part of what you're searching for?"

Toren almost rolled his eyes but held back. "Like I just told you, I thought she could give me answers about what I've been going through. And I know she can shed light on what I need to do next. All the clues I've been following led me to Friday Harbor, and then our mutual friend led me here. So I need to talk to her to find out what the next step is."

The woman nodded. "Might I make a suggestion?"

"Yes, of course."

She patted her chest again. "Try wrapping your heart around it instead of your mind."

Toren gave her his full attention. Hadn't Clavin Sorken and Eden said almost exactly the same thing? Toren thought about this. Why would Eden have used those words?

"What do you mean by that?"

The woman nodded as if responding to a voice he couldn't hear, then moved to a

288

small table and picked up three pieces of dark wood interlaced with lighter streaks. The wood made him think of the golden tigereye stones he had collected over the years.

"Those are stunning."

"I agree." The woman picked them up and laid them in her palm.

The pieces were two-and-a-half to three inches high. All were curved and twisted, each in a slightly different way. They were polished to such a high gloss they seemed to throw off light.

"Can I show you something?" The woman held them closer to his face.

"Sure."

The woman turned her back. In less than two seconds she spun around and held out her hand. The pieces were no longer separated. They had somehow become a solid piece of wood.

Toren tilted his head from one side to the other as he studied the wood.

"Do you like it?"

"It? Or them?"

"It depends on your perspective, doesn't it? In the end it is all about perspective. Everything is."

The woman's quizzical look was in perfect harmony with the playful sound of her voice. "When they are apart, they are three, but as you have just seen, when they are together, they are one."

"Yes, I do see that. They are, or it is, beautiful."

"Thank you. I just finished them this morning." She gazed at them as if they were her children.

"You made them?" He cocked his head. "You have quite a talent."

She ran her finger over the surface of the carvings. "Would you like to hold them?"

The woman held the three objects out to Toren, and he took them as if they were finely spun glass. They fit together so perfectly he had to squint to see the seams where they came together. He held them up close and peered at the wood. There. He could just barely tell where the pieces joined each other. He held the object out at arm's length. From that distance it was impossible to see that the objects weren't one solid piece. Toren ran his finger along the seam but couldn't feel it.

"Amazing." He smiled at the woman. "What are they supposed to be?"

"They are, of course, whatever you want them to be."

He frowned at her and she laughed. "I'm not trying to be elusive with my answer. It

290

is an answer from the heart. I think everyone will see something different. Just like with a piece of music or a poem or a story or a painting. Perspective again, yes? Each person will interpret the melody and the rhythm and the words through their own experiences, their own views of life, sorrows, triumphs. Through their own filters of the soul if you will. And what reaches their hearts will be unique, because each soul has been crafted so very differently from every other soul."

He studied the pieces as he tried to make sense of the woman's rambling explanation. "Okay."

"So what do you see?" She continued before he could answer. "You don't have to answer now. It will likely take you a good amount of time to discover your response."

"I see the Trinity. Father, Son, Spirit. Three pieces that are separate and distinct, yet they are also one."

She nodded as if this were the only acceptable answer. "Then that's what they are."

"My answer doesn't surprise you."

She didn't respond.

"I would love to buy these." Toren glanced at the table she had lifted the pieces from. "Do you have others? I don't see any —"

"No. These three pieces are unique. But they are not for sale."

Toren's heart sank, and he realized how drawn he'd become to the woman's creation. "Not for any price?"

"No, they cannot be sold." She smiled, and her eyes seemed to be laughing at him. "They can only be given as a gift to the one they were made for."

"I see."

"No, you don't, Toren. Your eyes are so clouded. For a time you thought you saw clearly, but now you know you did not see with as much clarity as you thought you did."

He started to ask what she meant, but once again she answered his unvoiced question. "I will explain what I mean someday."

"In other words, you think I'm coming back here at some point."

"Of course you are!" She laughed. "We both know that."

"Who are you?"

"My name is Alena, and it is so good to meet you."

He smiled at her, and an inexplicable peace settled on him.

"Good to meet you as well," he said. "Do you own the store?"

"I do."

"Since you've actually answered two of my questions in a row, do you want to tell me who the wood pieces were made for?"

Alena looked at him as if confused, her head tilted, a frown on her face.

"What I mean is, who are you going to give the pieces to?" He held them up.

"I just did." She smiled and pointed to the pieces in his hand.

He stared at her. "You can't be serious."

"Deadly."

He saw by the look in her eyes that she was.

"Why me?"

"Do I need to keep repeating myself that we were expecting you?"

"We?"

"Yes."

"Who is we?"

"I think you're bright enough to know I'm not going to answer that question. In fact, I've already gone over that, haven't I?"

Yes, she had. Maybe not that bluntly, but he'd gotten the message. He turned the gift over in his hands. It was one of the most beautiful things he'd ever seen. "I don't know what to say. Thank you."

"Thank you is more than enough."

"Do you mind if I take it apart?"

"Of course not. It is yours." Her smile

returned as if she had given a child his most wished-for Christmas present, and it delighted her.

He squinted, found the seams, and slid the first piece apart. Then the second. As he stared at the pieces, two on one palm, one on the other, he couldn't decide whether he liked them better apart or together. If he was forced to choose, it would probably be together.

"As beautiful as they are individually, I think I want them to be together." He smiled at the woman.

"I long to see that."

Strange words, and strange tone of voice. Alena said it exactly as if it had been a cherished desire of hers for many years. Toren gingerly aligned two of the pieces and tried to ease them together, but they wouldn't fit. He squinted at them. This was the way they should go together. Toren set down the piece that looked slightly bigger and picked up the third piece. There. He saw where the piece would go. But when he tried to slide the third piece into the second, it was as resistant as the first piece.

He glanced at her. "Not as easy as it looks."

"No." Alena tilted her head down and looked at him from under her eyebrows.

"Most times it isn't."

"You wouldn't want to give me a clue, would you?"

"Do you really want me to?"

"Probably not." He had tried every combination possible and wasn't any closer to seeing how the pieces fit together. "You didn't tell me you were giving me a puzzle."

"It is much more than a puzzle. But I suspect you knew that already."

"Do I at least get some instructions on how it's done? You know, in case I never figure it out on my own?"

"It's impossible to figure it out on your own."

"Then will you help me?"

"I hope so."

"You hope so?"

"Yes."

"Then do you mind if I leave the pieces here?"

"Why would you do that?"

"Because it gives me a reason to come back and get your help at the point you're willing to give it."

The woman nodded. "A good answer, so yes, I will hold on to them for you till you're ready."

"You wouldn't want to start now, would you?"

"It was so wonderful to meet you, Toren." She smiled at him. "There is such light in you. Step into it, yes? Align with it, yes? Become the light, yes? Release it in all its glory and power, won't you?"

Something in her words, or maybe just the way she said them, surfaced a memory from the time he'd been at The Center. He was with a group of people outside — it was warm, he was in a T-shirt — and Sorken was standing in front of them, teaching them something about . . . and then the memory vanished.

Before he could stop himself, he blurted out, "If you were expecting me, then do you know about the time I was gone?"

Her only response was to stare into his eyes until the intensity in her gaze forced him to look away. What was it about her? He didn't really need to ask himself the question. She seemed to see to the back of his mind and into the closets of his soul, where he'd always kept the hidden things.

He looked back up at her. "You know about The Center, don't you? And my time there? You're connected somehow." Toren leaned forward. "Tell me. Please. Are you part of it?"

"Answer me this first, Toren. What do you want? More than getting back to the NFL,

296

more than for your friendships to be truly healthy, even more than for your children to love you — and yes, even more than having your wife return to you — what do you want?"

Alena didn't wait for an answer. She smiled, turned, and ambled away from him toward a door tucked into the back corner of the store. Toren stood stunned, but only for a moment.

"Wait!" he called after her as he made for the back of the store. He was determined not to lose her until he got a few more answers, but a moment later a thick, older man emerged from the door and blocked his path. Toren slid to the left to go around the man, but he glided in front of Toren.

"Hello, might I assist you with something?"

Toren pointed at the door. "Yeah, I was just talking to —"

"To Alena?" The man arched an eyebrow.

"Yes, and we didn't finish the conversation."

The man rubbed his chin. "If she left, it seems at least for one of you, the conversation has concluded."

"She asked me a question. I want to give her the answer."

"It's curious that you want to give her an

answer to the question when you don't know the answer. How will you accomplish that?" He frowned and cocked his head. "I'm simply interested in your method." The man smiled. It wasn't warm.

Toren started to ask how the man knew he had no clue how to answer Alena's question, but he didn't have time for that.

"Listen, I need to ask her a few more things. I don't think she'll mind."

"I'm sure she would enjoy seeing you again sometime. But she's done working for the day."

"But she just left, and like I said, I have to ask her a few more questions."

"You have to?"

"Yes. It will only take a moment."

"I'm sorry."

"Then can I get her cell number or e-mail address?"

"Have patience. Stay in the moment, Toren. Next time will come." The man's eyes grew intense, and Toren knew no matter how insistent he was, he wouldn't see Alena again that day.

One ferry ride and two hours of driving later, he pushed through the front door of his rental home and pulled up Alena's store's website on his computer. There was little to look at. A splash page with a panoramic shot of the inside of the store, the address, and a phone number. A Google search revealed nothing more than when the store was incorporated — four years ago — and the grand opening, which was three years ago. But it was a start.

Two days later — days when Toren continued to strive to eradicate Hyde from his life through hours of prayer, study, and worship — it became more than a start. He got a text from an unknown number, asking him to come to the San Juan Islands — Friday Harbor — the coming Saturday afternoon.

I believe it is time for you to visit again. Saturday 2pm. Your life is about to change. Possibly for good. But ultimately, that will be up to you. Alena.

CHAPTER 32

When Toren stepped inside the store on Saturday, Alena wasn't there. Only the man who'd rebuffed him.

"I'm here to see Alena."

"Yes." The man smiled, warmer this time, then motioned toward the door at the back of the store. The one Alena had escaped through the day he'd met her.

"I get to find out what's behind the door?"

"Do you think you're ready?"

Toren wanted to shout, "Yes, I'm ready!" but he wasn't, so he spoke the truth. "No, I don't think I'm even within sight of ready. I feel like I'm stepping off the end of a dock blindfolded, with no idea how far down the water is."

"It is wonderful to hear that, Toren." The man smiled again. "You're closer to being ready than you know. I believe the scales will fall."

"What scales?"

The man tapped his forehead just above his eyes, then pulled a key from his pocket. "You'll need this. Please don't lose it. It's my only copy."

"I'll try really hard not to. But I can't make promises." Toren smiled, but the man didn't return it.

He motioned again in the direction of the door, and Toren walked toward it. Before twisting the knob and stepping through, he turned and offered his thanks.

Toren wasn't sure what he expected to find — probably an office, or a storage room for all the inventory not ready to be on display in the shop, or a room with a circle of chairs and dark wood and books for deep discussions revolving around spiritual mysteries, but instead he found himself at the top of a steep staircase that led straight down to a dimly lit concrete landing three feet by three feet at most. A weathered steel door stood guard at the bottom, and as he stared at it, the back of his neck pricked.

The two lights on either side of the staircase flickered, and images from cheesy suspense movies flashed through his mind. But his feelings of fear weren't cheesy. They were all too real. His hand started to ache, and he realized he was still clutching the doorknob. He turned back to find the man staring at him, hands clasped behind his back.

"It's your choice, of course. To continue on."

Toren nodded, let go of the knob, and started down the stairs. By the time he reached the midway point, sweat had broken out on his forehead, and he wiped it away with an equally sweaty palm. As he stepped onto the concrete landing area, he heard the door at the top of the stairs slam shut.

"Thanks, old pal," he muttered. "Now it feels like I've been buried alive."

He slid the key into the lock in the door, turned it, and the metal door opened without resistance and without sound.

"Wow."

After uttering that one word, he stood in stunned silence staring down a long hallway made entirely of sweet-smelling cedar. Floor, ceiling, walls. Recessed lighting, warm and soft, created an ambience of simple luxury. He took a hesitant step forward, then another, his shoes on the wood far quieter than he expected.

There were no doors in sight, so going back or straight forward were his only options. After sixty or seventy yards he expected to see a sign or some indicator that he was going the right direction. Nothing.

This didn't bother him until he'd gone what felt like the length of a football field. When he'd covered another two football fields, he pulled out his phone. Toren scrolled through his apps and opened the one that tracked distance traveled.

At a quarter of a mile, the hallway took a forty-five-degree turn to the right, and one hundred yards later another slight turn to the right. The wood here darkened, apparently because a different stain had been applied. He stopped and ran his fingers over the wood. The finish was gritty, as if the craftsmen hadn't sanded a final time before putting the wood up. It was easy to understand why. Already, the board footage of lumber used on the hallway had to be in the thousands, and it kept going as far as he could see.

He kept walking. In a follow-up text, Alena had suggested he block out the entire afternoon for their time together, but he thought it would be for time to talk, not to hike. Another quarter mile passed.

Now, for the first time since Toren started down the hall, he spotted something in the wood. Writing. Every few feet he spied a name etched into the wood with a wood-burning tool. He walked on. Hundreds of names now. Toren skimmed them, searching for someone he knew. He wasn't sure why. The odds of finding a familiar name were infinitesimal, but it would have given him assurance he was doing the right thing, as if a friend had gone before him. No one.

He ran his fingers along the paneling, feeling the texture of the names under his fingertips as they became fewer and farther between, and then —

Toren stopped and staggered back a step. There, illuminated by the soft overhead light, in elegant and precise lettering, was a name he knew: Eden Lee.

What? Eden? He stared at her name. A woman of secrets. He'd known that from the moment they'd met. When he saw her again he'd find a way to get her to reveal a few of them.

A half mile later, he finally reached the end of the corridor, and he stared with admiration at what loomed in front of him. Another staircase. This one started out straight, then curved after seven or eight steps. The steps looked like acacia wood, stained dark with a gleam that made them look like they were polished yesterday. The undulating swirls of dark and light wood were like rivers on some of the stairs, like a map of another world found in the front of a fantasy novel. The craftsmanship and beauty were stunning. Every other stair was inlaid with a lighter wood that formed what looked like words from another language.

He hesitated, then reminded himself they were stairs, meant to be stepped on, and he started up. It didn't surprise him to find no creak in the stairs as he placed his foot on the first one, then eased his weight onto the second, then the third. After the eleventh stair, the words — if that was what they were — stopped and his pace quickened and the spiral of stairs tightened.

It was a strange sensation, as if the walls of the staircase were closing in on him. In a sense they were, simply because of their construction, and yet the sensation was caused by more than the space growing smaller. It was as if the air around him had grown thinner and was pressing in on his mind and body as well. Toren forced his breathing to stay steady.

As he reached the thirtieth stair, he spotted a landing above him. Ten or so more steps to go. Toren hesitated as an unfamiliar voice inside his mind cautioned him against going farther. Not a chance. He clipped up the rest of the stairs and found himself on a small landing, maybe six by six, with a single door to his left. Narrow. A thin stream of light came from a small spotlight embedded in the wood above the door. He didn't recognize the timber. The wood was so white it seemed to throw off its own radiance.

He knocked even though he'd been invited. An instant later, Alena's muted voice invited him to come in. He took the knob and turned it, but where he'd expected the knob to turn smoothly, it turned with difficulty, as if taffy were gumming up the hardware. He pushed the door open as if he were about to walk into the treasure room of an ancient castle and stepped through the doorframe.

Alena stood in the center of the room. She wasn't alone.

Right beside her stood Eden.

CHAPTER 33

Toren stared at Eden, dumbfounded. She smiled and nodded once.

"Hello, Toren."

"What? What are you . . ." He trailed off as his mind vanished.

She eased over to him and finished his question. ". . . doing here?"

"Yeah."

"I'm so glad you made it."

"I don't get it. I don't understand. Why didn't you tell me you're part of this?"

"It is the glory of God to conceal a matter; to search out a matter is the glory of kings."

"But I'm not a king."

Eden only raised her eyebrows.

"When you told me to . . . How'd you know I'd pick Friday Harbor?"

"Odds were good."

"What if I hadn't?"

"I don't know."

"But if I hadn't come here, everything would have been delayed and —"

"I'm not in a hurry, Toren."

"I am."

"Yes, I know, which is why I'm glad you chose Friday Harbor." Her eyes laughed at him.

"What are the odds of Friday Harbor being the place this . . . whatever this thing is, is built, and where Sloane and I . . ."

"Yes, what are the odds?" Eden gave a thin smile.

"How did you know?"

"I know far less than you give me credit for. I listen to the voice of the Spirit, and sometimes I get it right. That is all."

A streak of light seemed to pass through him. In the next moment he believed it was the most natural thing in the world to have Eden standing before him.

"But we could have saved so much time if you'd just —"

"If I'd just what? Led you here from the moment we first met? Robbed you of the chance to rekindle your relationship with Colton and Callie? Told you about The Center so you understood in your head but not your heart?"

"Who are you really?"

"I am your friend. One who has longed

for you to come to this place." She motioned around the room. "You've made my day being here."

"I'm not sure I had a choice. My friend Alena here can be fairly persuasive."

"So she decided for you?"

He studied Eden. Was she playing with him?

"No, I chose."

"Good, good, good. I wouldn't want you to be here unless you wanted to. But now that you are here, I believe astounding revelations can be yours."

"I see."

"No, Toren." The corner of Eden's mouth turned up. "I'm afraid you see very little. But there is hope that you will. For you have come and you are now here. You are most welcome in this place. And with all that I am, I hope you remain till the end."

"I'll leave you two now." Alena came close to Toren and took him by both arms. "I wish you well. You are light, Toren, for God is light and you are in him. We will see each other again soon."

Eden motioned around the room again. "What do you think?"

Alena exited, and Toren eased into the room with cautious steps. The space was octagonal, maybe forty feet in diameter.

Each of the eight walls was painted a different color: one white, one a cobalt blue, one a forest green, one deep gold, one black, one crimson, one nut brown, and one purple. Toren's mind said the colors should clash, but his heart instantly embraced the contrasts.

Each wall — except one — boasted a four-by-four window that filled the room with natural light from the sun, still hours away from its descent into the ocean surrounding the island. The effect on the room was one of vast openness. The windows were framed with thin strips of wood, intertwined and stained with a high-gloss finish.

The one wall without a window was directly to Toren's right. Instead of a window, a wooden door took up most of the space. It reached almost to the ceiling and was at least four feet across. What looked like eastern white knotty pine had been stained dark. Intricate patterns were carved into the door's surface, patterns that looked like a language to Toren's untrained eyes. Emotion surged through him, as if what was behind the door had the power to both inspire and destroy.

Above and below the windows were photos, artwork — everything from exotic paintings to sketches in pencil and charcoal.

Wood pieces bearing Scriptures hung from a few of the walls. Others showed small mirrors etched with quotes. The room stirred an image in Toren's mind of Alena's store, but it also evoked a far deeper feeling of the unknown and hidden ideas.

"Where am I?"

"Do you like it?" Eden asked.

"I must have walked for two miles."

"Just under two."

"Why would Alena build this place so far from her store? Why not make it more accessible?"

"There are many reasons, but only three that matter. First, she did not build this place. We discovered it — or I should say, those before us discovered it. Yes, in years past, we have made some enhancements, improvements we hope, but it was here long before us."

Eden strolled to the front of the octagon and ran her fingers down the wall painted cobalt blue. She continued to speak, her gaze fixed out through the window on the sea.

"Second, if we had been the ones to build, I imagine we would have chosen this very spot. The octagon is a place we prefer others do not discover. If you were to search for it by hiking the area, you would not find it. It is on the side of the island least traversed, with treacherous terrain. And the octagon is walled in on three sides by a thick forest and high cliffs. The tower we stand in has been camouflaged so that even from fifty yards away, it would be challenging to see."

"Haven't you been spotted by boats passing by?"

"Perhaps. But the octagon is built into the rocks. And considerable money was spent to make it blend in with the trees to our right and left. Even if someone were to spot us, we would be a curiosity at best, and with the difficulty in getting to us, we feel quite safe. Most people who walk this earth give up seeking long before they reach the end of a mystery."

Toren peered through the window straight ahead and spotted two sailboats on the water. Beyond them, a white Washington State ferry was pulling away back toward Anacortes. He turned back and surveyed the room. Anticipation shot through him. He felt like he was twelve again, at his first real football practice, in his oversized pads and slightly too small helmet. The room itself seemed to vibrate with hope and light. Yet a tinge of danger seemed to lurk in the corners of the room, even though there were no shadows. He tried to shove the thought from his mind.

"This place astonishes and terrifies me at the same time."

"Yes." From behind Toren, Eden's voice floated toward him. "This is a very special place. It is a place of wonder where the mind is of little use. In fact, your mind will almost certainly be a stumbling block here if you're not careful. This is a place of heart, of spirit, of truth. A place where there is much to discover if you can let go of your intellect."

"If you didn't build it, who did?" Toren turned to face Eden.

"Those who did the work before us."

"The work?"

"You didn't think we invited you here only to play, did you?" She laughed, and the sound filled the room and his head.

"No."

After staring out through the window again, past the point of being rude, Toren fixed his gaze on the woman he knew but didn't know. "Thank you for inviting me here."

"Ah, yes, the thought that your life is controlled by another." Eden strolled toward him.

"What?"

"You invited yourself here, Toren. Long ago."

"I'm guessing you're going to explain that statement?"

"Of course I am, if you need me to."

Toren stared at the closed door that led to the staircase — a sensation of dread and expectation filling him.

"Are you quite well, Toren?"

He spun to find that tiny smile once again at the corner of Eden's mouth.

"You're going to explain more of what this room is, what the training is, what exactly we're going to do here, yes?"

"Of course."

"But you're probably not going to explain any of those things when I'd like you to. Or you might."

"Of course."

Her face seemed to radiate light. She was having fun, and yet underneath the exterior was a solemn foundation that he found impossible to ignore.

"Will you join me?" Eden motioned to the two chairs and table behind her.

"Of course." He winked, and she smiled at his weak attempt at humor.

They sat, and she poured him a clear dark-red liquid from a teapot. It steamed as it swirled its way into the cup.

"Tea?"

Eden gave a tiny nod. "This is a tea that is not well known outside of a small area in the Himalayas. There it is plentiful. Here it comes at a price that is steep, but it is needed for what we are about to accomplish."

"And what is that?"

"To continue on your journey, of course. To go deeper. To concentrate your energy on the central point of this path. It is my point as well. The point of everyone who has chosen to traverse this passageway."

"To learn to open our eyes."

"Go on." She handed him his cup of tea.

"To learn to see clearly. To gain perspective. To see the truth."

"Yes, Toren." She picked up her cup, brought it to her mouth, and blew.

"It will open you, if you believe it will."

"The tea or the journey?"

"Take a sip. Then we will start to explore the greatest lesson of life. The only lesson that ever truly matters."

"To learn to love."

"Yes. To love. So simple, isn't it?"

Toren took a tiny sip of his tea. It tasted hot and cold, sweet and bitter at the same time. A second later, an image of The Center shot into his head, then the scene of him losing it with Sloane, and the plate smashing into the glass cabinet, and the tiny scar on Sloane's beautiful neck.

"I don't think learning how to love is simple at all."

"Nor do I. It is a state most of us find impossible to attain."

"You just said —"

"No, I didn't. Knowing the path — which can at times be simple — and walking the path — which is often the most challenging adventure the soul will ever go on — are two extremely different disciplines."

Toren took a longer sip of the tea this time, and immediately a tingling sensation sprinted down his throat, then expanded into his chest. The expansion slowed as the feeling spread down his legs and into his arms. Peace, thick and warm, filled him. By the time it reached his feet and hands, the tingle moved like molasses. He mentally begged the tea to work its way to his extremities faster.

Minutes later — it felt like hours — the sensation crept up his neck into his face, ears, head, and finally his hair. Then every cell in his body seemed to explode like the finale of a July Fourth fireworks show, and new images flashed across his mind: Sloane and him rappelling down a sheer rock face, working together to hand out meals deep in the heart of Seattle, sipping tropical drinks on an island halfway across the world, and holding young children in Africa who melted into Sloane's arms.

In that moment Toren wanted nothing more than to drink that tea for the rest of his life. After staring into his cup at the liquid that seemed to swirl of its own volition, he lifted the cup for another sip. Eden stopped him.

"No, Toren, we need to start slow. One drink is enough for now. If you choose to come again a week from tomorrow, we will sip together once more."

He felt like a teenager who'd kissed a girl for the first time, then learned he'd have to wait another year for his next chance.

"What is in that tea?" He set the cup back on the saucer without taking his eyes off his host. "What just happened to me?"

"I don't know." She placed her own cup back on the table. "Please understand, I'm not evading your question. You see, the tea affects each person who drinks it differently based on what they believe it will do for them. For some it does nothing. For others — much more than I can imagine. So why don't you tell me what it did for you? What you felt, or sensed, or saw."

"My past. My future."

"And what does that stir in you?"

"Hope."

"What hope?"

"That the things I saw, that I imagined, can become reality. That the visions are what God has for me. For Sloane. For us."

"Excellent. It is wonderful to hear that."

"So how do I make those things happen? How do I bring them into existence? How do I fix things with Sloane? How do I take tomorrow and —"

"Tomorrow?" Eden laughed, light laughter that seemed to hang in the air like a subtle perfume. "You do not take tomorrow at all."

"Why? If what I saw is real, or has a possibility of becoming real, then I have to —"

"There is no tomorrow, Toren. It does not exist. The same with the days behind us. The past is gone. There is only now. As Jesus put it, tomorrow has enough worries. As Isaiah wrote, you must think no more on the things of old. Let us live in this moment instead of living in our memories, or living in the imaginary days that are coming, the places and dreams and yesterdays and tomorrows that can exist only in our minds."

"But what about making plans? Setting goals? Telling Sloane what I saw, what God is telling me?"

318

"It is an honor to be on this journey with you, Toren." Eden steepled her hands. "Before you go —"

"Before I go? I just got here."

She smiled, her dark eyes almost disappearing into her face. "Before you go, allow me to answer one of your questions. If you have any, that is."

One? He had thousands, but the one that demanded first rights was about the ornate door.

"I want to know what is behind that door." He pointed.

"Yes, most of the souls who come here do."

"I'm drawn to it. I want to know why."

"I would want to know the same." Eden looked at the door for a few seconds, then turned back and fixed her eyes on Toren. A mixture of intensity and delight filled her gaze.

"It is a very special room, a special place. A place to let go of what you know *about* your Father so you can *know* your Father. It is a room of prayer. A place of peace, a place to be silent, a place to scream, a place of solitude and thunder. A place of visions and hope and worship. A place to celebrate and rail at life, to weep, and a place to be bound to others with a love you cannot imagine —

the love of the Christ in all, unified. And it is a place to be utterly alone."

"Can I see? Can I go inside?"

"That's not a concept we use here often."

"What concept?"

"We don't use it at all."

"I'm not following."

"You want permission."

"Yes."

"There is never a need to ask permission in this room, because all things are permissible here, as Paul says in the Scriptures."

"Except for taking another sip of my tea."

"No." She clapped her hands like a little girl. "That is the glory of God's grace. You *can* have more, right now, if you'd like. However, though all things are permissible, not all things are profitable."

"And another drink of tea would not be profitable."

"No, it would not be. It is a wise choice to embrace the truth of the Scriptures."

Toren gazed into Eden's eyes for a long moment. A message of challenge and love and wonder and unseen worlds flowed past his mind and into his spirit. The hair all over his body tingled as if the room pulsed with static electricity.

"Are you well, Toren?"

"More than."

"Good." Eden rose and strolled to one of the windows, her back to him. "I'm looking forward to our next time together."

"Can I go inside?"

"The room I just described?"

"I'd like to take a look."

She turned halfway and motioned to the door. Toren waited only a moment before easing over to it. When he reached it, he spun back. Eden stood motionless, still gazing out over the water. He turned back and started to reach for the knob, then stopped. Everything about the room had been giving him a singular message from the instant he'd stepped inside, but it didn't present in a way his mind could understand till that moment. As certain as he'd ever been, he knew that this room, this octagon he'd been invited to, or led to, or maybe in some weird way brought himself to, would at some point bring about his redemption — or his death. The thought didn't scare him. He embraced its truth, because without question it was the only way out of his prison of fury.

He slid his fingers onto the dark wood handle and was only slightly surprised to find the handle warm. Toren would have been more astounded to find it a normal temperature. He glanced once more at Eden, but she hadn't moved. Toren counted to three — it just seemed as if this moment needed a countdown — turned the doorknob, and pushed.

The door didn't move, not even a shudder. He pushed again, harder this time. Again nothing. It felt like shoving a boulder.

He spun and stared at the back of Eden's head. "What am I doing wrong?"

"Nothing."

"It won't open."

"Yes, it will, Toren. The door most certainly will open. I've done it many times. As have many others. It is the most important room here."

He turned back, tried again. Same result. In four long strides he was across the room and standing next to Eden.

"I can't get the door open."

"Yes, you can." Eden laughed. "Did you not hear me?"

"I heard you, but it's not happening." Toren mashed his lips together. "Tell me. What am I doing wrong?"

"In this place" — Eden spread her arms wide — "there is no wrong. Only right. Don't try to accept that. It flies in the face of most of what you believe. We will have time to talk about that later. Right now all you want is to know how to open that door, so let us concentrate on only that task. The reason you cannot open the door has nothing to do with the door and everything to do with you. Something is holding you back."

"Nothing is holding me back except the fact that the door won't budge."

"Why won't it budge?"

"I don't know! If I knew that, I could open it."

"What is holding you back, Toren?"

"I just told you, nothing is holding me back."

Eden closed her eyes and drew in a deep breath. Her arms hung loose at her sides and a subtle smile crossed her face. "Close your eyes, if you will, and answer a question for me."

He did as she asked. Five seconds. Ten. Thirty. *Patience.* Finally Eden said, "Remember what we just talked about. Do not think about what came before you got to the octagon — that is gone. Do not think about what the future might or might not bring. It does not exist. No. Let the thoughts of the past go. Let thoughts of the future go as well. Instead, concentrate on this moment. This place. Where you stand right now. Think about the floor beneath you. Feel the wood pressing up into your shoes. Ponder whether you can feel a breeze against your face in this moment. Consider the idea that your skin or mind or soul still maintains a hint of the tea you drank. Or contains none of it. Yes?"

He nodded.

"Now go to the deep place inside yourself, beyond your body, beyond your mind, beyond all the images you brought into the octagon when you stepped inside ten minutes ago. Go into the place where the Spirit of God dwells, into the temple, your heart, and tell me what you find there."

"There's nothing. I think —"

"No. Don't think. Deep calls unto deep. Don't think, Toren. What is there? Don't think. Simply go there."

"Okay."

"There is no time, for he is outside of time. There is no yesterday, there is no tomorrow, for the Spirit holds all moments in his hands, yes? And where are you?"

"I'm in —"

"You are in him. You are in Christ."

"He's in me and —"

"You are in him." Eden's fingers settled on Toren's shoulder. "He is in you. You are in him."

"Yes."

"Yes," Eden echoed. "In that place. You are there?"

"Yes."

"With him. In him?" Her voice grew softer.

"Yes."

"Now bring the door into that place, the one you stood before a few minutes past. Do you have it?"

"Yes."

"What do you feel?"

"Hesitation."

"What do you feel?"

"I told you, hesitation."

"What do you feel, Toren? It is profitable to be honest in this place."

"Fear."

"Yes." A laugh almost too soft to hear floated up to him. "Tell me more. Fear of what?"

"Fear of not being able to open the door. Fear of opening the door and knowing I don't belong. Fear that I've done too much to Sloane to be worthy enough to step over the threshold. Fear that being here will bring nothing and I'll be trapped with Hyde forever. Fear that I'll never be rid of him. That I'll never get control. That he'll destroy me."

"Yes, yes, yes."

Her gentle touch became like one of the forty-five-pound plates he used in the gym, and he staggered under the pressure and wanted to open his eyes.

"No, keep them closed." Eden's voice was soft but filled with steel. "Stay with me."

"Okay," Toren sputtered out.

"Soon the weights will be lifted. Soon you will fly as you have always been able to do. Soon you will be free of the darkness. I promise you."

The pressure of her fingers lessened, then an instant later it was completely gone.

"Is there anything else, Toren?"

"No."

"Anything else? Are you sure? This place is safe. There is no law here, only greater law, the greatest law against which nothing else can stand."

"The law of grace."

"Yes, that is right. Keep your eyes closed just a little longer. Now, if you would, stop fighting those fears. The lies that batter you. Stop trying to talk yourself out of them, or to overcome them. Stop pummeling yourself for having them. Instead, embrace what you know in that place you are now. That the law of grace is the law that condemnation cannot stand against. That nothing can separate you from Christ. Nothing. For Christ is in you. And you are in him. In his power. In his mercy. In his kindness. All of it. You are in it. And all of it is in you."

"Yes." Toren whispered the word so softly he doubted Eden could hear it.

"Now, stay in that place deep inside you, and speak truth to your spirit. No shame for feeling the way you did. No shame for believing the lie. No shame for embracing the fear. Condemnation does not exist here. Judgment has no place. There is no atom small enough into which darkness can scurry and try to hide when light streams in, yes?"

"Yes."

"Speak the words now, words of truth. Right now. Of power. Of grace. Of forgiveness."

As he spoke words of forgiveness, as he stopped fighting the fears, as he offered himself tenderness, Eden kept saying, "Yes . . . Good . . . That's it . . . Yes, good . . . Well done, Toren." Less than sixty seconds later the fears had faded — not disappeared — but settled so deep in his soul he couldn't touch them any longer.

Toren opened his eyes to find Eden smiling at him, her eyes moist.

"Why are you crying?"

"You're my brother. Who wouldn't get emotional seeing her brother take a step closer to discovering who he truly is? Stepping into the man he's always been? Stepping away from the man he never was?"

Toren laughed. "Don't tell me you're into that whole calling people in your life 'brother' and 'sister.' "

"Not really. I'm much more into calling others an extension of myself, but we'll probably need to explore what I mean by that another time."

"Probably?" Toren arched his eyebrows.

"Definitely."

With one hand she motioned back toward the door, and with the other she gave him a light shove. "Now go, go to the door and open it."

This time he spied another handle, much smaller than the one on the side of the door, embedded in the center of the panel. It was barely a half inch across and a quarter inch wide and blended in with the wood. But still, how had he missed it?

He took the bigger handle in his right hand, pressed down on the tiny piece of wood with his left forefinger, and pushed. The door glided open a quarter inch, then stopped. Toren pushed again. Again an inch or two. He didn't push hard each time. He didn't need to. The door offered little resistance, but each time it stopped after

moving only a sliver. Toren didn't care. The
door was opening.

CHAPTER 34

Toren pushed again. Again a few centimeters. As he continued to push, a thought struck him like a hammer. He wanted to know — needed to know — what was behind the door before he stepped inside. Not sweeping feel-good statements from Eden, but clarity. Not generalities, specifics. A fear of not being ready, not being worthy to step inside, rocketed through his mind.

"What will I find in there, Eden?"

"I told you already, Toren."

"I need more."

"You need less. It is a place where your mind will only hinder you. I see it in your eyes — you are letting the lies creep in. Do not. If you allow your mind to freeze you in place, you will never discover what your heart has come to find."

"What am I going to find in there?"

"Is that a question of your mind, or your heart?" Eden asked, turning toward him.

"Is that a question of a man, or a child?"

"It's the question of anyone who has a brain."

"In other words, it is a question of the intellect, from an adult."

Toren sighed. "Everyone standing in my shoes would ask the exact same question."

"A child would marvel at a room that promised untold adventures and mysteries. A child would want to explore this mystery. A child's eyes would widen and his pulse would quicken with anticipation of what he would find if he stepped inside the room and began to explore."

"Okay, I get it."

Eden approached him. "And a child would not be asking a question of the mind — 'How is this possible?' He would be asking, 'Can I go in?' " She smiled at him and said, "Put your mind aside. Bid it sleep."

"I'm trying."

"Good, good, I know you are." Eden patted his arm in the exact way his mom had done when he was little. "When you're ready, when your mind is at rest, tell me what your heart is asking, Toren."

"I already know. It's exactly what you just said. I want to know if I can go in."

Eden narrowed her eyes.

"But I don't need to ask that question

again, because it's already been answered, because here, in this place, all things are permissible."

Eden dipped her head and motioned toward the door, but not before Toren caught the smile on her face. He started through the door, then hesitated. The place was holy. Too holy for him to step into. It felt like he was invading someone's home or, at the least, a private museum.

As if reading his mind, Eden spoke close behind him.

"Go in."

He stepped over the threshold. Whether it was his imagination or something more, a hint of the tingling sensation he'd felt when he drank the tea pervaded his body. Peace. Joy. Love. Toren brought his other foot into the room in slow motion, then took in the room with all his senses.

He was home. This was a place where God dwelled. As he turned to his left to study the room, he caught motion in his peripheral vision. He turned to find Eden standing a few feet from him.

"You're coming with me."

"For a bit."

"I sense the Spirit's presence in this room."

"Or maybe you have put your mind away

in such a manner that you are sensing what has been inside *you* all along. Christ, living inside you, you living in him."

Toren smiled and turned back to survey the room. It was larger than the octagon, at least forty feet by sixty. The walls were painted a forest green, and in the center of the far wall a fire burned. The floors were a dark wood, perhaps mahogany.

Three windows were set into the wall facing the water. Two more windows were placed to the left and right of the fireplace. The glass in the windows was so clear Toren had to focus to be sure there was glass in the frames. The same wood that graced the door to the room framed the windows.

In front of the ocean view, two wide brown leather chairs were angled slightly toward each other, providing the perfect spot to have an intimate conversation. Two identical wood tables with spiral legs sat next to the chairs, with large round candles in the center, burned about halfway down.

But what captivated Toren more than anything else was what sat on the shelves built into the wall opposite the ocean. Carvings of wood and stone, more exquisite than he'd ever seen. Small paintings in watercolor and oils. Sketches in pencil that looked almost like photographs. Long and short poems recorded on light-brown parchment paper.

"The sculptures, the carvings, the paintings . . ."

"Spectacular, aren't they?" Eden's gaze meandered around the room, and she shook her head slowly as if seeing the offerings on the shelves and walls for the first time.

"Truly," Toren said.

"I'm glad you like them." Eden fixed her gaze on him.

"You created all these things."

"Oh no, Toren. A few, yes, but only a few. My students have created the majority of them."

Eden glanced around the room again, satisfaction etched on her face. "I play with the layout, trying to find the perfect place for each creation. They're all part of a tapestry that fits together when you look at the parts and when you look at the whole. It's never complete, because a new piece is always coming in. Which I love. It's a chance to exercise my creativity, even when I'm not creating, you understand?"

He stared at Eden. The way she'd said "you understand?" wasn't rhetorical. It was as if she really did want to know if he understood what it meant to use his creativity. As if she could read his thoughts, she followed up with a question that went to the center of Toren's soul.

"What kind of creativity fruit are you squeezing the juices out of these days, Toren?"

"I've been working with wood for the past three years. It makes me come alive."

"Then my hope is you follow that path."

Eden strolled farther into the room and Toren followed. "And then, one day when you're ready, perhaps you'll create a piece for this room."

Eden spun as she finished the last word, and Toren looked into her eyes, eyes so playful and so full of affection, he couldn't stop a laugh from spilling out of him. This was indeed a room of peace, joy, and the presence of the Spirit. If Eden told him he could stay here for the rest of his life, Toren would agree instantly.

Toren wandered deeper into the room and spied another door at the back. How had he missed it? It led into a small room, not more than six by six, with one overstuffed black chair and bookshelves against three of the walls, all filled with books both large and small.

A gold-framed picture hung on the wall to his left, a portrait of a man with dark eyes and long dark hair parted in the middle. A mustache extended beyond his cheeks. His countenance was at once playful and intense. Familiarity danced in Toren's mind, but he couldn't place the man. He slowly eased over to the portrait and studied the man's face. Again Toren was struck by the mischievous look in his eyes, but also by the sadness behind them.

He turned to Eden, who had moved to the center of the room, and asked, "Who is it?"

"It would benefit you to meet him, I think, if it were possible. He shares your pain and your longing. The pain and longing in every son and daughter of God. But he never found the answer, from what I know."

"Who is it?"

"Robert Louis Stevenson."

"The author of Jekyll and Hyde."

"Yes."

"Why is his picture here?"

"A reminder."

Toren took in the man's eyes. "For him, the dark dog won."

"I'm not sure if he embraced who he truly was."

"But you're going to show me how to destroy the dark dog forever."

Eden only smiled in response and motioned Toren out the door of the small room and to the chairs in front of the window. They settled into them, and he gazed out as the wind churned up whitecaps on the water. Eden steepled her fingers and rubbed her hands back and forth briskly a few times before speaking.

"There's a story the second Adam told about a son who asked for his inheritance before his father had died."

"The story of the prodigal son."

"Yes."

"I know the story. Well."

"Do you?" Eden put one hand up to her mouth as if to stifle laughter. "That's encouraging to hear. Because I think that story tells us who your Father truly is, a truth I believe you need to understand. Possibly more than you do now."

"Okay."

"Good. Good." Eden turned away from him and seemed to be staring at something far out on the water. "I'd like to ask you, Toren, have you dwelled on the part of the story that says the father saw his son when he was a long ways off?"

"Maybe not fully."

Eden continued as if he hadn't spoken. "I like to think of the father pacing at his window, searching the horizon for the silhouette of his son every moment the sun provided rays to do that. I think of the father standing on the porch in the dead of night when all his household is asleep, straining his ears for the softest footstep on the fine dirt, straining his eyes as he peers into the darkness, wishing, hoping with all he has for his son to come home.

"I like to mediate on the fact that when the father finally spied his son — which could have been years, for if the father was rich enough to have servants and men working for him, he certainly would have given the son enough to be gone for quite a long time — the father sprinted toward his son, that he fell upon his neck, and rained down kiss after kiss after kiss after kiss upon his son's face and shoulders and head. I like to imagine the father wrapping up the son in his arms and giving him the fiercest of hugs as tears washed over his cheeks."

Eden paused and stared into Toren's face with such kindness and understanding that a sensation of utter acceptance surged through him. Yes, acceptance. And passion. And love. From a father. A dad! Images of Toren's father sliced through his mind. The scorn, the disgust, and, maybe worst of all, the indifference his dad had always shown him without a hint of remorse. All he'd wanted was his dad to say, "I'm proud of you." Just once. He could have built a world around that. Created a belief that deep down his dad loved him.

But he did have a Father who had given him all those things. He'd been there all along.

"And then we come to the issue of sin, don't we, my dear brother Toren? The son is destitute. He's slogged his way back to his father, hoping, praying his father can find the grace to make him a slave. That is his greatest hope, that he could be a servant in his father's house. It's too much to ask, he knows it is, but it is his best and only hope. He's prepared a speech, memorized it, probably rehearsed it in his mind a thousand times over the days it took him to come home. And as he gives it, dread and hope course through him.

"How does the father respond, Toren? What does he say about his son's great sin?"

Toren stared deep into Eden's eyes as a realization filled his mind.

"He doesn't say anything about the sin."

"Nothing? But doesn't he say, 'I forgive you, son'?"

Toren paused even though he knew the answer, a chance for the reality of the story to sink into him. "No, he doesn't."

"You're right, the father does not. He

never addresses it. His response is what? To call for his ring to be put on his son's finger. His shout is for his robe to be brought and drawn across his son's gaunt shoulders. His cry is for the prized calf to be killed, for a feast must begin. The celebration cannot start too soon."

Eden dropped her gaze from Toren's eyes but leaned in till their noses were almost touching. Her voice was now a whisper. "This is who your Father is, Toren. That is how he loves you. That is the way in which he longs to be with you. In celebration. Every day. A feast of delights. Every day. Everything he has is yours. Everything. His affection for you is beyond measure. His love for you is infinite. His mercy and grace are light-years beyond anything you can imagine that would steal away his love. His love for you is greater than the length and breadth and depth of the universe. Now. Always."

They sat in silence for an age, maybe two. Finally Eden stirred and said, "It's time for me to go."

"Go?"

"Yes, for me to allow you the gift of solitude in this place. Be with him. In speech and prayer. In song and silence. In imagination and wonder. In laughter and sorrow."

Two emotions immediately battled for supremacy in Toren's soul. Exhilaration at what would happen if he were in this room alone, and a fear that he could be destroyed.

"I don't think I want to be in here alone."

"You will not be alone. The father of the story Jesus told is the Father, the Abba, the Daddy who is calling you to join him right now. His arms are open. He is inviting you into the house, to the table, to partake of the feast he has created for you."

"I get the story. I do. I get what you're saying. But . . ." A nervous laugh popped out of Toren's mouth. "It still feels a bit intimidating."

"You understand the story, but you don't believe it. It seems too good to be true."

"Yeah." Toren peered around the room. "God is that Father, but he's also a consuming fire. Right?"

"There is that perspective, yes."

"And the fire has always given me pause."

"I understand." Eden nodded knowingly. "But while in one way God is such a consuming fire that no man can stand against it, he is also a place of such radical, unquenchable love that you'll long to float as a speck in that ocean of love forever.

"God is the ruler of angel armies so

majestic you'll faint at the sight and sound of them, and at the same moment he is the Daddy who longs for you to crawl up onto his lap and bury your face in his chest forever and a day.

"According to the Scriptures, he's a Father and fortress, a rock and a lamb, an eagle and a shield and a hen and a mother with her child and a thousand other things. And he's everywhere. Throughout every galaxy, even those that the most powerful telescope on earth can't show us. He is in every atom, every quark. All at the same time." Eden winked. "He's never had a problem with the finite like humans do."

"God is Spirit."

"And not limited by a body, correct?" Eden tilted her head.

"Yes."

"Nor restricted by our feeble attempts to define him."

"Probably not."

"Do not fear, Toren. How many times will you need to hear that perfect love casts out fear? All fear. And he is love. And he is perfect."

"Two thousand four hundred ninety-five more times and I think I might be good."

She laughed and stood up. "I think you will be delighted. And, yes, maybe terrified.

I don't know. But don't worry. I believe in your ability to step into love, and once again — we cannot hear it too often — love, pure, true love, casts out all fear. Only two thousand four hundred ninety-four more times to go."

Toren had become enamored with Eden. And even though he'd already asked once, he stood with her and asked again, "You won't stay?"

"As I said, this must be a solo trip." Eden pointed at the door. "I'll be out there when you're ready to rejoin me."

Eden walked backward into the octagon and pulled the door shut. Toren turned to look out the windows, and immediately a kaleidoscope of colors streaked through the windows in front of him and exhilaration shot through him. The room filled with a hint of jasmine.

After a few more seconds, the abundant light from the windows seemed to grow in brightness. And it didn't stop. After half a minute, the light was already almost too bright for Toren to look at. Thirty seconds more and the brightest spotlight he'd ever seen was like a dying bulb on a two-inch flashlight compared to the light that now surrounded him.

Soon the light was too bright for him to

keep his eyes open. He squeezed them shut and covered his eyes with his hand. He took a faltering step toward where he pictured the chairs to be, to grab hold, to steady himself. Still the light increased. The light was now blinding even through his hand and closed eyes. More than blinding. It tore through him, and for a moment he thought the light would rip him apart, but a second later it seemed to be seeping into every molecule of his body. In his mind's eye he saw a microscopic world where each atom that made up his body was now buried in the light, and then the light became waves of indescribable joy that washed through him like an ocean. A second later the light became a million tiny particles, like phosphorescence in the sea, chasing each other around the nuclei of his atoms.

As he watched in his mind's eye, the particles of light grew larger. Now they were the size of grains of sand, now pebbles, now stones, now footballs — ha! — footballs, of course! His body couldn't contain this part of the light, so it exploded out of him, then raced around him in ever-widening circles till it reached to the edges of the room.

But there was no less light in him than when the light had started its dance, because the light came from within him and its source was never ending. He sensed he was spinning and twirling in a kind of dance, and as he did, either the light dimmed or his sight adjusted to the brilliance. But it was not the light that utterly astonished him. It was the love, because the light was love, and the light was his Father, his Abba, his Daddy, in all his radiant glory. Joy poured out of him in great swirls of laughter as he found it impossible to feel any worry about Sloane, or Callie, or Colton. Impossible to feel sorrow or fear about the future. There was no future. No past. Only now, and the ocean of love in which he swam.

A few minutes later, the dance ended and his feet came to rest. Toren opened his eyes and looked around and was surprised to see his feet on the floor of the room. Had he been floating?

Cascading swirls of light still danced in the center of the room, shooting out then gathering again. The Presence of the light was still so strong that Toren closed his eyes again and sank to his knees and bowed his head in total surrender. There were no words to express the emotions rising out of him, so he didn't try to speak. He remained on his knees and worshipped, and without warning, sleep stole over him.

When he woke, twilight had seeped into

the sky outside the window, and the last moments of a red-tinged sunset were sinking beyond the mountains to the west. He rose and wandered out of the room.

"How was your time, Toren?" Eden sat at the table in the center of the octagon, her eyes expectant.

"You stayed." He glanced at his watch. "I was in there for almost three hours."

"Yes."

"Was that real?" He ambled over to the table.

"I'm guessing you had a chance to see some of the unseen that the apostle Paul tells us to focus our lives on."

"That might be one way to describe it. Did you know that was going to happen to me?"

"No, because I don't know what happened to you." She motioned to the chair on the other side of the table. "Would you like to tell me?"

Toren's encounter spilled out of him, and he relived it as he told Eden the story, and the love he'd experienced washed over him again with almost as much force as when it first happened. Eden's eyes were tender and thrilled and amazed as Toren told of how the Light had surged through him with power and tenderness unlike anything he'd ever known.

She nodded and smiled but said nothing, even after he'd finished.

"I've never felt his love like that before. Never."

"You can have this every day, you know. Not just here in the octagon, but back there, in your everyday world. You only need eyes to see."

"I believe that."

"It seems our Abba is quite delighted with you, Toren." Eden smiled, and a soft giggle floated out of her mouth.

"What's next?"

"I'll see you here a week from today — if you choose to come back."

"You know I'll be here."

"Good. Good."

"Want to give me a preview of what we'll be doing?"

He didn't expect Eden to answer, but she didn't hesitate.

"We'll be looking into why you have a temper that you cannot control."

"Okay."

"And you thought our first time together would not be much more than an introduction."

Eden strolled to the door he'd entered by and stood to the right of it.

"We have accomplished a great deal today. Well done, Toren. I look forward to next time."

Eden opened the door and let it swing wide. Toren stopped when he stood in its frame and looked at Eden. She smiled, and in that smile Toren found more hope than he'd felt in ages.

"Thank you, Eden."

She nodded, and he walked through to the landing at the top of the stairs.

"Toren?"

"Yes?"

"One more thing."

"Sure."

"The last steps up a mountain like Everest are always the hardest."

"What are you saying? More than a few people have died on that mountain."

Eden nodded but didn't speak.

"What are you saying?" he repeated.

"Many people turn back. They make a different choice at the end. Due to weather, due to their own will. Due to many things."

"I still don't get it."

"You will have to choose."

"Choose what?"

"There will be two mountains in your future. You will have to decide which mountain you want to climb the most."

CHAPTER 35

As Toren approached his car, he spotted someone sitting on the trunk. No. Come on. Did God think this was funny? It couldn't be. But another ten seconds confirmed his suspicion. Letto sat with elbows on knees, a crooked smile on his face, a finger pointed in Toren's direction.

"Hey! Toren," Letto called out when Toren was still thirty yards away. "You have a few minutes to talk?"

Toren slowed his gait and studied Letto. The man shifted on the trunk of Toren's car, what looked like a hunting knife in his hand, cleaning his fingernails. A surge of anger stirred inside Toren.

"What happened to us being finished? I thought you were done."

"Yeah, I thought so too. I tried, really I did. But it's not going to work."

"I'll help you make it work." Toren strode to within five feet and stopped, then slowly pounded his fist into his palm.

"Good, good, good, I appreciate that." Letto whacked Toren's trunk three times — far harder than was necessary — and said, "Have a seat. Let's have a good ol' talk, jus' you and me."

Toren stood like stone.

"Don't want to get cozy, huh?" Letto glanced from his knife to Toren's face, back to the knife, back to Toren. "What is it, Daniels?"

"What is it going to take to convince you?" Toren locked his arms across his chest. "I have no desire to get physical with you, but if that's what it takes to make you stay away, so be it."

"You like getting physical, don't you? I'm just curious: Who would win if you and Sloane really went at it? Huh? Her with the black belt, you with the size and muscles." Letto slid off the trunk and started bobbing and weaving. "Stick and move, baby, stick and move!"

He laughed, then shuffled back to the car and leaned against the trunk.

"Wonder who would win between you and me?" Letto pressed his teeth into his lower lip as he raised his eyebrows.

"That I can answer for you right now."

"I might give you a shot someday." Letto

ran the blade along his jeans.

"How 'bout right now?"

"Someday is not now, brown cow." Letto grinned and waved his hand in the direction Toren had come from. "What are you doing way up here in the islands? Long way from home."

"I'm starting to think there's no other way for the message to sink in."

He wanted to intimidate Letto, not fight him. Not that he was scared. Not even close. The guy was at least four inches shorter and seventy pounds lighter, and all of Toren's extra weight was muscle. But he respected the guy. He'd yet to meet a Special Ops guy — and Toren was convinced that's what Letto had been — over six feet. And their shorter stature was always an asset. They had swiftness, agility. Their fighting skills were far different from what Toren needed to take down a running back out in the flat. And knives were way out of Toren's league.

Letto's countenance shifted so quickly from a mocking, sarcastic scowl to abject misery that Toren blinked.

"I'm hurting, Toren. Life's gone crazy."

"I'm sorry to hear that. I get it."

"No, no, no. You're not sorry. Not at all.

You don't come within light-years of getting it."

Letto slumped forward, his hands on his knees, his face drawn. For a few seconds, Toren felt sorry for him.

"Where are you living these days, Letto?"

"In the pit." He looked up at Toren, a look of desperation in his eyes. "Dark, you know? Little trickles of brackish water always flowing toward me. Tough to breathe. I want to be free."

"I feel the same."

"Not like me. You have hope. Not me." He sputtered as if to continue, then fell into silence, his eyes cast down.

Toren didn't respond. The pity he'd felt a few moments back had vanished.

"I'm not stupid, Toren." Letto poked himself in the chest and held his finger there. "I know there's little chance we'll be friends again, but if you'd let me — we could help each other out. I will help you through this valley. I will stick closer than a brother, to borrow a verse from Proverbs, and you'll grow to appreciate me like no other."

Again Toren didn't respond.

Finally Letto shuffled off, and Toren watched him till he faded from sight. Then he got in his car and headed for the ferry.

After he boarded, Toren snatched a cup of bad coffee from the cafeteria, went to the front of the ferry, sat, and stared at the vast expanse of water, trying not to think about Letto. He tried even harder not to think about Sloane. He refused to think all hope for them as a couple was gone. She was dating a guy. So what. She hadn't said she loved him, had she? He rubbed his head. Yes, she had.

He wanted to call her, had to call her. Connect. Do something. But there were three good reasons for him not to call. First, it was getting late, eight forty-five, and Sloane liked to take Saturday evenings easy, and his call would definitely not put her at ease. Second, the last time they'd spoken hadn't been exactly tranquil, and third, she'd been ignoring his texts lately. What was he going to say if she picked up? *Hey, how's it going? I'm getting some kind of guru-like spiritual insight from the woman you hired to find me, but now I'm not even sure she's a true PI, but I have deeper insight into my temper, and, uh, how are you? Still dating that guy? Do you mind if I punch him in the face if I lose it again?*

The pros of calling were just as clear. One, he was still in love with her. Even if all he got was her voicemail, hearing her speak was water to his parched life. Two, if they talked, there was a one in a googolplex chance she would agree to coffee. Three, same as number one. The cut of not having her in his life was deeper than any he'd ever known, and he was bleeding out.

If he did call, it would hurt. If he didn't call, it would hurt. Odds were, she wouldn't pick up the phone. He'd have to leave a message. Right. No idea what to say in that scenario either. His excuse could be to warn her that Letto was still around, but he couldn't see her being concerned about that.

He wandered back to his car, not wanting to be in public. Less than a minute after he settled in, his cell phone vibrated. Unbelievable. It was Sloane. His heart rate shifted into a higher gear as he answered.

CHAPTER 36

"Hey, Sloane."

"I'm sorry I haven't responded to you. I've been busy."

"I see."

"What do you want?"

"Nothing, I just —"

"Nothing? Good." She sighed. "Neither do I, which means there's no reason to be having this conversation."

An idea flashed into Toren's mind. "Wait!"

"What?"

"Do you remember us talking about building some birdhouses for out back? Long time ago. A couple of years before I disappeared."

"What about them?"

"Let me come over tomorrow and build them for you," Toren said. "I won't even come inside. The kids will love them. So will you." He paused. "I think."

"I think you're right."

"Are you serious?"

"Yes."

"Okay. Maybe the kids could help me."

"We'll see. I have tentative plans."

"Leave the kids with me. And maybe you and I can talk for a while when I'm there."

The phone went silent for ten seconds. "Maybe. And, Toren, of course you can come inside."

Sloane's voice was more tender than he'd heard it since his return. It was true. Hope did spring eternal, because it was exploding inside him right now.

At just after ten thirty the next day — a radiant Sunday morning — Toren pulled off the street and onto the long driveway that led to his onetime home. A house that would be his home again. If faith was the substance of things hoped for, the evidence of things not seen, then Toren was slowly building up a solid supply.

Sloane and he and Callie and Colton would be a family again. It was happening. And the fire of Sloane's and his love would be rekindled and blaze brighter than it ever had before. This morning, this moment, was the next step. Sloane said they'd get a chance to talk after. Toren was ready, knew exactly what he was going to say. He would win her back. First the birdhouses, then the conversation. *Yes, Lord.*

As he swung around the last turn blocking his view of the house, a car he didn't know filled his vision. Who? No idea. But Toren didn't have time to run through the possible suspects because before he brought his car to a stop, the front door of the house opened. Colton stepped out. Then Callie. Then Sloane and a tall man with wavy blond hair. Heat shot up Toren's neck into his head, and deep in his gut the heat began turning into a raging fire.

The boyfriend. Had to be.

Colton had a glove on his hand. So did Sloane's guy. Of course he did. Colton scampered to the edge of the driveway and tossed a pitch to the tall man. He caught it, tossed it back, and after it smacked into Colton's glove, said, "Nice catch!" loud enough for the words to seep through Toren's window. The smile on Colton's face burned through Toren's mind.

Calm. Control. He would not lose it. Not here. Not now. Not ever again.

Toren rammed his car into park, shot up a prayer, stepped out of his car, and stood next to it, arms pulled tight across his chest.

Sloane strolled toward him as she waved the man over. When he reached her, Sloane took the man's hand as if it were the most natural thing in the world.

"Hey," Sloane said. "Perfect timing."

"Yeah." Toren didn't move. "Perfect."

"Toren, this is my friend Levi. Levi, this is Toren."

It took all of Toren's resolve not to crush Levi's palm in his during an awkward handshake. Neither man told a lie by making some inane comment about how good it was to meet the other.

Levi backed away and looked only at Sloane. "I'll give you two a chance to talk."

"Sure," Sloane said. "Be there in a few seconds."

She turned to Toren, her eyes hidden behind her sunglasses.

"Where are you and that guy going with my kids?"

"I'm not going anywhere with *that guy.* I'm going somewhere with Levi."

"Where are you going with *Levi*?"

Sloane shifted her weight. "I told Colton and Callie about the birdhouses. Callie seems more excited about them than Colton, but I still think he's secretly looking forward to seeing what you come up with."

"Tentative plans, huh? Isn't that what you said? Not so tentative now, are they?" Toren ground his teeth together. "You and him and my son and my daughter, huh?"

"Do you really want to get into this right here? Right now?"

Toren stared over her shoulder at Levi as the man seemed to be teaching Callie a new handshake that involved fist bumps and making their hands into birds. Her laughter sliced across Toren's heart like a serrated blade.

"Often? The four of you? You go out often together?" Both hands inside his jeans turned into fists.

"Thanks again for building them, Toren. We'll be back in about three hours."

With that, Sloane turned and sauntered to her car. The one he'd bought for her and surprised her with four years ago on a wet Christmas morning.

By noon he'd finished the first of three two-story birdhouses. By one the second was finished. At this pace he'd have the third done by the time Sloane and the kids and the guy stealing his family got back from wherever they'd gone to. What had Sloane said? Three hours? Half an hour to go before he'd watch the four of them shatter his life into even more pieces than it already was.

Do not go there!

He pushed the thoughts from his mind and focused on the final birdhouse. No one said reentry would be easy. She didn't love the guy. She couldn't.

Toren centered the roof of the final birdhouse on its four walls and set the first nail. On the second smack of the hammer the wood split. Ruined. A moment later, thoughts of Sloane with Levi overwhelmed him, and the darkness lurking inside him erupted.

A guttural scream roared out of him as he swung the hammer in a wide arc and brought it down on the birdhouse with all his strength. The wood splintered as he brought the hammer down on the house again. And again. And again.

Seconds later the rage had vanished and Toren slumped to the floor of the garage, head in hands, willing himself to forget what had just happened. It wasn't real. It was a dream. He hadn't lost it. That was impossible. He was the man he'd discovered at the octagon.

He shifted onto his knees and reached for the pieces. Had to clean up before Sloane and the kids and Levi got back. Couldn't let her see this and start asking questions. As he reached for the piece closest to him, a low sigh split the air. He looked up.

Sloane.

Standing just inside the garage door, her eyes not angry, but unquenchably sad.

"How long?"

"Plenty. Long. Enough." She raised her head to the ceiling, gave a tiny shake of her head, and walked back into the house.

CHAPTER 37

"Let it go, Toren."

"How can I let go of the fact I blew up any progress, any chance I had with Sloane?"

"You can't be certain of that," Eden said.

"The look in her eyes told me everything I need to know." Toren pressed his knuckles against his forehead. "I want to kill that part of me. I have to. Show me how. If you know, you have to show me how."

Toren sat with Eden in the northwest side of the octagon, gazing out over the water. A hard wind kicked up whitecaps, and few boats had ventured out.

"What is love, Toren?"

"What does that have to do with Sloane and me?" He scowled.

"I won't mock your emotional or intellectual intelligence by answering that question." Eden glared at him. "What is love, Toren?"

"God."

"Love takes no offense at one's actions. If something is done wrong, no account of it is recorded. Can love ever be provoked? Impossible. Love is kind. Always. Love is patient. Always. Love believes all things, endures all things, hopes for all things. Always."

Eden leaned in toward Toren. "You cannot overcome evil with evil. The only way to overcome evil is with good, with love."

"Yeah, sure, 'cause that's such a gosh darn easy thing to do."

"It will not be possible for you to love Sloane until you love the person you find the most impossible to love."

"You're talking about the degenerate who held the greatest three people he's ever known in the palm of his hand and lost them because he's an idiot of epic proportion."

"That's quite a descriptive self-assessment."

"The shoe fits nice and snug."

"We'll see." Eden sat back in her chair and took a sip of the hot tea she'd prepared. "Yes, Toren, we will see."

"Then who am I if not the person I just described?"

Eden turned back to him, her eyes bright.

"That is the good news. You are dead. As am I. We have been crucified with Christ, and we no longer live, but Christ lives in us. The life we now live in this flesh?" Eden plucked her arm and frowned. "We live it by faith in the Son of God."

"You have something against yourself?"

"This body?" Eden laughed and plucked at her arm again. "This isn't me. It's decaying. Soon it will be dust."

"What do you mean it's not you? Looks exactly like you."

"These are just molecules formed in a particular way for an infinitely short amount of time that we call a body. Paul called them tents." Eden patted her knees. "So temporary! Just costumes we put on for a flash till we take them off forever. You are not your body at all."

"Yeah, I kind of get it, but if I'm not this" — Toren thumped his fists against his chest — "then what am I?"

"Think of a jar of peanut butter. The jar isn't the peanut butter, is it? When someone says, 'I think I'm going to make a peanut-butter-and-jelly sandwich, I'd better get the peanut butter,' they're not really thinking about the jar. Yes, the jar holds the peanut butter, so they might picture the container in their mind, but what they really mean is they're going to get what's inside the jar and spread it on their multigrain bread. So when you ask what you really are, don't think about the container, then ask yourself the question again."

"I'm . . ." Toren couldn't find the words. "This jar seems pretty important while we're here." He flexed his arms. "A lot of who I am. Pretty solid."

"Actually, there's very little that's solid about you. You're almost completely made up of space."

"Oh really?"

"If all the space were taken out of all the atoms in the eight billion people who live on this planet, we would fit into a rather small area."

"Like the size of a small country?"

"Smaller."

Toren peered at her. "Tiny like the size of Washington state?"

"Think tiny."

"Seattle?"

"Tiny like inside one cube of sugar."

"You're not serious." Toren stared at her, dumbfounded.

"Yes." Eden's eyes sparkled. "I am. The molecules we're made up of are not us. The teachings of Jesus and Paul are true. This" — she patted her arms — "is a shell. We are far, far more than our containers."

Toren sat stunned.

Eden folded her hands, brought them to her face, and bumped her fingers against her lips as if trying to decide how to continue.

"Will you take my hand, Toren?" She didn't wait for an answer and took his fingers in hers. "Close your eyes."

"Do you feel my fingers touching yours?"

"Yes."

"And yet your eyes cannot see this. So is it still real? Of course. What if you lost your sense of touch? Would we still be holding each other's hands?"

"Yes."

"So even though you can't see it, and wouldn't be able to feel it, would it be true that I was touching your fingers?"

"Of course."

"Then is it possible that your true self, your authentic self, your eternal self, is not the one you've thought of as your body, but one that will go on forever? One that perhaps you're not in concert with as much as you thought you were?

"Can you consider the possibility that these senses are lying dormant within you, the eternal you, just waiting to be awakened? Ask yourself if it is possible that there are things all around you, right now in this moment, that you can't see or touch or feel or perceive in any way."

"You're saying I can do that if I have faith."

"No. It is not a matter of faith. It is a matter of science. This is not a new idea. Any high school graduate who took a rudimentary physics class knows that anything we see, taste, touch, feel, and hear is only a small part of reality. There is a far greater reality that exists right now, not in the words of the poets and dreamers of this world, but in actual fact."

"What are you driving at?"

"You're trying to fix something about yourself, Toren, through limited physical means, by doing. More prayer. More worship. More meditation. More study. More duty. Memorizing a set of truths. These are not bad things. In truth they can bring life if used correctly, but if they are done without love . . ."

"They're worthless."

"Yes, dear brother. The way of love, true love, is a narrow path, and few find it. You must open your eyes."

"How do I do that?"

"Your time is coming."

"Explain that."

"I think you know." Eden's face grew earnest. "Do not rush this. The moment will soon be here for you to choose the narrow path of love."

"No, I don't know," Toren said, frustration mounting inside him. "What moment?"

"The moment you need to choose to do what you need to do."

"Could you be any more cryptic?"

She smiled.

"When is the moment coming? I'm losing Sloane. I need answers now."

Eden's eyes were on fire now. She clapped her hands together three times, the sound like tiny firecrackers going off.

"I know you do. I understand that. But trust your perfect Father. Trust his perfect timing. You can't force this."

Toren gritted his teeth as he rose to his feet and shuffled toward the door.

"Toren?" Eden's voice floated over his shoulder as he reached for the doorknob.

"Yeah?"

"Be careful. Be on your guard. The enemy prowls like a lion, out to shred you."

CHAPTER 38

On the ferry ride back to Anacortes, Toren did nothing but stare at the dark water of the Sound and try to figure out Eden's words about love. Yes, he knew what Eden was steering him toward. He couldn't love Sloane truly until he loved himself. But what did that look like? And what did she mean his time was coming?

As he walked off the ferry forty-five minutes later and up the long asphalt walkway toward his car, he was still wrestling with the questions and couldn't pin anything to the mat. He hadn't driven onto the ferry this trip. Wished he would have. Something about the air made him feel uneasy. Only a few cars in the lot. Shadows filled the concrete, the last vestiges of day slinking away into dusk. And the man Toren was beginning to hate more than anyone else in the world stood beside his car once again. This was getting ridiculous.

"Hey, pal."

Toren stared at Letto, the sinister sensation that emanated from the man snaking along his back.

"How was your trip to the islands this time? Same place? Whaddya got going on up there? Ready to tell me?"

"Get away from my car."

"Learning how to get Sloane back? Is that it?"

Toren's hands formed into fists.

"You need me."

"No, I don't."

"Yeah. You do." Letto jabbed a finger at him. "You want Sloane back, you gotta change. How do you do that? You dig in. Work it, baby, work it. Focus. Discipline."

"I tried that."

"Yeah, did you? With who, Toren? Who was beside you challenging you, encouraging you, pushing you hard? Huh? Give me their names. Or did you work it all out on your own? There's a reason you have coaches. There's a reason people get personal trainers. You know this stuff. You're an athlete, for crying out loud."

"I don't need help from you."

"It must be a shredded mess inside your soul." Letto shook his head and sniffed out a laugh. "Brutal. You show up after eight months, and not only does she not want anything to do with you, but she's seeing someone else. Not fun, is it? That has to get the heat going, yeah? Tick you off to high heaven? Want to punch something? Huh?"

Toren stepped toward Letto. "I'm going home."

Letto pushed off Toren's car and paced back and forth as he jingled his keys at the end of his forefinger. After six paces to his right and six back to his left, he stopped and jabbed his finger at Toren.

"You are a cockroach."

"Who?"

"You are, brother." Letto grinned. "Learning the way of love, but the way you treat me? An old friend trying to get on the straight and narrow. Yeah, cockroach. The only thing I could think of that can survive a nuclear blast and keep going, same way you survived going to that Center place, learning the truth in the Scriptures, then seeing it wear off like a bad paint job seconds after it went on. You come away after eight months of work as much of a disaster as when you went in."

"What is your problem?"

"Mine? My problem is you. You need me, I need you, and it's really ticking me off that you think you're too good for me."

Letto stopped pacing and grinned. "So because I love you, I'm going to help you out."

"Oh really?"

"Yeah. Right here. Right now. You. Me. No one else, just one brother to the other, speaking truth and helping him grow."

"You want to tell me how you're going to do that?"

Without a hint of warning, Letto thrust his hand toward Toren's face, far too fast for Toren to move, and ripped his keys across the back of Toren's neck. Then Letto danced back on his toes like a pro boxer, a grin splashed on his face.

Toren staggered, put a hand to his neck, and felt blood.

"Like that, buddy? Huh? Feel good? It should. Now you and Sloane can relate, something to compare notes on, yeah? Matching scars will be really cool."

Toren wiped the blood from his neck on his jeans as a flamethrower deep inside ignited a rage stronger than any he'd ever known. He fixed his gaze on Letto's dark eyes and strode toward him.

"Yeah, buddy. That's it. That's it. I'm giving you the chance. Fight it, Toren. Right now. I can see the rage. I feel it. I feel it deep in my gut. Now is the time. Not tomorrow. Not next week. Let's end this, douse the anger in love. Don't give in. Be stronger, you can do it. I believe."

The words registered in the most distant parts of Toren's brain but slipped out of his consciousness. He'd never experienced a loathing like this. A thought flitted through his mind that he could kill Letto, but he brushed it aside as he reached the smaller man.

Toren swung for Letto's nose, but he ducked faster than Toren thought possible, then slugged Toren on his right side, just under his ribs. Toren had tensed at the last second, and while the blow shot pain through his chest, he didn't lose his wind. Or his sense of attack.

He launched an elbow that grazed Letto's ear and his enemy danced back.

"Nice, Toren. Really, really nice. Felt the wind of that one." Letto gestured toward himself. "Come on, you want more? Or is Mr. Cockroach going to take the path of love instead? Time to choose . . . tiiiimme to choose."

Toren stepped back, hands still raised. Everything in him wanted to grind Letto into the ground. Yes, the man was quicker, but Toren was far bigger and far stronger. All he needed to do was get one grip on the man and the fight would be over. But Letto was right. That was not the way of love. He did need to choose. Choose life. Choose love. Chose patience, kindness, not the way of offense. Not the way of provocation.

Toren took another two steps back and dropped his hands.

"Well done," Letto said as he continued to dance in a slow circle. "Couldn't have been easy to make that choice. I mean, think how many times you weren't able to make it, like when you shredded Sloane's heart again and again and again before you went away. Hundreds of times. Right? And then just when you're seeing hope . . . boom! You detonate right in front of her once again."

Letto snickered as the rage Toren had subdued began to rise again.

"Yeah, but it's all good now, oh yeah, nothing to worry about. I'm sure she's getting a lot of love right now, all snuggled up in Levi's tender, loving arms."

Full-out laughter burst out of Letto's mouth at the same moment the rage inside Toren took over. His feet pushed off the concrete and he sprinted toward Letto. The man mocked Toren even now, his fingers wiggling as if to beckon Toren closer. With a primal scream he slammed his shoulder into

Letto's chest and they both went down, rolling, punching, tearing at each other.

Toren wound up on top of Letto and rained blows at the man's midsection, but Letto fought back with a ferocity Toren had only seen on the field in men who seethed fury out of every pore of their being. And he was skilled, more than Toren had imagined. If he didn't have the weight and strength advantage, this fight would have been over seconds after it started, with Letto the victor.

He drove his hands through Letto's flailing arms, grabbed hard on the man's throat, and began to squeeze. Knock him out, render him unconscious. Had to do it before his strength ran out.

"You like that?" Toren clamped down harder. "Huh, you like that?"

A stupid grin appeared on Letto's face and he rasped out an answer. "Yeah, I do. I love it."

Toren dug his thumbs deeper into Letto's throat and at the same time slammed his knees into the man's stomach. Letto gasped and air whooshed out of his lungs. His arms went limp. Toren's gaze flickered to Letto's face, but the man had closed his eyes. It was almost over.

But a moment later Letto rasped, "Really

love it, but enough."

With a strength the man shouldn't have had left, he clutched both of Toren's arms and head-butted him. Light exploded in his eyes as pain reverberated through his skull. Toren loosened his grip slightly, but it was enough as Letto pulled Toren's arms away and then, in another lightning strike, jabbed his fingers into Toren's throat. Toren fell away onto his back and clutched at his throat as pain streaked down his chest and up into his head.

Letto rolled to his side and staggered to his feet. "You're tougher than I thought."

He slammed his boot into Toren's ribs three times, then backed away, grinning.

"This isn't over." Toren rolled onto his side, pain shooting out from his ribs like a lightning storm.

"Don't worry, I'll give you a rematch someday."

"I'm coming for you, Letto."

"Whatever you want, Toro." Mocking laughter again. "And by the way, I have to compliment you. You got it going on, all right. Lots o' love. Turning the other cheek. Not getting offended or provoked. Nice display just now of keeping it locked down. Keep it coming. You should tell Sloane all about it. And please say hi to her for me."

With a final throaty laugh, Letto loped off. Toren heard the sound of the man's shoes crunching on the parking lot long after he'd left.

CHAPTER 39

Toren woke the next morning to pain ringing in his ribs and the doorbell ringing in his ears. He pulled his phone off the nightstand. Nine thirty. Late. But not surprising given the beating he'd taken last night. Next time Toren would take Quinn along for a talk with Letto and things would turn out different, Special Ops training or not.

The doorbell rang again. Toren staggered to his feet and stumbled to the door. He opened it to a familiar face. It was a young man who had delivered pizzas to him and his family five or six times during the year before Toren went to The Center.

"Freddie? It's a little early for pizza, and I don't think I ordered anything." He glanced at Freddie's hands. A manila envelope, no pizza.

"Mr. Daniels?" Freddie glanced at the envelope and frowned. "What are you doing here?"

"I could probably ask you the same thing."

"I got . . . I got a new job. Just a month or so ago."

"Oh yeah, what's that?"

Freddie looked down and muttered into his thick stomach as if Toren wasn't standing right there. "This isn't right, is it? It can't be, can it?"

"What can't be right, Freddie?"

He started to point at the envelope in his hand, then said, "Is Mrs. Daniels home? I mean, did you guys move? You and Mrs. Daniels are doing good, right?"

"Why are you here, Freddie?" He asked the question even though Freddie had just tipped him off to exactly why he was there. As the kid stumbled to answer, the bomb in Toren's gut exploded in slow motion, and for the rest of the conversation he felt as if he watched it from above, as if it were happening to someone else.

Freddie stopped looking at him and fiddled with the zipper on his jacket while he spoke.

"I just go to the address, right? See, I always, one hundred percent of the time, make it a point never to look at the names, you know what I mean? I figure it's none of my business and it's pretty painful. I'm guessing that because I've never been in a position to —"

"Freddie. Stop."

Freddie handed the envelope to Toren. He didn't need to look at it to know what was inside, but even so, Freddie's next words tore into him like a dull blade.

"I'm sorry, but I gotta say this part, Mr. Daniels. You've been served."

Chapter 40

"She can't do this." Toren glared at his steak and baked potato, neither of which he'd touched.

"Sounds like she figured out a way to do it somehow anyway," Quinn said.

"Thanks for the brilliant insight. It's a huge help."

"You're welcome." Quinn stuffed another popcorn shrimp into his mouth and mumbled through his food, "Have you talked to her?"

"I've talked to her voicemail. Three times. I was calm. Controlled. I told her all I wanted was the chance to talk."

"But she hasn't called back."

Toren glared at Quinn for stating the obvious, and for being able to eat. Toren's stomach had gone into hibernation since he'd been served ten hours earlier.

"What are you going to do?" Quinn said after taking a gulp of his iced tea.

"Fight it. Try to talk her out of it. Tell her what's been going on with me up in Friday Harbor."

"You mean your spiritual thing, counseling thing, looking at God different thing."

"Yeah."

"So how's it going?"

"It's driving me nuts." Toren jabbed at his steak. "Eden says answers are coming, that my time is almost here, that I have to learn to love. But none of that is helping. He's still inside me and getting stronger."

"He? You mean this whatever-you-call-it? Mr. Hyde, your dark self, the shadow, the dark dog?" Quinn stifled a laugh.

"This is real, Quinn. My control is slipping."

"Yeah, I know." Quinn locked his fingers together. "So what you're saying is that the training is going good on one level, you're better, but the puppet master that has the strings on your temper is still renting a room in your brain."

"I want to kill him. I'm going to kill him. It's coming."

"And that has you down. I get that, and not getting to see your kids without jumping in the car and clearing it with Sloane has you down, and getting served has you down, and —"

"I really don't need a headline recap of where my life is."

"All I was about to say is that it seems like you could use some good news."

"Yeah? I don't suppose you have some."

"As a matter of fact . . ." Quinn leaned back, elbows on the back of the booth. "I was going to let it be a surprise, but I'm going to blow it because I want to talk you through it and tell you to wait to call him about it."

"Call who about what?"

"Take a guess. Wild. Way out there. Dream come true for you."

"I'm totally in the mood for a game like this right now, Quinn."

"There's a serious rumor going on that Prinos is going to the Dolphins."

"What?"

"Defensive coordinator."

"You're serious."

"Yeah, you can't say anything. I heard it through a few sources I'm not supposed to talk about, but it sounds pretty real."

Toren sat back. This could be it. "He could get me a tryout."

"You said it, not me, brother." Quinn stuffed another three shrimp into his mouth at once. "But yeah."

"I gotta call him."

"That's my point, why I told you before it hits the Internet. You can't. Let him settle in a bit. Lay things out for himself. Then call. Give him a few weeks to get in there. You ping him right away and it's going to be an immediate no." Quinn held up a palm. "Just my opinion."

The dream becoming reality.

"You said you talked to him a while back, right?" Quinn asked.

"Yeah."

"Told him you had control now and all that."

"I told him everything."

"Good." Quinn pushed his now-empty plate toward the center of the table. "Then I agree with you, Tor. I think he'll try to give you a shot. Go to the wall for you with the brass at the Dolphins. No guarantee of anything, but at least get you a tryout and an interview."

Toren slumped back in the booth, two voices screaming at him. One said he should call Coach immediately, that this was God's way of giving him the hope he needed to plow through the insanity of facing divorce and figuring out how to destroy Hyde.

The other voice told him Quinn was right. He had to be patient. Wait. Wait. Wait. The overarching pattern of his life right now.

After saying good-bye to Quinn, Toren lingered on the restaurant's front walkway, glancing between the darkening sky and his phone. Call Coach now? Or wait? As it turned out, he didn't have to decide.

Toren's cell rang and he glanced at the caller ID. Coach. Yes. Hope front and center. *Thank you, God.*

"Talk to me." Toren grinned.

"I got news for you, Torrent."

"Yeah?"

Coach told him about the job with the Dolphins, that it was a done deal except for the ink, that he'd be flying down to Miami in the morning to sign.

"I want you there, Toren. Without question. It's my call but not my call. Got it? It will take some pushing, sure, but I know I can at least get you down there. You've kept working out since we talked?"

"Every day."

"Excellent." Coach coughed. "Can't promise a thing other than a chance to talk to them, let you give 'em a workout. You up for that?"

"More than."

"Good. I'll call you the second it's set up. You gotta be ready to go with a few days' notice. You okay with that?"

"No worries. I'll be ready." Toren grinned.

"Anything else?"

"Yeah." Coach hesitated. "You say you got a grip on your temper. I believe you. Hundred and ten percent. But the Dolphins won't. They'll more than likely jab you with a red-hot poker during the workout and the interview. See if you go off. You get me?"

"I get you."

"Good. If you show 'em everything's under control, and you're in the kind of condition you're telling me you are, then there's a good shot —"

"I get invited to training camp."

"Bull's-eye."

"I owe you, Coach."

"Not yet you don't."

"Thank you."

"Torrent?"

"Yeah?"

"You're going to have a great workout when you come down here, so good you're going to come to camp, where you're going to show everyone else what I believe you still have. You're going to make the team; you're going to finish your career in three or four years the way it should have ended."

Toren slid his cell phone into his pocket and trundled toward his car. He gripped his arms, shoulders, thighs. He was ready. Right now. Sure, a little sore in the ribs from

Letto, but nothing that would slow him down. He glanced to his left at the huge window of a furniture store, caught his reflection, and studied his body, then looked at his face for a second as he passed. Instantly ice shot down his back. It wasn't his face that had been reflected back at him.

His momentum had taken him past the storefront, so Toren staggered back and stood panting in front of the massive twelve-foot windows. What was that? His face, nothing more, now stared back at him. But it hadn't been him a moment ago. Had it? No, he'd seen the reflection. It wasn't a trick of the light or his imagination. He'd seen a face looking back at him that held a thin smile, malevolent eyes.

He stepped toward the window, close enough that his reflection was now less than two feet away. He turned and looked behind him, as if the face he'd seen wasn't his but someone else's. Of course no one else was there. Of course it had been his face in the reflection. Who else could it be? But it wasn't him. So it had to be someone else. He argued with himself, but there was little point.

Toren knew this couldn't be settled with his mind, only at the heart level, and once he surrendered to that truth, he knew instantly who the man in the window was. It was himself. It was Hyde — who seemed less and less inclined to hide from him, and more intent on stepping up, front and center, and turning his life into a living hell.

Ten minutes later, Toren's breathing was still unsteady. He needed to get control. Had to trust Eden that his time was coming. The chance to take out Hyde. It was coming. Soon. It had to if there was any hope with Sloane. Any hope for his tryout in Miami.

Chapter 41

Two days later Toren finally reached Sloane.

"Hey." Sloane's voice was quiet, but not soft. There was an edge to it, sharper than he'd heard before.

"Thanks for calling back."

"Uh-huh."

"I've been leaving you messages."

"Yes, I know you have. I've listened to all of them."

"Why, Sloane? Why the no-fly, no-talk zone? We gotta discuss this."

"I needed time."

"Time for what?"

A heavy sigh came through the phone. "What can I do for you?"

"You filed."

"Yes, Toren, I filed."

"Why?"

"You can't seriously be asking that question."

"I am."

"Take a guess, a guess so wild it will surprise even you."

"The thing in the garage, the bird-houses . . . You can't . . . It was —"

"What? A onetime thing? Will never happen again? You want to go down the list or just trust me when I say I have it memorized?"

"I won't let you go, Sloane."

"You want to hear the crazy thing?" A bitter laugh floated through the phone. "I was starting to go insane. I was actually starting to believe you'd changed. I actually wondered if there was a future for us. I did. Really."

"There is a future. I know there is. I've got a tryout set up with the Dolphins. Miami, Sloane. We could start over and —"

"Yes, you're right. There is a future. I believe it. Just not a future where you and I are in it together."

"It was one time, Sloane. You can't scrap it all on one time."

"Once?"

"Yes."

"Tell me that again, Toren. Tell me that's the only time you've lost it since you got back. That you haven't felt anything else going on inside you since you got back from this Center place. Tell me."

Toren went silent.

"That's what I thought."

"I'm seeing a . . . counselor. I'm working through it. Breakthrough is coming, Sloane. I feel it. I know it."

"Mm-hmm."

"I'm serious, Sloane. It's up in Friday Harbor of all places, where you and I —"

"I remember, Toren."

"Something revolutionary is going on inside me that I can't even explain. I've experienced God in ways —"

"Revolutionary? Like what happened to you down in Arizona? That kind of revolutionary?"

"This is different. This is . . . I want to tell you about it. At least let me describe why this is so different from last time. These are people who know what went on at The Center, and what's happening in me now is going to truly get rid of my temper forever."

"I hope you got a money-back guarantee on that, 'cause your next wife is going to want a refund when it all comes crashing down."

The words ripped Toren to the bone. He paused, struggled to form a coherent thought.

"I love you, Sloane. There will never be anyone else." Promises would do nothing at this point. Even showing her he'd changed wouldn't do much.

"Sloane?"

"Unless you have some pressing concern about the kids, I need to go."

"This conversation isn't over."

"I think it is, because if it's only going to consist of you telling me how you're going to fight me on the divorce, I don't need it."

"I can't let you go through with it." Toren paused, shot up a prayer. "I want to tell you what I've been doing, learning. That's all."

"Fine. Go ahead."

"Can we do it in person, please? Coffee. Ten minutes."

"Why do I feel like I'm watching a show I've already seen? One where I know the ending."

"Please, Sloane."

The hum of the phone filled his ear for ten seconds.

"Are you free right now?"

Hope rose inside him. "Yes."

"Good. So am I. Talk."

No. Not over the phone. But what choice did he have?

Toren explained to her about Eden, the octagon, the insights he'd gained, the experience in the room off the back of the octagon, what love was and could be. He told her how The Center wasn't a solution, but this time the solution would be a true answer. How he'd already experienced the Father's love like he never had before. When he finished, more than twenty minutes later, Sloane said nothing for an age. Finally she spoke in a whisper.

"I'm happy for you, Toren. Really, I am."

"Is that all?"

"No." Again a long silence. Then, "Levi and I are getting serious. I'm going through with the divorce."

No. Please, God, no.

"I need a little more time, Sloane. I'm changing, really, truly changing this time. Please wait for me."

"He's asked me to marry him."

Toren's body went numb. This couldn't be happening. Not now. Not when there was hope. True hope. Not hope propped up by a series of mantras and conditioning and starvation of a part of him that couldn't be starved, but a process of coming into a relationship with the Father that was unlike anything he'd ever experienced. A process that would teach him to love Sloane like she'd never been loved before.

"What did you tell him?"

"It's none of your business."

Cold sweat broke out on Toren's forehead.

"Did you tell him yes?"

"I'm done with this conver—"

"No! Sloane, don't hang up. Please. Listen to me, you can't marry him."

"What I can't do is believe I'm even having this conversation."

"Sloane, don't do this to me."

"You're kidding, right? *You* did it, Toren. You. All by yourself."

His phone went dead and instantly seemed to gain twenty pounds. His hand fell to his lap and he stared at the maple leaves being tossed by the wind.

The next three days were as vicious as Toren could ever remember. Remorse, guilt, and shame pounded at him like an unending hurricane. The only bright spots were milkshakes with Callie and a game of chess with Colton. But his chances of restoring his marriage? Zero to nonexistent. Sloane would marry Levi and his world would be ripped apart. But he would fight it with everything inside. There had to be a way to save their marriage.

As he walked the long tunnel that led to the octagon the next Sunday, a sliver of hope stirred, then died just as quickly. God was moving. Toren was changing. But it wouldn't be enough. Maybe Eden was right

— he would find a way to destroy Hyde, but to what end? Without Sloane, what was the point?

After he caught her up on the recent explosions in his life, Eden poured him a cup of tea as they sat at the table in the center of the octagon and began speaking.

"We cannot love till we know we are loved. You've heard this many times, I'm sure, Toren, but hearing is vastly different from knowing it in the core of your being. And we cannot truly love till we believe that perfect love casts out fear. Not some fear. Not ninety-nine percent of fear. All of it."

Toren set his cup on the table. "You told me the story of the prodigal son earlier. And ever since then all I can think is that I've never known that kind of love. Not even close. My own father? Well, he was the type to beat fear into a kid and then, for a bonus, brand it on his back."

"And so you have made God in your father's image," she said. Toren frowned. "You think God is no better than your earthly father?"

"No, I know he's better. Way better." Toren squeezed the back of his neck.

"Where do you know it?" Eden pointed to her head. "Here?" Then pointed at her chest. "Or here?"

"You know what I've done. Who I've been. I'm never going to measure up to what God requires. At least not for a million years or so."

Eden leaned back in her seat. "Was that the nature of the love you experienced in that room?" She pointed at the door to the sacred space. "Think. If you fear God, if you are scared of him, then you do not know his perfect love. If there is even a shred of your consciousness that feels the need to perform, or come through, or measure up, or do all the right things, then you feel your father's wrath, but that father is the one of lies, not the one who rushes toward you when he sees your silhouette on the horizon, not the one who kills the fatted calf, throws the robe around your shoulders, puts his ring on your finger, and rains kisses down on you."

Eden paused again, allowing time for her words to sink deep.

Toren pulled in a deep breath and let it out slow. "It's too good to be true."

"Only if you believe it to be so. In which case you will reject it."

"I can't possibly deserve that kind of love."

"Who said anything about deserving?" It looked like Eden was stifling laughter. "Did the prodigal deserve his reception?"

Her words sparked fresh hope in Toren's chest. "So how do I do it? How can I believe that love is for me?"

Eden tilted her head to the side. "Perhaps begin by forgiving yourself for believing the lie that this love is not for you."

Eden continued speaking, but most of her words flitted out of Toren's reach, his mind turning over that word again and again: *forgive.* And as the ferry pulled away from Friday Harbor that evening and chugged across the dark-green water, he had an idea that had never occurred to him.

Toren pulled out his cell phone and stared at it. Thirty seconds stretched into forty-five and then into a minute thirty. He asked himself why he was waiting to make the call. He wanted to. Deeply. Which surprised him. Maybe he was waiting to see if the desire would wear off. Nah, he knew without question it wouldn't. Which surprised him even more. And then it didn't surprise him at all.

He finally tapped in the number he hadn't dialed in almost a decade. The man had probably moved, or disconnected his phone after all this time. Five rings. Six. Nine. No answering machine kicked in. Twelve rings and Toren was about to hang up, but halfway through the thirteenth ring, the phone on the other end of the line was picked up.

"Yeah?"

Toren's heart slammed against his chest. "Dad?"

"Who is this?"

"It's Toren."

A pause.

"Ain't funny."

"It's me, Dad. Really."

His dad's heavy breathing was the only sound for ten seconds.

"You . . . you died. They tracked me down . . . told me."

His dad's voice was raspy. Weak. Toren listened for a hint of the old fire and anger that had been in his dad's voice every minute he'd known the man. Wasn't there.

"No, I didn't." Toren swallowed. "I was away for a while, and they thought I had. But I'm alive."

"Oh." His dad coughed. "That's good, I suppose. I mean . . . it is good to know that. Really good."

Tenderness? Maybe it was just Toren's imagination. Didn't change what Toren wanted to say.

"Something's happened to me, Dad."

"Yeah? What's that?"

"For the first time in my life I'm starting to figure out what love is. Real love."

"Huh?"

"And I wanted to let you know I forgive you for what you did to me. What you did to Brady and Mom."

"I didn't ask for your forgiveness," his dad growled. But the growl had little strength behind it.

"I know you didn't ask." Toren smiled. "But I needed to tell you that. I realize maybe you just didn't know how to be the dad you wanted to be. Or didn't think you deserved forgiveness for not being that man."

A loud cough. Then, "Anything else?"

"Yes."

"Spit it out then."

"I love you, Dad."

A silence began between them that lasted for more than twenty seconds. Finally, Toren's dad broke it.

"Even after all these years, huh?" A rasp of laughter.

"Uh, Dad, I'm not . . . What do you mean 'after all these years'?"

More hacking laughter. "Even after growing up big and playing football in the pros, underneath all your he-man muscles, it turns out you're still just a wussy, pretty-please pansy boy. Aren't ya? Huh? Yeah, that's what you still are!"

His dad laughed once again, then swore.

A second later the line went dead.

Heat smothered Toren. He dropped his phone, and it clattered to the floor of the ferry. He bent over and pressed his fists into his forehead and drew hard breaths through his teeth. That's what came of forgiving? That was the way of love? A second later he lost it.

Toren rose up and slammed his fist against the window of the ferry three times as hard as he could. Then three more times. The glass shook. *Boom! Boom! Boom!* The sound filled the back of the ferry. Followed by a scream of anguish that lasted more than ten seconds.

By the time security arrived a few minutes later, his rage had settled. Toren apologized profusely and gave a lame excuse for his behavior. They let him off the hook after studying his driver's license, taking down his information, and giving him a stern warning.

The rest of the trip he stared at the water with one thought. It was over. He couldn't love. Wouldn't ever be able to. Wouldn't ever get control of Hyde. No matter how many times he met with Eden and heard her words of wisdom, he was never going to change. Sorken was right. Sometimes the dark dog wins.

CHAPTER 42

Monday morning, Toren's cell phone rang at six thirty. He rolled over and groaned. He hadn't slept, felt like he'd been run over by a dump truck. He was still sore from the pounding Letto had given him and exhausted from the emotional tsunami of recent days. He glanced at the caller ID and didn't recognize the number, ignored it. But he was awake. He rolled out of bed and took a hot shower. It helped. A little. He studied his body in the mirrors. He looked ripped, but his ribs were still painful and right now he needed a serious pain reliever along with a shot of java. After his first cup of coffee, his cell rang again. Same number. Same reaction from him. *If I don't know you, I'm not answering.* But when the third call came in five minutes later, sheer curiosity made him answer.

"Yeah?"

"Are you ready?"

Toren knew the voice. Was it . . .

"Eden?"

"Yes, are you ready?"

"This isn't your usual number."

"I know that. I'm calling you from the store." She sounded irritated. "Are you ready?"

"For what?"

"To become truly free. Not in man's way, but in the way of your infinite Father."

Truly free? It wasn't possible. That was the truth. Last night proved it. And the truth had not set him free.

"There's no point, Eden."

"With God, all things are possible."

"It's over. I called my dad, and he —"

"Did you forgive him?"

"I tried."

"Did you or didn't you?"

Toren bit his lower lip, then whispered, "I did."

"Then it is not over — it has just begun," Eden said. "You forgave him. Do not dismiss that act lightly. You have done well, dear brother."

Her words somehow stirred a hope he didn't know was still inside. "Pretend I believe you. What would I have to do?"

"You know what you must do." Eden's voice dropped to a whisper so soft Toren had to strain to hear the words. "It's time. You must face him."

"Who?"

"You know who, Toren."

"Hyde. But I don't know how to face him."

"It is the only way."

"Why?"

"Again, you know the answer. At The Center you were led to believe you could destroy Hyde — or at the least, bring him under full submission forever. Through your power. Your will. Your determination and sacrifice. But you cannot control him. This you know. He will reemerge. Always. No matter how hard you try, how far down you press him, he will find a way to escape."

"Yeah."

She paused to let out a slow breath. "You've seen him recently, haven't you?"

"How do you know that?"

"Where?"

"A reflection. In a window."

"It is time. I told you it would come, and it has." Eden's voice sounded tired. Older. As if she hadn't slept for days.

"So I have to kill him." Toren spoke the words more to himself than to Eden. "Starving the dark dog is not enough. He will never fully die that way. I must kill him, destroy him once and forever.

"I have to fight the Hyde inside me." Toren whispered the words to himself. "I have to be willing to die to myself to have any hope of destroying him."

"I believe in you, Toren."

"But I don't know what that means. I don't know how to do that." Toren stood and went to his window, fixed his gaze on the dark clouds rolling across the sky. "What do you mean I must face him? How?"

"You know exactly what I mean, and it scares you because you don't know if you'll win."

"I don't know how to fight someone who doesn't exist except inside my soul."

Eden sighed. Not with judgment, but as if she'd heard that said many times before. "Now you understand why I said few people finish the journey. It is not an easy one. The end of this journey is for you, yes. But it is for Sloane as well. It is for Colton. It is for Callie."

"Will I live?"

"I don't know." A long pause. "The better question is, are you willing to die? It is not easy to surrender one's life."

They sat in silence as the question echoed in Toren's mind. Was he willing to die? Surrender all that he was in order to have the chance to destroy his dark half once and for all? But there wasn't a choice, not really. Toren would face him.

"I hate him. With everything I am, I hate him. He's destroyed my life, and now I will destroy him. Where does this battle take place?"

"It happens in a place of peace, a place of triumph, a place of solitude. A place where you will not be disturbed."

"The octagon."

"Of course."

"When?"

"I've been praying for you, Toren. All night."

"When?"

"You do not have much time." The sound of her labored breathing came through the phone. "Six days from now. Saturday. Noon."

"I'll be there."

Eden didn't respond.

"Did you hear me? I said I'd be there."

"I hope so."

As Toren pulled into the gym parking lot two hours later, his cell phone rang again and his pulse spiked. This time he knew who it was. Coach.

Tell me something good.

"Hey, Torrent. Want some great news?"

"I don't want it. I need it."

"You're in."

"The tryout?"

"Not exactly."

"They're not giving me the tryout? I thought you said —"

"Yeah, they are, but that's the great news. The blow-your-mind kind of news. The workout is nothing more than a formality. They're bringing in a few of the guys. They'll watch you put a few hits on 'em. Hard hits, please. Not the time to hold back, you hearing me? They need to see you rock some bells on those boys. Just like old times."

"What are you saying?"

"They're going to invite you to training camp. Doesn't mean you'll make the team — not even close — but you'll get a decent shot, a legitimate shot to show why you deserve a spot on the roster."

"Unbelievable."

"I'm not saying it's all 'cause of me, but it's all 'cause of me." Coach's laughter echoed through the phone. "And yeah, you owe me like you've never owed anyone in your life."

"Are you . . . What are . . . they . . . Why . . ."

Coach hacked out another thick laugh. "Spit it out, man!"

"I'm stunned. I mean, I thought it was possible, but now that's it happening . . . I'm . . ."

"Yeah, I get it. Like being a rookie all over again. Like I said, this is only a shot. Even if I was head coach, you're going to have to rock it out of the park to make the team."

"I don't . . ."

"Know what to say? Here's what you gotta say. You say, 'Coach, if the sun rises, I'm standing in Florida on the day you tell me to be.'"

"If the sun rises, I'm there."

"Excellent. Glad you're ready to rock and roll."

"When?"

"Sunday."

"What?" Heat buried him. No, not this Sunday. Couldn't be.

"This Sunday?"

"Yeah, you fly out Friday afternoon. That'll give you Saturday to acclimate to the time change, get a little rest, and be ready to destroy the world on Sunday."

"Coach, I . . ." Toren trailed off.

"You what?"

"I don't know if I can."

"I'm going to pretend you didn't just say

that. Whatever it is, you cancel it and get your butt down to Florida."

Eden's call echoed in his mind. *You do not have much time.*

"I have to —"

"Are you high? This is your dream. This is my neck. Way out there. Stuck it out there for you." Coach's voice was just under a roar at this point. "And you're saying you don't know?"

"I'm in the middle of —"

"I don't care if you're in the middle of the Amazon jungle with malaria and three broken legs, you get down here." Through his phone, Toren heard Coach spit, and he didn't have to imagine the look on the man's face. "Friday."

The line went dead.

Chapter 43

"Quinn, call me back!"

Toren tossed his cell phone onto his passenger seat and gripped his steering wheel like he was choking Letto in a rematch. He had to talk to Quinn, get someone other than Eden or Coach to referee the most insane decision of his life. How ironic that the one person he wanted to get counsel from more than anyone else was the woman who still had his whole heart and was in the process of shattering it forever.

He glanced at his speedometer. Sixty. In a forty. Not good. He slowed, and just as he was about to pick up his phone and try Quinn again, his cell rang. Quinn. Yes. Maybe God really did like him.

"I need your counsel on how to make an impossible choice."

"Talk to me."

"Where are you?"

"Having lunch."

"Where?"

"At Sassy's." Quinn chuckled. "Where else?"

"I'll be there in seven minutes."

"Are you kidding me?" Quinn smacked his palms on the table. "Why would you even consider not going?"

"You don't get it. My time is this Saturday. Eden says —"

"No, your time is not this Saturday. It's this Sunday. Under the Florida sky. You getting your dream back. You getting your destiny back."

"I trust this woman. She —"

"I get it, Toren."

"No. You don't."

"Yeah, I do. We all have a dark side. Even me. And you want to destroy this imaginary Hyde person dark side of you. Good. Way to go. You call him Hyde, I call him your temper, whatever, huh?"

Toren blew out a sigh.

"You do this, you'll be able to get control of your temper while you're figuring out the other thing. That's good, right? This is your answer, Tor! The outlet! You go down there, hammer some guys, you're back to being you. The old you. But not the old you, because, whatever that Center place did for you, you have control of your temper most of the time, right? A flare-up now and then is about it. So this is perfect. Now you're gonna get that outlet for the little flare-ups and be right back where you belong."

The idea struck Toren like he'd been blindsided by a pulling guard. Quinn was right. If he could get back on the field, hit some people, he could get control.

"I don't know."

"I do. So do you. I can see it in your eyes."

"I get control for a time. Maybe. But think." Toren slapped his chest with both hands. "This thing is aging. Fast. Even if I make the team, I can't play forever. Three seasons, maybe four if I'm extremely lucky."

"Don't worry. You don't have forever. You don't even have six months. You have three months before you have to go to court and the divorce sails through whether you want it to or not. Then she gets a ring from this other guy welded to her finger. I'm not saying you don't come back and do your swami guru lady thing next week, but right now? You don't know when your temper is going to explode, do you? Do you have any control over it? No. So get it under control long enough to figure out how to get it under control forever, or time to do the rest of this octagonal training or whatever it is . . . Are you tracking with me?"

"Yeah."

"I'm just saying, this octagon thing sounds like it's been around for a long time and will probably be around for a long time, but this shot with Coach? It's going bye-bye unless you jump on it now, and it ain't ever coming back."

Four days later, late on Friday morning, Toren cruised down 405 on the way to Sea-Tac Airport and tried to choose a winner in the debate going on inside his head. Call Eden? Or just not show and explain things to her when he got back from Florida? The right choice was to call her. But he didn't need that battle right now, her telling him he needed to come to Friday Harbor instead. Yes, in a perfect world he'd be there. But Quinn was right. Odds were pretty high that the octagon wasn't going anywhere, and neither was Eden. It wasn't as if she'd refuse to let him come see her even if he was a few days late.

As he pulled into the airport parking garage twenty minutes later, there was still no clear victor. He shut off his engine and stared at his phone. Call. Don't call. Call. Don't call. Wasn't there a middle ground? Yes, there was. And for the moment, it was the best choice. He'd call her tomorrow, when there was no going back. For the moment, he'd make it short and sweet.

Toren picked up his phone and pulled up her number.

Eden, this is Toren. Something's come up that I have to do this weekend. No choice. I'll call you tomorrow to explain.

By the time he'd checked his bags and sat at gate N17, waiting for Alaska Airlines to wing him to Miami, the little voice inside him had sung the same refrain at least ten times: he'd taken the coward's way out. If he knew with conviction he was doing the right thing going to Florida, he'd have no problem talking to Eden about it on the phone.

"Shut up!"

The elderly man two seats down raised his eyebrows and scooted a few inches away.

"No, sorry, I wasn't talking to you. I was talking to myself . . . I . . ."

The man returned to his book without glancing up at Toren. Toren glanced at his watch. The plane was supposed to start boarding in five minutes. Too long. Once he got in the air, the struggle would be behind him. The choice made. But the next half hour wouldn't be easy.

Ten minutes later he was settled into his seat, watching the other passengers board, willing them to move faster. Just as what looked like the final stragglers boarded, his cell phone buzzed but he didn't look. He knew. A text message, had to be. From Eden, telling him the mistake he was making. But whose life was it? Hers, or his?

Toren fought the urge to look until the flight attendants finished their safety routine, then he pulled up the text. He read it. Looked at the picture that came with it. Once. Twice. Three times. Heat shot through him and he unbuckled his seat belt.

"I have to get off the plane," Toren said to the flight attendant standing near the cockpit door.

"What, sir?" The attendant leaned forward, a frown on her face.

"I have to get off. I can't take this flight."

"Sir, I'm sorry, we've already closed the cabin door and been cleared for takeoff."

"I'm the one who's sorry to put you through this trouble, but I absolutely have to get off."

As Toren strode back through the concourse ten minutes later, he studied the text again and again. It wasn't from Eden. Not from Coach, or Quinn, or Sloane.

It was from his daughter. It was from
Callie.

CHAPTER 44

Toren reached the door to the octagon at noon on Saturday, knocked once, then stepped inside, still not sure if he'd made the right choice. But when the Spirit surged inside, when hope shot through him, when he saw the look in Eden's eyes — one of radiant joy for him — all doubt shattered and faded into nothingness.

"You're here," she said.

Eden didn't say it as if she were surprised, but as if she knew with absolute certainty he would be standing in front of her on this day, at this hour.

"Yes."

"Why?" She strolled toward him, hands extended. When she reached him, she took his fingers in hers, squeezed once, let go, and repeated her question. "Why did you choose this over your dream?"

"How did you know that's where I planned to go?"

Eden invited him to sit with her at the table. After he'd sat down, she repeated her question for the third time. "Why did you choose this?"

"Callie."

"Oh?"

"She sent me a text. On her mom's phone. I didn't even know she knew how to do it." Toren pulled out his phone and pulled up Callie's message. "I was on the plane, doors shut. Decision made. My phone buzzed. I thought it was you arguing why I had to come here — I wasn't going to look at it till we were in the air — but for some insane, not-insane reason, I couldn't stop myself, and I looked down and there it was."

"I see."

"For her fifth birthday I made her a wooden box."

Toren had given it to Callie that night after her party was over, after he and Sloane cleaned up the cake crumbs and sticky fingerprints, after friends and family went home and the stillness in the air was thick and warm with memories.

He walked into her room to tuck her in and settled on the edge of her bed.

"I have something for you."

"What is it, Daddy?"

"For you." Toren pulled the box out from

behind his back and set it in front of her.

"It's so pretty."

"I'm glad you like it."

Callie sat forward in bed, her pink covers bunched up around her like snowdrifts. "Is there anything inside?"

Toren laughed. "Why do you think there's something inside?"

"There has to be something inside pretty boxes. Everyone knows that."

"Why don't you open it up and see?"

Callie lifted the lid and pulled out twenty or so folded pieces of paper. "What are these?"

"They're promises. From me."

"What kind of promises?"

"I've written something on each piece of paper. Some are silly, some are serious. Some are for now, some are for when you get older. But the important thing is, you get to decide when the things written on the papers get done."

"So like when I want to, I give you one of the papers and then you read it and have to do what it says."

"Yes."

"Can I look at some of them now?"

"Sure!"

For the next ten minutes they read through a few of the coupons together.

- I promise the biggest milkshake you've ever had, ever, ever, ever!
- I promise a super-long bike ride together.
- I promise to make sure any boy who wants to take you out is worthy of you.
- I promise to let you stay up two hours past your bedtime.
- I promise to always be available to talk about anything you want to talk about.
- I promise a movie night together with popcorn and way too much butter and salt and whatever movie you want to watch.
- I promise nighttime prayers and morning tickles.
- I promise to teach you how to drive a stick shift car.
- I promise an overnight campout together in a tent in the backyard.

"Can I make you promise to do a promise tomorrow, Daddy?"

"Of course!" He laughed.

Toren pulled himself away from the memory and fixed his gaze on Eden.

"There were a few times when she gave me one of those papers and I meant to make it happen, but I kept putting it off until . . ."

"You broke the promise."

Toren nodded.

"But this time you are going to follow through."

"Yes."

Toren pulled out his cell phone and looked at Callie's text message again. A picture of one of the papers he barely remembered writing filled his screen.

I promise to _____. (You get to fill in the blank, Callie, with whatever you want.)

She'd saved it. And filled it in, in green pen: *I promise to love Mommy again more than anything else with God's help.*

"I am thankful to Callie for sending that text," Eden said. "I believe by the time you leave the octagon today, you will be as well."

"I already am."

"May I offer a thought before you face him?"

"How do I face him? I don't even —"

Eden held up a finger. "Trust."

"Yeah." Toren ran his fingers through his hair. "Sorry, what were you going to say?"

"There is nothing that can separate you from the love of Christ. Nothing. There is no storm that can harm you, for you are hidden in Christ. There is no fear that can overtake you or even touch you, because the love of Christ is perfect and it casts out all fear. All."

"Thank you."

"I love you, my dear brother."

Eden nodded and stood. "I have to leave you again now, Toren. This is another part of your journey you must take alone, but know that I am with you as your sister in Christ, and since he is in me and I am in him, I am also in the Christ part of you."

Toren gave a soft smile. "Someday I think I might even understand that."

"This will not be easy."

"That part I do understand." He paused. "But do I get any clue how I'm supposed to do this?"

"The Spirit will lead you. Trust, Toren. Trust him. Trust who you are in him, trust who he is in you."

They stood together in the silence until a noise from the far end of the room shattered it like a stone against glass. Toren heard a voice he knew far too well.

"My main man! Yes! It's rematch time. You wanted the rematch, you got the rematch. Rock and roll, baby."

Letto Kasper strode out of the room at the back of the octagon, muscles twitching, a sick grin splayed on his face. Toren's heart hammered and he shook his head in disbelief.

"You have got to be kidding me. What are

you doing here?"

"Here we go, brother, here we go now. Ready, Toren? You wanted this, remember? Rumble time. Battle of the ages. But doesn't look like Quinn could make it. Pity. Jus' you and me."

He stopped his bobbing and weaving and shuffled over to a chair near one of the far windows that overlooked the water, sank down into it, and waved his fingers.

"Take your time, say good-bye to the guru, give her hugs or whatever it is you do, no rush. We'll start whenever you're ready."

Toren's adrenaline kicked into fifth gear. He jabbed his finger at Letto. "Stay right there. Do not move."

"Okay."

Toren spun and in six long strides reached Eden, who had moved to leave the room. He took her by the shoulders. "What have you done? Why did you invite him here?"

Eden reached up, took his hands in hers, and slowly lowered them between them but did not let go. She glanced to where he'd pointed, at Letto, then turned kind eyes to Toren. "Your oldest friend will help you with what you must do to Hyde. I promise you, this is the way."

"You can't be serious."

"I am."

"He's not my friend."

"I see."

"So I'm missing the part where he's going to help me. At all."

Eden squeezed his hands and whispered, "Remember your greatest weapon."

She let go of his hands, walked through the door of the octagon, and shut it tight behind her. The sound of the door shutting resounded like the shot of a cannon. He stared at the door. Closed his eyes. Prayed for wisdom, strength, and control. But all he could think about was how unprepared he was, no matter what Eden said. Toren turned and faced Letto. If his help had to come from a man he now fully detested, so be it.

"Eden says you're going to help me face Hyde. Is that true?"

"Yes, it is." Letto rose from his chair and started a slow bobbing shuffle, a half-speed version of the one he'd done during their fight in the parking lot.

"You can't do it without me. Impossible. She understands that. I see by the stupid look on your face that you clearly have no clue about the truth of that statement."

"Enlighten me." Toren stepped toward him.

"Idiot."

"Yeah, let's say I am. Educate me."

"I really am going to help you though this. I am. But not in the way you want me to. Or the way she wants me to. That part I'm guessing you *have* figured out. I'm going to kill you this time." He grinned, his eyes flashing a darkness that shot through Toren like ice.

Blackness seemed to seep from the floor and ceiling of the octagon and from Letto. It met the light coming in from the windows as if a solid wall stood between dark and light. Fear snaked up Toren's legs and arms, into his shoulders, into his mind.

He staggered back, his gaze locked on Letto, his eyes straining to see through the growing darkness. After another few seconds the darkness was complete and Toren saw nothing. The silence was so deep, the sound of Toren's heartbeat filled his head.

"Kasper!"

No response. Nothing. But Toren felt him. Evil. Malevolence emanated from him in waves. How could he take Letto in total darkness? He couldn't. Couldn't take him even in the light of day. But he had no choice.

How long the darkness and silence pressed down on him, Toren didn't know. Might have been minutes, although his mind screamed it had been hours. He didn't risk stepping forward, not until his eyes adjusted. He'd seen how fast Letto was. And Toren had no doubt the man's knife was already in his hand. So why hadn't Letto moved? Already attacked him?

Toren stumbled farther back, his hand groping for the door to allow the light from the landing at the top of the staircase to fill the room. A few seconds later he found it and grabbed the knob, but his sweat-slick hand slipped off.

Toren wiped his palm on his pants, grabbed again, and twisted. It didn't budge. No! Why would Eden lock him inside?

Letto's voice slithered out of the darkness. "Come on back and play, Toren. What's wrong with you?"

Toren closed his eyes and thought of Sloane and Colton and Callie. He could do this. Yes, he was willing to die if it meant saving them. Even if he had no idea what being here, fighting Letto had to do with it, and even though he couldn't fathom what this battle had to do with facing Hyde. He would press on. He trusted Eden, trusted his heavenly Father.

Toren felt the air shift. Close by. Move! Too late. Letto's steel fist slammed into his ribs. The air rushed out of Toren's lungs as he keeled over. A slam to Toren's head. He dropped to his knees as a groan eked out of his mouth.

"Come on, Toro ol' buddy, you gotta do better than this. You did last time. Kinda sorta anyway. Yeah? Don't be a pretty-please pansy boy like when you were a kid. At least take a swing at me."

Rage surged inside Toren, and he flailed at the sound of Letto's voice, snagged one of his legs, dug his fingers into his calf, and drove his shoulder into the smaller man's thigh. But Letto slammed his other foot into Toren's shoulder blades. His grip loosened.

"That's better, Toro, but still, giving my leg a little tickle isn't going to get you too far."

Letto was dancing again. Had to be, based on his voice, the sound coming as if the man were circling Toren. In his mind's eye he saw the mocking look on Letto's face.

Wham! An elbow to the back, so hard Toren collapsed. Then a kick to his ribs. Felt like two broke. Maybe three. Then another boot to the same spot.

Father, I need you like I've never needed you before. I need your power.

An answer came an instant later. *You have my power, for you have Christ in you. You are in him; he is in you.*

Another boot to his ribs. This time the other side. Just like his father had done a thousand years ago. Hot pain. Worse than he'd ever felt on the field.

"Get up, big man! At least make it interesting. You're a big football star. Let's rock and roll, Toren!"

Toren closed his eyes even though it made no difference in the darkness and spoke with a belief that came from a part of him so far down in his soul he barely heard the word inside his own mind.

"Light." He opened his eyes. "The light of Christ. Here. Now."

Before he'd finished the last word, a dim light appeared in the far corner of the room. Miniscule, yet radiant and hot, it shot hope through Toren even as it illuminated Letto from behind, casting him in silhouette.

"Nicely done, Toro, baby." Letto shook his head as if the accomplishment meant nothing.

Toren held no weapons, had no idea how this battle could be waged so he would win, had no thoughts other than the certainty that he had to beat Letto, and the certainty that it wasn't going to happen.

"I love the way you think, Toren." Letto's thick laughter stabbed him through the darkness. "Beat me. Save them. Yeah, right.

But you are right that you have no shot at beating me. I'm stronger. Faster. You want me to just get it over with? Put you out of your misery? Just give the word."

Anger and fear buried Toren.

"Who are you?"

"You seriously cannot be that stupid, can you?"

"Tell me."

More laughter. "I suppose you can be that stupid."

"Tell me."

"Think, idiot. Anyone else would have figured it out ages ago. I mean, yeah, maybe not back in junior high, but really? Even now?"

An instant later he knew, and the truth almost sent him to his knees.

"The other night, in the window," Toren whispered. "Impossible . . ." Toren trailed off, the weight of the revelation landing on him like an avalanche.

"No, it can't be." Toren pressed his palms into his temples. "It can't."

Letto snickered. "But it is."

Toren's lips barely moved as he stared at Letto. "This whole time."

"Yeah, brother. The whoooole time."

Toren spoke, but the word slogged out of

his mouth as if coming from someone else's tongue.

"No." Toren's breaths grew shallow. And fast.

"Oh yes." A leering smile from Letto.

"You're Hyde."

CHAPTER 45

Sick laughter sputtered out of Letto's mouth as he slowly clapped his hands once, twice, three times. "Such an idiot. But now you've grown just a fraction smarter. Congratulations. But you're still an idiot. I mean, come on. How could I have known about Sloane's scar? And that she had a black belt? And a million other things? Huh? Huh, idiot?"

Toren stared into his own eyes but didn't recognize them. These weren't the eyes that had looked back at him in mirrors all his life. These were eyes he didn't know, yet ones he knew intimately at the same time. Eyes he must have had when he'd screamed at Sloane or his kids, eyes he'd had when the rage took him.

"You're right, you do know my eyes."

The realization that Letto would know Toren's every thought struck hard.

"I am you, Toro. Of course I know your

every thought. Well, not every thought. Sometimes you shut me out. Just like I shut you out sometimes. But most of the times I can get through." Letto grinned. "You stupid, snot-nosed, idiot kid. Still the wee-nie little pansy boy after all these years."

Toren knew him, loathed him, and yet in a bizarre twist of reality he realized that Letto was a very real part of him. But he couldn't admit it to himself.

"You're not me."

"No?" Letto placed his hand over his chest. "I'm so hurt that you think so."

"You're part of me, yes, but you are not me."

"I am you, and it terrifies you. Because you know I'm stronger. You know how this story ends, thanks to your friend Robert Louis. I win."

"That was fiction; this is real life. My life."

"Story imitates life, Toren." Letto laughed, a cold sound that iced Toren's mind.

"Not this time."

"How? You want to explain how? You can't take me. You know this. Your strength, your size, even your will mean nothing here."

"You won't win. You'll never take control of me."

"Are you kidding? Won't? I already have. From the moment you gave in to me at age ten, lying on your bed, the beating from Dad still throbbing through you, I've had control. That vow has ruled you your entire life. You think you're going to get rid of it after decades of feeding it? Tell me, mighty Toren. Who is in control when you go off on Sloane or your kids? You suppressed me for a few weeks after we went to The Center. Wahoo.

"All the years you indulged me have given me a strength you know nothing of. I've got a resilience that will bury you again and again and again. Forever.

"You wonder how I flicked off the training you got at that Center place in Sedona? It was nothing more than a mask, paint made of fool's gold that couldn't stand the crucible of real fire. But now you're feeling the heat, brother. And it's real."

Letto paced slowly back and forth, five steps to the right, five to the left, the sneer on his face growing.

"Why are you even here in this place right now? It's because you're desperate, you're clutching at anything you think will save you. But nothing can."

Toren racked his brain, searching for an answer.

"There is no answer, Toro, baby." Letto circled again on his toes and bobbed his shoulder toward him at random intervals like a boxer appraising his foe.

"Come on. Let's go." Letto threw a mock jab toward Toren. "This will be fun. Killing this part of me and taking full control once and for all."

Letto circled faster now, jabbing and kicking at him in the style of an MMA fighter. He was still too far away to reach Toren, but he moved far quicker now than before.

Toren pressed his fists into each other. What he saw in front of him wasn't real. Wasn't a physical entity. But what had Eden said about Toren's own body? That it wasn't him? That his body was only a shell, a container for his real self? But if his body wasn't him, then what was he? What was Letto? What was he about to fight?

It didn't matter. He had to win. Toren shivered.

"Cold? Need the heat turned up, brother?" Laughter poured out of Letto.

"This is all in my head."

"You keep telling yourself that, Toro."

Father. Holy Spirit. Jesus.

An image of Sloane filled his mind. He wished for just one more chance to tell her he loved her if this didn't go well. One more.

Toren closed his eyes, shot up a plea, then opened them.

"Mistake."

Letto stood six inches away, and before the word faded, he slammed a fist into Toren's stomach just below his rib cage.

"Ughhhh!"

Toren's air whooshed from his lungs.

"Shoulda kept 'em open, Doctor."

Toren arched forward and Letto's knee slammed into his face. Pain rocketed through his nose. *Wham!* A shot to his ribs and Toren went down, hands and knees on the floor propping him up, blood dripping from his nose.

"That feel like it's in your head?" Letto laughed. "Or does it feel *reeeeal*?"

Toren glanced to his left. Letto's legs were a foot away. Letto was quick, but Toren wasn't slow. He faked a cough, then lunged for Letto's legs. Wrapped his arms around him and launched himself up, his shoulder burying itself in Letto's stomach. Lifting Letto high. *Wham!* Slamming him onto the floor, Toren's full 235 pounds landing on Letto's chest.

Now the grunt of pain and stream of air came from Letto's mouth. Fist to Letto's ribs. Another. Another. Anger surged inside him as he pummeled the smaller man's body. Faster. Blow after blow. He was winning.

"Argh!"

Letto's blade sliced across Toren's forearm. Idiot! Should have seen it coming. He rolled to his right an instant before the knife would have slashed into his other arm. Toren wrestled himself to his feet and lurched backward, eyes not leaving Letto, who now stood grinning again as he tossed his knife back and forth between his hands. Toren risked a glance at the cut on his arm. Long, but not deep.

Considering Letto's speed and knife, Las Vegas probably would have put Toren's odds of winning at 5,000 to 1. But Toren refused to give up. Letto wouldn't walk away from this. If there was any hope for him and Sloane, Toren had to destroy this part of him. Not through rules and discipline and checking the right boxes the right number of times a day. No. The only answer was to overcome his dark side through one-on-one combat.

He could do this. He'd battled like this on the field most of his life. Be stronger. Be quicker. Be smarter. Head fake one way, get your opponent to bite, then make your move and bring the hammer down.

Toren began to circle, fists up, eyes flitting from Letto's knife to the man's eyes, searching for an opening, the moment when he would attack. Wrest the knife from Letto's hand and drive it through his heart.

"Thank you, old pal." Letto continued to toss the knife back and forth. "I thought this thing was going to be over without a real fight."

Toren rose and wiped the blood from his face.

"After this? After I take over completely, you know what's going to happen? I see it in your eyes that you know. So why should I bother to say it out loud? For the drama, of course."

Hacking laughter spilled from Letto's mouth, then the laughter halted like a door slammed shut, and he narrowed his eyes.

"I'm going to take care of Sloane. Then Colton. Then your lovely little daughter."

Deeper anger than Toren had ever known flooded his soul. Multiplied with exponential growth. And still it grew, infusing him — his arms, legs, torso, all of him — with strength far greater than what mere muscles could wield. He strode toward Letto, the volcano inside surging out of him. A blow to Letto's wrist. The knife popped out of his hand, spinning high in the air, clattering to the floor. A fist to Letto's midsection. Then to his face, the smaller man staggering under the onslaught. *Wham!* Another blow to the face, his ribs, the crunch of fist on bone filling the octagon.

Letto up against the back wall. Covering his face. Trying to strike, but none of his parries coming close to reaching Toren. And still the rage inside Toren grew. The end was coming. He felt it, knew it. He would be free.

But an instant later, Letto's fingers slipped through Toren's arms and stabbed into Toren's throat like iron bars. Pain tore through him and he reeled back, clutching his throat. Faster than light, Letto was on him. His heel cracking into the side of Toren's knee, taking him to the floor once again. Then a blow to his head. Another. Toren tried to draw breaths, but whatever Letto had done to his throat made the air feel like fire.

A foot to his ribs forced Toren onto his back. He peered up at Letto staring down at him, grin bigger than ever.

"Now that was fun. Come on, you gotta admit we both had a good time."

"I'm going to kill you."

Letto frowned. "You know what I've been saying about you being an idiot? I didn't think you really, truly were one. But now I'm beginning to doubt."

He wiggled his fingers at Toren. "Stay

there. I want to finish this with the knife."

As Letto strolled toward the knife as if he were walking down a sandy beach with nowhere to go, the truth hit Toren like a waterfall. He couldn't win. Couldn't kill Letto in a million lifetimes. Because Toren's rage not only made him stronger, it fueled Letto's power as well. And no matter how strong or how fast or how enraged Toren became, Letto would always be a little stronger, a little faster, a little angrier. Letto was right. Toren could never destroy him.

Letto sauntered back over, pressing the tip of the knife into the fingers of his other hand one by one. "Are you ready to die?"

It made no sense. Why would Eden invite him here if he had no chance of victory? Why put him in a scenario where Letto could take over completely? Why had she told him he had a weapon when there was no weapon that could prevail?

Letto knelt beside him and raised the knife over Toren's throat.

"I know you wanted to love her. But you're just not there. And you'll never get there. You'll never be able to love Sloane fully. It's just not inside you. Never will be. And no amount of study or discipline or penance or anything else is ever going to make it happen. We both know the truth of this, but I'm the only one who has accepted it. It tears you up inside to fight that reality. So really, I'm helping you by taking over. I'm going to help you say good-bye to so much emotional agony."

As Toren stared into Letto's eyes, a revolution swept through him. He realized the truth his dark half had just spoken. Letto was right. Even if he did kill or subdue Letto, or escape, he could never love Sloane fully until a radical shift happened — until he himself knew he was fully loved.

But he *was* fully loved, by a Father who held no account of his wrongs. No record. A Father who was not offended by anything he'd ever done or ever would do. Any part of him. A Father who was never provoked. Never. His Father was the father at the ranch, searching the horizon for him, waiting with a ring and a robe and a feast. Not for the light Toren. Not for the dark Toren. For all of him.

And Christ, the Father's Son, had come to show him the mind-shattering truth that the Son was in him, and he was in the Son. Hidden in the shadow of his wings. And perfect in his Father's sight, because he was in Christ and Christ was in him.

Love your neighbor as yourself.

He was to love himself. How? As God

439

loved him. No offense. No record of wrongs. No provocation. Showing kindness and patience. Believing all things.

What he believed, what Toren now *knew,* was that he wasn't either man. The good man or the evil man. *Neither* side of the old Toren was alive any longer. The true him was hidden in Christ.

"Any final words, Toro, baby?" Letto waved the knife back and forth, now just inches from Toren's throat.

Toren patted his chest, his stomach, his legs. This was only his peanut butter jar. The true Toren was hidden with Christ, *risen* with Christ, loved by a Father who loved him with a love unquenchable. A love that kept no ledger and invited him to partake of a love that was perfection. A love in which fear could not exist. A love that nothing could defeat. A love that banished all darkness like a wind sweeping every cloud from the sky.

This costume, this temporary container he now inhabited, was not his truest self, was not him at all, according to the Scriptures. The old man was dead. Crucified. The true Toren was risen with Christ. A new man. A new being. Holy. Perfect in his Abba's sight. He no longer lived, but Christ lived in him. The Christ who had the power to love anyone. Even his greatest enemy.

He stared at Letto as revelation after revelation swept over him. How had he missed it? He laughed as the realization of how he could beat Hyde, the *only* way he could beat Hyde, crystalized. Toren smiled and closed his eyes for a few seconds before opening them, fixing his gaze on his enemy.

"It's okay, Letto. Everything you've done. Everything you're going to do. All the pain you've caused me. All the pain you've brought Sloane and Colton and Callie."

"Shut up," Letto snarled as he fell back.

"You're forgiven. I forgive you. It's all okay." Toren rolled onto his side, then to his knees. "Really. It's okay. All of it."

"Shut the hell up."

"That's it, isn't it?" Toren raised himself to his feet. "There is no room in hell for love, is there? There is no room for fear in God, for God is love. And love casts out fear. All fear. All of it."

"I said shut up."

"I don't hate you." Toren shook his head in disbelief, as if he couldn't believe he'd spoken those words. "For so long . . . but no longer. No, I don't hate you, I pity you. You are in a war you cannot win. For he has overcome. 'It is finished.' And I am glorified now. Perfected in Christ. Loved by the Father without reservation. How can you come against that?"

As Toren spoke the words, a sensation stole over him that he couldn't express, and then he could. "I can't believe I'm going to tell you this. This is crazy."

Letto stepped back, eyes narrowing, teeth grinding.

"I love you, Letto." A swell of joy formed in his stomach and he laughed. "Not with my love — are you kidding? But with his. With the love of Christ, with the love of the Father, who is the very essence of love, I love you."

Two things happened simultaneously. The joy inside Toren bubbled up and forced itself out in gentle laughter. And Letto started to fade. Toren stepped toward him, gazing at the astonishment in Letto's eyes. Toren reached up, his fingers almost touching Letto as the man faded completely from sight.

As Toren stared at the now-empty space in front of him, he whispered, " 'The Light shines in the darkness, and the darkness did not comprehend it.' "

During the long journey back through the tunnel to Alena's shop, gratitude and awe and worship poured out of Toren's mouth.

There were words and then no words, and communion with Abba God, Jesus, and the Holy Spirit with such power that it felt like floating more than walking.

When he reached the stairs that led up to Alena's store, he stopped, smiled, and shook his head. His life would never be the same. And in seconds he would stand before Eden and Alena, no doubt as the true Toren, the authentic Toren, the man he'd always been.

At the top of the stairs, he hesitated just a moment before opening the door and stepping into the store. Eden was there, yes, with a smile as wide as he'd ever seen. And Alena. And standing next to them was the last person he ever expected to see.

CHAPTER 46

"Hello, Toren."

Next to Eden, with a wide grin on his face, stood the leader of The Center, Clavin Sorken.

"What in the world . . . What are you . . ."

Another voice, behind him. "Good to see you, Toren."

He spun. Collette Engleton, known to the world as Dr. Ilsa Weber, stood behind Sorken and to his right. Next to her was the tall woman he'd first met at the birthday party who'd told him he had to accept his death. He had — oh, how he had.

He stared at them, dumbfounded, wanting to ask a thousand questions at the same time.

"You know each other . . . You're not . . . What . . ."

They all laughed and gathered around him.

Eden slid her arms around his waist and

squeezed tight. "Well done, brother."

Alena nodded at him, her eyes bright, then motioned to some wooden chairs set in a circle toward the front of the store. "Why don't we all take a seat and then we can try to answer a few of Toren's questions."

"I have more than a few," he said, which brought another round of laughter.

After they'd settled in, Eden said, "The summit is yours, Toren."

He glanced at each of them, then settled his eyes on Clavin.

"Even I've figured out that you're all working together, but why The Center, then? What is the point? If you knew it wasn't going to work, that it would eventually lead here, why the charade?"

"Because I knew it wouldn't work." Clavin steepled his hands, then pointed them at Toren. "But you didn't. You are an accomplished athlete and have competed at the highest levels of competition. You've seen what discipline and focus and determination can accomplish. You did not have help from your father by his choice, and due to circumstance your mother was not able to assist much either. Yes, you had your coach, but largely you were a self-made man, Toren. One who got it done. You played the role of professional football player well. But it made you think you could do life on your own. So when it came to your Christianity, you thought you could win the civil war inside you in the same way you achieved success on the field. You thought the law would save you.

"You needed to go down that path — all the way to the dead end — until you would be willing to admit you cannot do it in the natural man. You needed to see that the good man inside Toren could never win. You needed to see that in order to find freedom, you needed to find your true identity as a son of Abba, and in that identity realize not only how much you are loved but that you must love yourself in like manner."

Toren sighed as the truth of Clavin's words poured through him. "I had to embrace the way of love. I had to embrace Love, who is my perfect Father. Then love my greatest enemy — and forgive my greatest enemy — myself."

"Yes."

He studied each of them for a few seconds. "So you're a team that brings people to their lowest point so they can reach heights they never knew existed. You watch them. Then when they're ready, you bring them here, to the octagon."

Eden waved a finger. "Not exactly. Yes, we

watch, but we only give an invitation. It is they who choose to come."

"I have no words." Toren nodded and smiled. "Thank you. All of you."

More questions, more stories, more laughter.

Alena said, "Do me a favor, Toren." She handed him the puzzle she had given him the first day he'd come to the shop. The puzzle he'd asked her to keep there for him. "Try your wooden puzzle again."

"Now?"

"Yes."

Toren turned the puzzle pieces over in his hands and immediately saw what he'd missed the day Alena had given them to him. His alignment had been wrong. Toren smiled. Of course it had been. Not now. With light pressure he slid two of the pieces together, and a second later the third piece joined them.

"Thank you," he said to Alena. "This will be a treasure forever."

Finally it was time to leave, though Toren desperately wanted to remain with them.

"Will I see all of you again?"

"Without question," Clavin said.

"So what now? What do I do from here — where do I go?"

Eden smiled. "First, we get you cleaned

up. Then, of course, you must write your name into the wall down in the corridor. Then? Go anywhere. Do anything. All things are permissible."

"But not all things are profitable." Toren grinned.

"This is true." Eden tilted her head to the side. "So I suggest doing the most profitable thing for your heart, soul, and spirit. That is what you do. That is where you go."

"I know exactly where I go." He rubbed his lower teeth against his lips. "I go to Sloane. I find a way for her to sit down with me. And I talk to her like I've never talked to her before."

CHAPTER 47

When Sloane got back from a short run on Sunday afternoon, she checked on Colton and Callie, showered, then took a salad sprinkled with blue cheese dressing onto the back deck. But before she could sit and eat, the vibration of her cell phone on the granite countertop just inside the door stopped her.

She set the salad on the deck table and stepped back into the kitchen to see who was calling. She closed her eyes and clenched her teeth. Toren. All she wanted was a lazy Sunday afternoon to relax and enjoy the sunshine, not another debate over the divorce papers. How stupid did he think she was? Toren was stalling. Trying to prove to her that this time he'd really changed. Digging for some argument that would change her mind. Why couldn't he accept the fact it was irrevocably over?

For a moment she considered picking up.

But what would be the point? He wasn't going to budge. He would run through his same old list of convincers again. How the past weeks at the cult up at Friday Harbor had changed him, but this time it wasn't a Band-Aid, but deep surgery on his soul. How he'd discovered a way to be free of the dark side of himself forever. How it could help her too. And how God was more real to him than he'd ever been before.

He would tell her he truly did know how to love, not with a formula, or with a steely determination to do right, but with a love that flowed from the Christ in him into everyone who came into his world. He'd probably tell her how he'd forgiven his dad for what he'd done to Toren's mom, his brother, and himself. Probably a long speech about how he'd finally gotten control over his temper.

For brief flashes of insanity, she'd believed his words about what was happening at this . . . what? Compound? Spiritual training center out at Friday Harbor? But then the memory of him smashing his hammer into the birdhouse in her garage, fifty feet from where she now stood, thundered into her mind, and she made the wall between Toren and her thicker and stronger than ever.

She turned and walked back out onto the deck and ate her salad as two birds cavorted overhead in a sky that held only wisps of white clouds. The image took her back to the days when her life was sky blue most days and the occasional cloud was an anomaly. Yes, deep down inside, where no one was allowed to go — and rarely even her — she wished that whatever the change Toren claimed to have slipped into was real. Yes, if she could wave a magic wand, she would turn him back into the man he was before his football career ended.

But that wasn't going to happen. On top of that, Levi was a good man. Solid. He loved her. And she loved him. And she knew within a few months, maybe a few weeks, they would set a wedding date.

She sighed and thought about the kids. Should she wait till they were older? No. Yes. Maybe. There was no right answer because whatever she chose would set up land mines for Colton and Callie, not only as they grew up, but for the rest of their lives. And then there was her. Didn't she have a right to have a life? To think about her own wants and desires?

A robin landed on the peak of the chair across the table from her, cocked its head, and stared at her.

"Take me with you," she told it.

A moment later her cell phone rang again and the bird flew off. She finished her salad, strolled back inside, and looked at her phone. Toren again. Sloane cleaned up, checked on the kids, and finally ambled back over to her phone. One voicemail from him. Might as well get it over with. Adrenaline had kicked in already and the only way to get it out of her mind was to listen to what he was spouting today. She put her phone up to her ear and hit play.

"Hi, Sloane, could you call me when you have a chance? There's no rush. Thanks."

Odd. His voice was more relaxed than she'd ever heard it. At peace, even. Without thinking she dialed him back. He picked up on the first ring.

"Hey, thanks for calling back."

Again his voice was different.

"Yes, Toren?"

"I've signed the papers."

"You've . . . you've what?"

"I'd simply like to give them to you in person."

"You signed them?" The words lurched out of her mouth.

"Yes."

There was a smile in that simple word, *yes*. Not of laughter, not of gladness, but

452

of . . . what was it? Peace. So strange.

"Um, okay. I, um . . ." She frowned. She'd been so ready to fight, she didn't know what to say.

"Sloane?"

"Yes, sorry. I just didn't expect . . ." She trailed off again, all the adrenaline from the last few minutes seeping out of her.

"I know. I've been fighting you so hard. I'm sorry."

"That's . . . that's okay."

"Far from okay."

Silence stretched from a few seconds into ten.

"Toren?"

"Yes."

"When?"

"You tell me," he said.

"Half an hour?"

"Sure. I'll see you then."

He hung up and she dropped her arm and stared at her phone as if it were someone else's, as if she'd only been a witness to the call that had just taken place. He'd signed. Did he actually say that? Yes. He did. She believed him. It would finally be over. After all the struggle of the past three years, she would have a new life. She would be free. Sloane stared at the stove where she'd made a million meals for him, practicing on him often in her early days because she'd never really learned how to cook growing up.

"What would you give that one, on a scale of one to ten?" she'd asked him once, in the early days of their marriage.

"Nine. Nine point five, maybe." Toren smiled at her with a mouthful of a casserole she'd pulled off the Internet earlier that day.

"Really?"

He nodded.

"You can be honest. It won't hurt my feelings."

"It's good."

"Toren, look at me." She leaned forward in her seat. "I want the truth."

He gave her a pretend ecstatic smile. "Maybe a five point nine?"

She had promised it wouldn't hurt her feelings, but it did. After she'd pouted for forty minutes or so, he came upstairs and gave her a back rub that only stopped because she fell asleep. Two days later she tried a chicken dish and he rated it a nine point two. And she knew he meant it.

Her gaze wandered to the table where he and Colton and Callie had carved ten thousand ugly pumpkins that were some of the most beautiful creations she'd ever seen. And the seed fights. *Oh my gosh, the seed fights we've had.* Every year, Toren had spent the better part of the day after a seed fight scrubbing the kitchen till the seeds and smell of pumpkins were no more.

"Mom?"

Sloane looked up to find Colton standing at the bottom of the stairs.

"Hey, Colton."

"What's wrong with you?"

"Sorry, I was just thinking about some things," Sloane said.

"I'm going over to Griff's house for the afternoon."

"You'll be back for dinner?"

"Unless they ask me to stay." He grinned.

Colton, her boy, so close to becoming a man, looking more like her husband each day.

"Just let me know."

"Sure, Mom." He strode to the front door, long, loping strides making her think of Toren even more. "I love you, Mom."

"Love you too," she said as the front door slammed shut.

She needed that wand. The one that would reverse time to when Colton and Callie and Toren and she had no idea that dark years were coming. As the fantasy circled her mind, a voice called from the top of the stairs. Callie.

"Hey, Mom?"

"Yes, sweetheart."

"What are you doing right now?"

"Well, your dad is going to come over for a little bit."

"Right now? Yes! When?"

Callie's happy smile brought out a sad one of her own.

"In a few minutes."

"Really?"

"Yes."

"To see me?"

She bounded down the stairs, but by the time she reached the bottom step, her smile had faded.

"I know you don't like him anymore, Mommy. So I'm sorry he's coming over, but I'm not sorry he's coming over, do you know?"

"I don't dislike your dad. It's just that . . ."

"What? It's just what?" She peered up at Sloane, so much still a little girl, so much a young woman.

She kissed Callie on the forehead and said, "I'll let you know when he gets here."

Sloane went to her bathroom, brushed her hair, and started to touch up her makeup. Halfway through, she looked into the mirror.

"What do you think you're doing? Stop it!"

Makeup? For him? She should be washing all her makeup off. Attack her hair till it looked like a dilapidated rat's nest. Smear dirt on her face. Make herself as unattractive as possible. He didn't deserve to see her looking good.

A knock at the door came seven minutes later. Always a knock. Toren never rang a doorbell — something about a knock harkening back to an earlier time when life was simpler. A funny little quirk she'd always loved about him. She went to the door and opened it wide, but he didn't step over the threshold.

"May I come in?"

He looked at her and time stopped. He was different. Radically different. Not physically, although he looked in as good a shape as she'd ever seen him. His eyes. Sharp. Clearer than they'd ever been. So bright. They spoke of a dozen emotions at once. Peace. Joy. Kindness. A childlike playfulness. A splash of mischievousness, and more that she couldn't name.

But most of all, his countenance radiated love. Unvarnished, deeply grounded love. If she didn't know better, Sloane would have sworn waves of love were surging out from him, wrapping themselves around her, playing a complicated game of tag as they swirled around her body.

She stared up at him as he smiled and pointed to the hardwood of the entryway and repeated, "May I come in?"

"Yes, of course." She motioned with her hand and stepped back. "Sorry, I was . . . You, um . . . Sorry. Yes, come in, come in."

He stepped in, stopped just inside the door, and handed her a manila envelope. "Here you go."

She took it. The envelope, which couldn't have weighed more than a quarter pound, suddenly felt like a barbell.

"Are you okay?" He frowned.

"Yes, I'm good."

"Good."

She set the envelope on the entryway table and started for the kitchen.

"Daddy!" Callie screeched around the corner of the family room and launched herself into Toren's arms. He picked her up in a hug and spun in a tight circle before setting her back down.

"What did I do to deserve you?" He grinned at her.

"It's bio-o-logical. You couldn't help it."

"Where in the known universe did you learn a word that big?"

"TV."

He laughed. "How are you, pumpkin girl?"

"Really good."

"Are we still on for Wednesday night?"

"Yes."

"Sweet."

Sloane took Callie around the shoulders and gave her a gentle squeeze. "I need to talk to your dad for a bit, okay?"

"Sure."

She scooted off, giving Toren a quick wave as she went into the family room.

"Let's go out to the gazebo," she said. "I don't want Callie hearing any of this."

"You think I'm going to lose my —"

"No, I'm not suggesting that at all . . . I just . . ." She sighed and motioned toward the back door, and Toren took the cue.

They walked to the gazebo and settled into chairs on opposite sides of the table inside. Sloane glanced at him, but there was no point in staring into those eyes. Just let him say what he had to say and get it over with.

"I was so blind, Sloane. So blind." He rubbed the surface of the table. "I couldn't see, but now I can."

It wasn't his words, not even the tone of them that flooded into her heart. It was something else, something she couldn't name, but it was more real than anything she'd ever known. Whatever had happened to him was more solid than anything had been in his life for a long, long time.

"I know what I want." He took in a deep breath and held it for a few moments before continuing. "I want you to be happy."

She blinked but said nothing. He looked at her, his eyes far brighter than they'd been even in the early days of their romance.

"Be with him, Sloane."

"Wha . . . what?"

"Levi. Be with him. I know you love him. From everything you've said, from everything I've heard about him and read about him — yeah, I did a little research online — he's a good man. A very good man. Be with him, spend your life with him. He'll treat you right. He'll treat Callie right. Same with Colton. We can work it out, the stuff with the kids. I know we can."

She stared at him, stunned. She'd been ready for him to give her the papers, then launch into all the reasons why she didn't have to do this, why she should reconsider, give it more time. She thought his signing was just a ploy to get her to sit down.

"You are the most stunning creation I've ever known. Not your outside, although you're more gorgeous than the day we met. I mean what's inside you. I was so fortunate to share your life in those early years, when spring was in the air every day of the year, and then when we lived in the heart of summer every evening.

"But fall came, because of me, and now it's winter. But there is a fire for you in your future, with Levi. So go. With my full blessing."

She stared at the tiny lines in the wood under her fingers. Her mind didn't know where to go. This was . . . This was . . .

She sensed Toren stand. Three seconds, five. Like a Greek statue he stood, till he stooped down, kissed her on the head, and said, "Good-bye, Sloane." Then he turned and strolled away.

Sloane wrenched herself out of the daze she was in and called out, "Toren!"

He turned and gazed at her, a smile on his face so tender she involuntarily pulled in a quick breath. But it was the sadness in his eyes that went to her heart.

A look passed over his face. Then he dropped his gaze, but she knew him too well not to know exactly what it was. He loved her. Period. Not for himself. Not for gain. Simply for her. But that wasn't the deepest part of what the expression was about. The deepest part was the fact he didn't want her to see his pain.

Finally he looked back up, but only for a

moment, waved, then turned and walked down the path to the house.

CHAPTER 48

Sloane sat at in the gazebo for ages, stunned, trying to wrap her mind around what had just happened. That was Toren, but it wasn't him. Not the man she'd known for the past year and a half, not even the one she'd known in their early days together. The man who had fixed his eyes on her soul just now was someone she'd always seen flitting around the edges of her husband.

When she finally stumbled back into the kitchen, Callie was sitting at a bar stool at the kitchen counter eating a grape Popsicle.

"Are you and Daddy getting a divorce?"

Sloane eased into the room and sat on a chair at the kitchen desk Toren had made for her when he'd first started working with restored wood. She set her elbow on the cedar, stared at its beauty for a moment, then rested her chin in her hand.

"Yes."

The word came out like lead.

"I guessed that's what you were going to do." Callie went to the window and gazed outside. "When are you going to be doing it?"

"Soon."

"I see."

"Sorry."

"It's okay." She turned. "I'll still see him lots, won't I?"

"Yes."

"Does he want to divorce you, or do you want to divorce him?"

"Me."

"Why?"

"Because."

Tears formed in Callie's eyes, and as Sloane stared at her daughter, it struck her that she'd answered Callie with one-word answers from the moment she'd stepped into the kitchen. It took her back to when Callie was just barely over age four and there'd been an almost identical conversation. But it hadn't been between the two of them; it had been between Callie and Toren.

"Who loves your mom more than the whole world?"

"You!"

"Who loves your brother more than the whole world?"

"You!"

"Who loves you more than the whole world?"

"You!"

"Who is loved by her mom and her brother and her dad more than the whole world?"

"Me!"

"Who will love each other forever and ever and ever and ever?"

"Us!"

"Will the four of us ever, ever, ever be apart?"

"Never!"

Toren started doing it every night when he tucked Callie into bed. Then it expanded to include Colton, and then her. It had become their family's unwritten slogan, whispered and shouted and laughed about for years. When had that tradition slipped out of existence? When had that memory faded from her mind?

Sloane stood, shuffled over to the entryway, and picked up the manila envelope she'd left there. She slipped the papers out and stared at Toren's signature. There was no yellow sticky note next to his name, begging her to reconsider, no final plea for her to change her mind. Just his signed name under the printed *Toren Samuel Daniels*.

A thought flickered in her mind and her

heart skipped. She flipped the papers over, knowing there would be a sticky note with words on it in his hand that would . . .

There was nothing but the clean white back of the papers that would change her life forever.

That night, sleep and prayers were mixed in equal measure, but by morning she knew what she had to do. After the kids left for school, she picked up her phone and called Levi. He answered on the first ring.

"Hey, babe, we still on for tomorrow night?"

Sloane swallowed hard and tried to sound normal. "I'm wondering if we can get together today."

"Sure, I suppose. There a reason?"

"There's something I'd like to talk to you about."

Levi paused before answering. "You okay?"

"Yes, I'm okay. But I need to —"

"You're not okay, I can tell. Talk to me."

Sloane closed her eyes and gripped her phone tighter. "Can we just get together?"

"Sure." Levi's voice was a mixture of concern and frustration. "What if we meet for coffee in an hour?"

"Or we could meet down at Juanita Bay Park."

"I like that idea. A romantic stroll among the flowers and water . . . see if we can spot the beavers while we listen to the songbirds? And did I mention the romantic part?"

"You did." Sloane scraped a laugh together, then said, "I'll see you in sixty."

She hung up and wiped her damp hands on her jeans.

She pulled into the parking lot at Juanita Bay Park fifty-three minutes later. Early, in order to get a chance to breathe, to sit in the silence and not worry about the fact she had no idea what she was going to say to Levi. A chance to walk down a path or two and back to the parking lot before he got there.

Thirty seconds later Levi's truck pulled in beside her. No! Why couldn't he be on time for once instead of always early? She glanced over, returned a weak smile in response to his wide grin, then yanked her keys out of the ignition and stepped out of her car.

"Hey, beautiful."

He came around the back of her car and seconds later slid his arm around her waist. Sloane spun away before his kiss could reach her cheek.

"Did I miss something, or did you just spin your way out of a smooch?"

"You don't like my new dance move?"

Lame. As if he'd believe that.

"No, not really." Levi was still smiling, but the dimmer switch in his eyes had been turned down. "You want to tell me what's going on?"

"Let's walk."

They wandered down the path to the narrow bridges traversing the northeastern edges of Lake Washington. The water was full of reeds and turtles and fish slaloming just below the surface. Levi reached out and took Sloane's hand. She gave him a quick squeeze, then pulled away.

"You want to tell me what's going on?" He tried to chuckle. "What? Are you breaking up with me?"

Sloane stared at him till tears started to rise, then looked away and watched a dark-green turtle slip into the water.

"That's a joke, Sloane."

She glanced at him, then back to the water.

"You gotta be kidding me." Levi's eyes went dark. "You are?"

"No."

"You're not breaking up with me then."

"I don't know."

"What?" Levi stepped closer, his eyes incredulous. "Talk to me, Sloane. What. Is.

Going. On?"

She didn't want to answer. He knew already. Had to know. It had to be scrawled all over her face. She turned, and they stared at each other long enough that the only thing left was to speak it out to make it real. But it wasn't real, was it? So much of her screamed it wasn't, but even greater was the whisper that said it was.

"I need time."

"For what?"

"You know what."

Levi kicked at a stone and sent it into the water.

"Do you want to be with him or with me? Which is it?"

"Something's happened to him. I can't explain it . . ." She trailed off.

"Let's cut to the chase. In fact, let's cut to the end of the chase. What does the car wreck look like? Is it his or mine?"

"Don't ask that," Sloane whispered. "Give me a moment to think, okay?"

Levi laughed bitterly, then turned and stared at her as his eyes slowly narrowed. "You promised me his coming back wouldn't affect you. Wouldn't affect you and me. At all. You promised."

"You're right, I did."

Levi pressed his lips together hard, eyes

closed. When he opened them, a resigned look filled his face.

"I get it." Levi stopped and shoved his hands in his pockets. "First love. There's part of you way down that hasn't ever forgotten that. And that part is wondering."

She stared at him for a few seconds, then said the words that would wound him deeply. "I'm not wondering."

"Ah. There it is."

Sloane nodded slowly, then softly said, "I didn't see this coming."

He didn't answer.

"I can't marry you now. I am so sorry. At this point, I don't think I'll ever be able to."

Sloane closed her eyes, took in a long breath, and released it slowly through her nostrils. When the air was gone, she took in another deep breath, opened her eyes, and looked around. Levi was disappearing around a corner in the path. She turned and roamed deeper into the park, thinking, praying, not thinking, staring at the water, the turtles, two beavers that came out to play. After forty minutes slipped by, when the time was exactly right, Sloane pulled out her phone and dialed. Two rings. Three. Then Toren's voice filling her mind, and quite possibly her heart as well.

CHAPTER 49

A year and a half later

"Let's do something crazy." Sloane's eyes flashed with the kind of light Toren had never been able to refuse. Never wanted to refuse.

He laughed as they sat in their gazebo watching the sky fill with gold. "Whatever it is, I'm in."

"This fall. Something certifiably insane."

"Tell me."

"Get married again." Her eyebrows rose.

"What?"

"Renew our vows. You and me and Colton and Callie. No one else, just the four of us."

"Are you serious?"

"Deadly. Let's fly to someplace exotic like New Zealand or Fiji or Belize and do it all over again." She paused, a playful smile on her face. "And maybe invite one guest."

"Eden."

"Yes."

Toren took Sloane's hand in his. "Crazy."

"Very crazy."

Three months later, Toren and Sloane stood on a tiny island off the north coast of Fiji, white sand under their bare feet, palm trees and lush jungle to their left, aqua-blue water to their right. A soft breeze brought hints of the ocean mixed with Sloane's perfume, Beautiful. She wore a sleeveless white top and a tropical skirt. Her hair was up, accented by a single flower. Toren sported a dark-green collared shirt with palm trees that matched her skirt and khaki shorts. Sandals? Not a chance. Bare feet all the way.

"You good?" he asked as he studied her eyes. "You still want to do this?"

"Without question."

He pulled her close and kissed her lightly on the cheek. A moment later she drew his mouth to hers for a long, long time.

"Oh, come on, knock it off!" Colton called out. They pulled apart to find Colton, Callie, and Eden strolling toward them.

"You guys are so gross," Colton continued. "This is a G-rated beach."

Toren turned to Sloane. "What, hitting twelve suddenly gives him the right to talk to us like that?"

"Precisely."

They laughed and watched the three of them amble over the sand.

"You ready, Mom? Dad?" Callie asked when she reached them.

"More than," Sloane said.

As they meandered toward the spot they'd picked out, Sloane asked Toren if he'd told Colton to conduct the service with reverence or a lighter touch.

"I told him to do whatever the Spirit led him to do."

"Oh boy."

Sloane squeezed his hand and smiled. When they reached the spot, Colton said, "I have to tell you, this feels so weird. I mean, me? Marrying you guys?"

It was the perfect statement to break any tension, and they all laughed.

The ceremony started with Callie singing "Brighter Than Sunshine" with more feeling and passion than had ever been recorded. Then she nodded to Colton, who stepped up to Sloane and Toren and asked them to take hands.

He tilted his head back and cried, "Mahwage! Mahwage is wot bwings us twogeddah today!"

All of them burst into laughter, and when they finally stopped, Toren said, "You had to bring *The Princess Bride* into this, didn't you?"

"You loved it, Dad, don't even try to deny it."

"True."

The breeze picked up and wandered through the trees and their hair as Colton led them in their vows and Eden prayed a blessing over them that was pure gold. After congratulations and hugs were given all around, Eden said, "I think we're going to give the newlyweds a little time alone before the skiff comes back to pick us up."

But before they could wander off, Sloane took Eden's hands. "What you have done for us is beyond priceless. I don't know how to say thank you."

Eden smiled and drew Sloane in for a long hug. When they finally parted, Sloane narrowed her eyes and smiled.

"I think you might be an angel."

"No more than you," Eden said.

Eden, Colton, and Callie strolled off, their feet scuffling through the white sand. As if preplanned, Eden moved between their children and took each of them by the hand. Colton and Callie turned to her almost in unison, then both put their arms around her neck and the three walked on as one.

"I'm happy, Toren. Truly happy. More

than I've ever been."

"I'm not perfect. I still get mad some-times."

"No, you're not, and yes, you do." Sloane's eyes grew serious. "And it took a while, but I finally admitted what I knew in the first month after your final time at the octagon: the change in you this time was not a fix, but a revolution."

"How did you know?"

Sloane gazed out over the ocean and tried to pull her hands out of his, but he held tight.

"Tell me, Sloane."

"I had to know. So I pushed every one of your most sensitive buttons, to see how you'd react."

Toren snorted out a disbelieving laugh. "You tried to get me to lose my temper?"

"A little bit maybe."

He shook his head and smiled. "Apparently I passed the audition."

"Flying colors."

They talked about the future, but mostly about now, and far too soon Toren spotted the skiff approaching to take them back to the mainland. A few minutes later, Colton, Callie, and Eden appeared.

Toren studied the woman who had trans-formed his life in every way and set him into a kind of freedom he'd only dreamed of. When they reached him and Sloane, Toren said, "I don't know how to show my gratitude to you for ushering me into a life I never knew existed, my dear sister."

He drew Eden to his chest, squeezed her tight, and kissed the top of her head, then stepped back and peered into her eyes. "You are a light of such incredible brilliance."

"You did it, Toren, truly. All I did was show you a path. You walked down it. You chose to see. To love."

"How can I repay you? Anything, tell me."

"In two simple ways." Eden smiled as she tilted her head to the side. "Continue on this journey. Continue to know who you truly are. Continue to step into the way of authentic love for yourself and for those around you in more and more moments throughout the day. Continue to shine as the light of the world, because that is what you are."

She stopped, and he couldn't tell if she'd decided not to make her second request. "And?" he said finally.

"Think about this idea. Seek the counsel of the Spirit as to whether you should or not. Will you do that for me, dear brother?"

She paused again so long that Toren finally laughed and said, "Are you going to tell me what the idea is?"

"I'm wondering if you already know. Do you?"

He didn't, and then he did, or at least he suspected what the idea was.

"Join you. Do the work."

"We could use another man on the team."

The idea overwhelmed Toren, but he said he'd think about it, pray about it, talk to Sloane about it.

Then Eden turned to Sloane.

"I'd like to give you something. A wedding present, if you will, although you might not see it that way. Which is fine. But not for both of you. Just for you."

Sloane's eyes glistened, her mouth trying not to smile. "I would trust anything you give me to be a gift of great value."

Eden nodded and reached into the tiny satchel at her side, but her hand stayed inside the bag. "Are you sure?"

Sloane glanced at Toren and laughed. "Of course."

"Good."

Eden handed Sloane a small square envelope. One side was a brilliant snow white. The other like onyx. She turned the envelope over in her hands and ran her finger along the edge.

"What is this, Eden?" Sloane said.

Eden took Sloane in a tender embrace and whispered in her ear. Toren didn't need to know what Eden had told his bride. He knew what was inside the envelope. He was certain of it.

It was an invitation to visit Eden at a certain spot in the San Juan Islands in a certain room with eight sides, where Sloane would be invited on a journey to a world of love and light and truth far beyond what she could imagine.

DISCUSSION QUESTIONS

1. What are the main elements you took away from *The Man He Never Was?*
2. What do you feel are the main themes of the novel?
3. I have the feeling many readers will anticipate the twist at the end of the book coming, even though they might not be sure till the climactic scene. Did you?
4. Do you believe we all have a dark side?
5. How does that dark side compare and contrast with the side other people see?
6. Has your dark side come out in different situations? What were they?
7. Can you put into words what constitutes your dark side?
8. In Romans chapter 7 (which was an inspiration for *The Strange Case of Dr. Jekyll and Mr. Hyde,* as well as my novel) we see a description of the two sides of ourselves, and the civil war going on inside each of us. How do you see that civil war

playing out in your own life?

9. In the end, Toren realizes he is not the dark man, or the good man described in Romans 7, but is "a new creature" in Christ (2 Corinthians 5:17). Do you think of yourself as good or bad, or do you think of yourself as the third option, crucified, the old you no longer alive, but Christ now living in you (Galatians 2:20)?

10. During Toren's final battle with Hyde, he realizes his only hope for victory (and his greatest weapon) is love, specifically loving himself. Many people find it extremely difficult to love themselves. Do you find that people have a tough time loving themselves? Why do you think it's so hard for them?

11. Many of us find it much easier to love and forgive others than ourselves. Do you? Why do you think that is?

12. Eden encourages Toren to focus not on the things that can be seen with our physical eyes, but on the things that can only be seen with our spiritual eyes. Is that easy or challenging for you to do? What does that look like in your life? In what situations is it easy? In what kind of situations is it hard?

13. Was there anything in the story that caused you to think differently about your

life? What was it? How do you think it will affect you and those around you?

14. Is there a question you'd like to ask me about the novel? I'd love to hear from you! You can e-mail me at: james@jameslrubart .com

ACKNOWLEDGMENTS

Darci Rubart, Taylor Rubart, Amanda Bostic, Erin Healy, Susie Warren, David Warren, Ted Dekker, Kevin Kaiser, Ron DeMiglio, Lori Roeleveld, and my team at HCCP, thank you with immense gratitude. Without you, this novel would still be languishing in my mind in a state of utter confusion. Because of you and your brilliance, there has come this story of which I am quite proud, and which I pray will help many step into freedom.

ABOUT THE AUTHOR

James L. Rubart is the bestselling, Christy, Carol, *RT Book Reviews,* and INSPY award winning author of nine novels. A professional marketer and speaker, James and his wife have two grown sons and live in the Pacific Northwest.

Want to stay in touch with James? Sign up for his newsletter (and an occasional freebie!) at JamesLRubart.com.

Facebook: JamesLRubart
Twitter: @JamesLRubart